# Rebecca Bloom

By

Eliel Luma Fionn

RESOURCE *Publications* • Eugene, Oregon

This book is a work of fiction. Places, events, and situations in this story are purely fictional. Any resemblance to actual persons, living or dead, is coincidental

Resource Publications
A division of Wipf and Stock Publishers
199 W 8th Ave, Suite 3
Eugene, OR 97401

Rebecca Bloom
By Fionn, Eliel Luma

ISBN 13: 978-1-55635-811-1
ISBN 10: 1-55635-811-3
Publication date 1/17/2008

## Chapter 1

Rebecca watched the people outside her window rushing about under their umbrellas as if they knew exactly what they were doing and where they ought to go. She wondered if one day she would be like them. Perhaps she would go to work every day and have fun on the weekends, take a trip now and then. Her days would fit a pattern like everyone else's. She knew that once the idea wouldn't have bothered her, since she had looked forward to college, a career, and a family just like her friends did.

Now, sitting in the room that no longer felt like hers, she felt as if she had turned into a person she didn't know and wasn't sure how to handle. Her parents kept telling her to give it time; she had been ill for weeks and needed to adjust. Rebecca wasn't sure that she wanted to go back to the way she had been, and she couldn't seem to explain how she felt so that her parents could understand. So she tried to pretend that everything was back to normal so as not to worry them, but alone in her room, she felt the change in herself.

"Here I am," she muttered to herself, "fifteen years old, almost sixteen, and I feel totally weird, only nothing around me has changed at all. I don't fit anywhere, not even my own room. I wish I could remember the place, the place I saw when I was ill. It seemed so much more real somehow."

School, which she used to like, had become torture. She noticed that classmates treated each other badly, and while that had always been normal before, now it gave her a stomachache. When the teacher picked on Ryan, the boy who sat next to her, she had felt like screaming. It seemed as if everything disturbed her more, like her skin itself were more sensitive. She spent most of school daydreaming. Her previous interest in boys had disappeared; the ones she'd had crushes on seemed to have turned into creeps.

She thought about what her father had said. "Rebecca, you need to do routine things until you feel normal; just keep trying to be your old self. You will be again." But so far it hadn't worked, and she felt more displaced every day.

She got up from her chair by the window and rummaged in the closet to find her raincoat. One of her favorite things to do when it was raining was puddle jumping, something she and her parents traditionally did on rainy weekends. Today was the first rainy Saturday since she'd been ill. Her parents were out helping some friends move, but she could certainly go puddle-jumping herself. Of course, it probably would be better if she didn't mention it to her parents; they wouldn't want her getting wet so soon after her recovery.

She pulled on her bright blue raincoat, grabbed her matching boots, and carried them downstairs, where she sat in the entryway to put them on. She stopped for a moment, looking around the house. They had three bedrooms, two upstairs and one on the ground floor. They'd put in hardwood floors and marble countertops. Her father was a well-respected architect, her mother a very successful interior designer. They both worked together at their own firm downtown, though they could also work from home when necessary. Their house was beautiful, elegant, and inviting. It was popular with her friends because she had her own refrigerator and bathroom. They were able to eat snacks and have as much privacy as they wanted. Now the house seemed too contained, too orderly, as if the walls had been forced to be square. She shook her head at her own thoughts, heading for the door.

She decided that her fever had given her parents such a scare it wouldn't be fair to leave without a note, so she scrawled a quick message on a napkin. She grabbed her house key, locked the door behind her, and stepped out into the rain.

The rain had lightened a bit and she pulled the hood of her raincoat off to feel the cool wetness on her face. She loved the rain. It always reminded her that even though people thought they owned the world, the weather did whatever it wanted, whenever it wanted. She paused for a moment, letting the rain sprinkle across her face like freckles, and set off down the street to find some good puddles.

She lived on East 29th in a old neighborhood that usually didn't get much traffic. She cut across the street, behind the church, and came out on 30th. As she had expected, the street had collected deep puddles in its potholes. Rebecca checked first to make sure she wouldn't be splashing anyone (one of her parent's rules), and then ran and jumped in as many puddles as she could without stopping. The water splashed up her legs as she raced through the puddles, leaving dark blotches all up and down her blue jeans. She laughed. For the first time in weeks, she felt alive. After dodging a few cars that were taking a shortcut away from the busiest traffic, she stopped for a moment to catch her breath. Looking up, she noticed her friend Lucy's mom, Mrs. Meyer, standing on her porch in the wet drizzle, laughing and waving.

"Rebecca," she called, her face barely visible under her raincoat hood, "you look like a little kid when you do that! Splash a big one for me!"

Rebecca grinned and waved back, then looked for a really deep puddle that would make a splash worthy of Mrs. Meyer. She soon found a promising one on the edge of the street. Wading in to test its depth, she noticed a strange reflection in the water.

At first she thought it was a floating photograph and reached down to grab it, but when she touched the water it disappeared. She waited for the ripples to subside, and there it was again, not her own face, with brown hair and blue eyes, but the face of a young man, about her age, with blond gold hair and green eyes. The reflection looked so real she felt she could reach down and touch him. He was smiling, but seemed somehow serious at the same time.

Rebecca crouched down to get a better look. The reflection grew larger and the boy's whole body became visible. He was wearing a long blue shirt, green trousers, and green shoes. He seemed to reach out a hand to her as if he could see her as well, but Rebecca shook her head in disbelief. "I guess that fever really did fry my brain," she thought aloud, glancing back to see Mrs. Meyer still smiling at her.

"It's okay," Rebecca called, "I thought I saw something in the water, but it must be my imagination."

"Water can play funny tricks on people," replied Mrs. Meyer, watching as Rebecca leaned forward once again as if to touch the water. The next moment Mrs. Meyer would never forget for as long as she lived. She saw an arm reach right out of the puddle, clasp Rebecca by the hand, and draw her down into the water. Then Rebecca vanished.

"I rushed out to find her," explained Mrs. Meyer later to Rebecca's parents, the police, and anyone else who would listen, "but I swear the water only came up to my ankles, and I'm a short woman. It was impossible, I tell you, impossible! And I saw it with my own eyes. She vanished right into that puddle like it was a deep pool. Someone grabbed her, I'm sure of it."

To Rebecca everything seemed to happen in slow motion. She reached down to touch the reflection boy's face, when she felt a warm hand come up to clasp hers. She felt a tug and was falling, falling past a swirl of colors and through an incredible warmth that was somehow not heat. She landed with a thump. She closed her eyes, half hoping that it was a dream and half hoping it wasn't.

"You can open your eyes now," said an amused voice. "You're not imagining things, although I suppose if you had no imagination you wouldn't be here. I'm not sure; I will have to ask Grandfather about that. I am Torin, and I'm happy to meet you, but it would be easier if you could see me so I could introduce myself properly."

Rebecca opened her eyes slowly, wondering if now that she was hearing voices she would have to go to the hospital like old Mrs. Appleby, who was convinced she had aliens in her cupboard. Rebecca saw in front of her the boy that belonged to the voice, so she supposed she wasn't crazy. Perhaps she was having a Dorothy Gale experience and would wake up to discover she'd only dreamed the whole thing after all. Though the boy certainly looked real enough. He was tall and well built, with welcoming green eyes and blond hair. He smiled, bowing gracefully.

"As I said before, I am Torin, of the Fire Folk. Welcome to my grandfather's dwelling. You have been expected, Rebecca Bloom. Everyone will be very glad that you have arrived at last. Are you hungry for some refreshment? I will bring you acorn cakes and leaf tree juice, if you'd like."

Rebecca, who was finally realizing she was truly not at home, not imagining things, and not asleep, burst into tears. Almost at once she felt warm arms around her. She was so frightened she didn't even worry about sobbing on the strange boy's shoulder.

"I'm sorry," he said a bit sheepishly, "I forgot you're probably not used to the idea of space-time traveling. You see; we saw you here in spirit so often over the past few weeks that I forgot you might not remember us. When you're ready, look around and tell me if anything here looks familiar. Here, have a fleecenest fern to wipe your nose. I am sorry if I frightened you."

It occurred to Rebecca that Torin was certainly unlike most of the young men she knew. Somehow she believed him, or she would have if she knew what he was talking about. She took the soft leaf-shaped handkerchief, blew her nose, wiped her eyes, and as Torin nodded at her encouragingly, she looked around his grandfather's house. House was probably not the correct term, for it certainly looked nothing like the houses she was used to. There seemed to be no wood or sheet rock, and if she'd had to guess she would have said it was made of hard-packed purple earth. The walls were smooth and rounded, with a polished purple sheen to them.

Even the roof was dome-shaped, as if corners were completely alien. The floor they were sitting on seemed to be made of black glass, like obsidian, with colorful, fleecy carpets placed here and there. On one wall was a series of shelves that looked as if they'd somehow grown out of the soil. On these shelves were assorted containers, thick books, and all manner of dried plants tied in small bundles. Circular windows let in light, although there seemed to be no screens to keep out insects or small animals. The ceiling was very high. Through a window in the roof came the sky and the sunshine. The room was cheerful considering the dark earthen walls. As Rebecca sat down on the soft, green carpet on which they'd landed, she felt a sort of humming vibration coming from the floor.

"What's that?" she asked. "It feels familiar, from when I was ill. A sort of tingling coming from the ground. I don't recognize this place so far, but the feeling underneath me I've felt before. What is it, Torin?"

Torin nodded at her approvingly, "It's the song of our planet, making you welcome. I'm glad you can feel it; it will make everything else so much easier for you. Grandfather will be happy to know that his farsight was accurate. Stand up; you'll feel it even more."

Rebecca stood up on shaky legs, as the humming grew more pronounced, traveling through her body in waves. When it subsided, becoming only a mild tingle, Rebecca noticed with surprise that she felt refreshed and quite recovered from her rather abrupt arrival.

"Yes," Torin said, "you are quite attuned now and will no longer feel a stranger here, or so frightened to be away from your world. Now I will give you a tour of our home. I'll show you the garden, the rest of our rooms, and the place we set aside for you. Please come with me."

"Wait a minute," said Rebecca, "I want to know why I feel so comfortable here when I've only just arrived. At home in New York I've only felt this way a few times and I've lived there my whole life. It makes no sense. I feel like a plant that's finally found the right soil."

Torin looked at her seriously. "There's nothing wrong with the ground on your planet, Rebecca. But if you had a song that few seemed to appreciate, would you sing as loudly, or as joyfully? Your Earth is merely waiting for a receptive audience, that's all. Now come.

I'll try to answer as many questions as I can, and we'll get you settled in."

As Torin led Rebecca down the hallway, she admired the glowing crystals embedded in the ceiling. She was surprised at how much light they emitted, especially when Torin said that they never needed to be replaced. He explained that the room they'd arrived in was the common room, where visitors gathered. He showed her the eating room, a beautiful space with low root tables, shelves piled with odd looking food, and the loveliest pink crystal Rebecca had ever seen. It was enormous, occupying a large amount of space by one wall. Torin explained that it promoted good digestion as well as being beautiful.

He took her through two resting rooms, his own and his grandfather's. Torin's room held a large bed; a fire pit that he said was for practicing his fire skills, a pile of books, and many shelves of clothes. His grandfather's room looked much the same. Rebecca was struck by how few possessions they had, the complete lack of clutter. There was a beautiful simplicity to the whole house. Most of the rooms were decorated with blossoming plants growing right from the walls. The floor coverings were woven from colorful vines, as were the clothes, and the furniture simply sprang from the ground as needed.

"My mom would love this place," Rebecca said. "It would sure make her job a whole lot easier."

She noticed the doors had anticipated their arrival by opening before them, like in grocery stores. "How does that work, Torin?" she asked, when they had reached the end of the hallway. "I don't see one of those things you step on to activate the doors."

"I asked them to open, so they did. We work in cooperation with the elements and ask for what we need. It's not that difficult, really. You can try it if you like. Ask this door to open for us." He indicated the large earthen door before them. "It will take us outside to the garden. I can show you the rest of the house later. We have only six rooms."

"What do I do, ask it out loud? Does it understand English?"

Torin laughed. "That's not necessary. Think the door open, only have the intent of asking permission first."

Rebecca looked at him hesitantly. At his nod, she concentrated fiercely, imagining herself standing in front of the door, asking it to open. She watched in amazement as it swung wide, letting in pink sunlight. She clapped her hands together excitedly. "It worked!"

"Yes, you'll soon become more accustomed to asking for what you need," Torin said, leading her outside the dwelling. "It's much easier than relying on mechanical things that need to be repaired. Although, there are other things that need to be mended here on Thianely. But we don't have technology here in the sense that you would know it."

Rebecca followed Torin into the pink sunlight along a soft earthen path. The ground was dark purple, like the walls of his home. She recognized none of the flowers that grew along the edges of the path, but the textures and colors were extraordinary against the purple soil. She looked up at the sky, noticing that the pink sun did not hurt her eyes as the bright sun on earth did. There were no clouds, just the subtle humming of flying insects and the mingled scents of flowers and earth.

The path opened into the most beautiful garden she'd ever seen. It was not arranged in rows like most gardens; the plants grew in a series of spirals, many varieties growing together in a way that appeared spontaneously harmonious.

"Wow!" Rebecca said, closing her eyes for a moment to breathe in the fragrant air.

Torin made a sweeping gesture with one arm, encompassing the entire spiraling profusion of plants. "I hope you'll enjoy it here. This garden is quite healing. Many Folk gather here when they are troubled, because Grandfather has such a strong gift with plants. His herb-drying room, the one he cleared for you, is a very powerful place.

My favorite spot is over there, by the Lalerosen tree. It bears much fruit, and its leaves are used for our garments. The leaves change color as the tree chooses, so they're always unpredictably beautiful." He indicated a tall, spiked tree with a thatch of yellow leaves clustered in bunches along its tawny branches.

"Don't you have seasons like back home?" Rebecca asked, somewhat confused.

Torin shook his head. "Because we often ask the weather to alter depending upon our needs, time becomes somewhat elastic. There are generally five seasons, but sometimes the intervals between them speed up or slow down. We have something like your spring, summer, autumn, and winter, although by other names, but there is also Yarwen. Yarwen is the time between times, when everything returns to complete balance. Right now we are experiencing a lengthy summer, but our previous season was a very condensed spring. Before that was Yarwen.

Thianely itself is really in charge of the seasons, for if it is not in the highest good of the season or weather to alter, it will not. If the elements become unbalanced in any way, the season of Yarwen will set it to rights. In this way, all Folk of Thianely work together with the elements to meet their needs and the needs of the planet. But lately, for some reason, Thianely itself has become unbalanced, which has affected everything.

I will explain more later, but for now let me show you the rest of the garden. You are always welcome here, Rebecca. If you long for your home or feel uneasy, the garden will comfort you if you wish."

They spent the next few hours wandering through the enormous garden, although Torin explained that they weren't really hours in the way that Rebecca might understand. Each day had an inconsistent number of hours, as the sun rose and set whenever it was most appropriate, so the hours themselves had various numbers of minutes. Rebecca couldn't see the logic in any of it, but Torin kept reminding her that on Thianely time was not a linear concept, so measuring it was not of much concern to anyone.

"Because our time is elastic, our hours and minutes are not set as yours are," Torin explained. "We call larger increments of time *morits*, and smaller *demals*. But think of them as hours and minutes in your mind; it will be less confusing."

Rebecca finally gave up trying to understand it, especially when Torin said the time to do things was when it felt like the right time, not an arbitrary moment determined by a technological timepiece. She looked at the place on her wrist where her watch normally was, wishing she'd put it on before she left home.

"Now come, let me show you the space we have set aside for you," Torin said, distracting her from her time confusion. "It's Grandfather's herb-drying room, but as I said, he cleared it for you some time ago."

"Wait a minute, or a demal, or whatever," Rebecca said, catching Torin by his sleeve. "How did you know I was coming? Why am I here anyway? This is like one of those books I used to read when

I was younger, with magic and stuff. The funny thing is, this seems more real than back home. It's weird."

Torin shrugged. "I could tell you that you are here, on Thianely, because you have special gifts, because you are an Elemental Master. I could say that you called to us for help, or that I pulled you here through space and time, but I don't think any of these explanations would help right now. You must wait until Grandfather returns, and he will explain. I know this must be strange. I felt very uncomfortable at first when I stayed on your planet, but I grew more used to it in time. Now come, you may start feeling the effects of traveling such a great distance. Let me show you your room."

Torin led Rebecca into the house, down the crystal-lit corridor. They headed back through the common room, rounded a bend, and stepped into a small room, which was almost completely filled by an enormous bed. The tall earthen platform was covered with a thick woven pad. A stack of colorful blankets lay on top. Nearby were several small tables with flowers and bowls of some sort of fruit. Round openings in the walls overlooked the garden, letting in the sweet scented breeze. Across one wall were more of the shelves that she'd seen in the other rooms. Her eyes were drawn to a clear oval crystal embedded in the wall, about a foot in diameter. The sun reflecting off of it made rainbows dance across the room. She went over to touch its cool surface, feeling it pulse slightly under her hand.

"What's this for?" she asked.

"It's a light crystal, like the ones in the hallways and eating room, though it has other properties as well. Grandfather often asks it to nurture the herbs to increase their potency. If it becomes too bright, ask it to dim for resting times."

"I guess if I can talk to a door, a crystal should be no problem." Rebecca stepped over to the bed to test its softness, and yawned. "Excuse me," she apologized. "I'm really tired all of a sudden. I think I'd better lie down."

Torin nodded understandingly. "It's perfectly normal to be weary. It takes a lot of energy to shift between planets, especially when you aren't expecting it. Before you sleep let me show you the waste room, and there are several fruits on the table here if you become hungry. I'll let you sleep for a while and check in on you later. Grandfather will be back soon. He'll be able to answer your questions when you awaken."

Rebecca used the waste room, which was basically a room with a small toilet-like chair formed out of the earth. After she sat down on the chair, a small hole opened up directly underneath and immediately closed over when she was finished. All waste was completely and instantly recycled. The leaf wipes were a soft, vibrant green, and so comfortable that Rebecca knew she would never appreciate Kleenex again. The walls were full of books with leaf bindings. When she asked Torin about them, he said that the waste room was a great place to find reading material. It reminded Thianelians that all information should be digested thoroughly and those ideas that were not useful should be let go.

Torin escorted her back to her room, letting Rebecca settle in. She was almost asleep when she felt a blanket tucked in around her cozily. Her last thought before falling asleep was that this was either the best dream she'd ever had or else life had become incredibly strange.

## Chapter 2

Rebecca awoke to the smell of something delicious. At first she thought her mother must be baking a pie, though it smelled of spices she couldn't quite place. "Mmm," she mumbled, rolling over and tucking her pillow more comfortably under her head, "smells great!"

"I'm pleased you think so," said a voice. Rebecca opened her eyes to see a very tall, slender man with deep brown eyes standing by her bed. He had silvery hair and a kind face, which appeared youthful except for a few smile lines.

"I have come to wake you for evening repast. The dorsani cakes you smell are nearly done. I am Torin's grandfather, Imanayon Rahalek, Village Centerian. Welcome to our world, and my home. May the Great Mother sustain you."

By this time Rebecca was sitting up. She would have felt more alarmed by the strangeness of her surroundings, but Imanayon's voice was comforting, somehow familiar. For a moment she felt as if her life on Earth was only a dream, and now she was waking up. As she stood, somewhat shakily, Imanayon reached out a hand to steady her.

"Your Earth experience is as real as we are," he said gravely, nodding at her startled look. "It is too difficult to maintain awareness of both worlds at once, so for now your own place will seem somewhat vague. Remember, it is also your home, and you are as welcome there as you are here. Come, let us eat, and I will tell you of our ways."

Rebecca smiled somewhat shyly, "Is it true I've met you before? You seem so familiar and even though I feel like I should be scared, I'm not."

Imanayon tucked Rebecca's hand onto his arm and led her from the room. "It is true," he agreed. "You have visited us here before, and as to the reason you have no fear, it is difficult to be afraid when you can feel the pulse of the planet within your feet. Here, Torin has already begun the blessing of the meal."

Rebecca and Imanayon stepped from the hallway into the eating room. The oval table looked like a root coming right out of the ground. The floor was smoothly purple with patches of moss and mushrooms, and the windows were open to the sky. Outside it was late evening. Stars were already visible in the dusk. In fact, as Rebecca glanced around the room, she realized that the starlight was so bright, the crystal light wasn't even necessary.

Torin stood by an alcove in one wall, doing something she could not see. He noticed his grandfather and Rebecca, and turned around with something glowing very brightly in his hand. He set it on the table. When Imanayon motioned for Rebecca to sit, she settled herself right on a clump of moss.

As Rebecca watched in astonishment, the glowing thing at the center of the table began to shimmer and hum. Light shot from it, bathing them all in alternating colors. Rebecca suddenly felt very peaceful, deeply happy in a way she had never before experienced. The ground tingled beneath her feet. She sat, her body pulsing, while Torin and Imanayon chanted before the strange glowing object.

"Thank you Father Telches for our sun,
And the moon and the stars in the sky.
Blessed be Mother Rhiate and her sacred breath of life
All have worth and purpose in her eyes.
Receive us fully creation's bounty
In the food we sup, the nectar we savor.
May all benefit from our feasting
In body be stronger, in spirit find favor.
Help us bless this former day,
Embrace the coming of the night,
Joy in moment, work and play
All now in rest, beneath starsight."

As Rebecca sat, listening to the chant, the light and sound and feeling of it washed over her. She felt thoroughly cleansed, as if she'd had a bath inside and out. At last, the chanting ended. The object began to glow more and more softly, until it barely glimmered at all. It looked to Rebecca like a small rock.

"What is it?" she asked in wonder.

Torin smiled, "It's a piece of star that fell to ground over in the meadow. It still hums the starsong of all creation. Because we have all come from the stars, we a song with it at evening repast, but only then since we are usually too hungry to make a long prayer during the day."

Imanayon said affectionately, "For someone who has stopped growing taller, Torin eats a great deal of food!" Torin meanwhile, had already helped himself from the tree bark dishes, and passed them along to Rebecca.

"Try everything," he suggested. "It's all good. I'm the cook."

Rebecca took a helping of everything with a broad yellow leaf utensil. As Torin had so modestly pointed out, the food was good, but she could not possibly have described the flavors to anyone back home. They were all unusual, with just the right amount of sweetness and spiciness, saltiness and sourness. Her favorite was some sort of thick round vegetable that reminded her a bit of potato, but with more flavor. Torin called it a Mangalan root, freshly erupted from the garden.

Rebecca ate until she was completely full, although she also managed to consume two dorsani cakes that had little pockets of honey inside them. At last everyone was finished eating, and Torin nudged Imanayon gently. "Aren't you going to tell Rebecca a story, Grandfather? Perhaps the one about the giant from her solar system, the one with a slice of moon, a cup of stars, a sip of Venus, a bite of Mars?"

Torin's grandfather shook his head, "Perhaps another time, Torin. Rebecca knows nothing of our beliefs, or why she is here. I thought to tell her our creation story and what we know of her purpose here among us. Lean back, and make yourselves comfortable, and I will tell you of the beginning of our world...

Once, long before this world was created and the night skies were full of emptiness, Mother Rhiate and Father Telches sang the universe into being. Father Telches created the galaxies, the stars and planets, while Mother Rhiate sustained them in the Great Pattern of her breath. All was fresh and bursting with energy. Father Telches and Mother Rhiate came together as mates, and from their union were born three daughters, the Princesses of the Universe, Teralina, Delaphina, and Niaphani.

Teralina, the eldest, was brilliant as the stars, patient as creation, and graceful as the motion of the spheres. Her hair and eyes sparkled with golden radiance, and when she spoke the galaxies whispered in awe. Delaphina, the second born, was deep and mysterious as space. Her hair rippled dark fire, and her eyes, black as obsidian, were wise beyond time. Niaphani, the youngest, had cascading emerald tresses and sea-blue eyes with the curiosity and richness of the universe itself. Each Princess had duties according to her abilities. Teralina assisted Father Telches with the creation of light and stars, Delaphina helped Mother Rhiate sustain the vast emptiness of space between and within all that exists, while Niaphani helped develop the lush greenery on the planets, the plants, flowers, and trees.

One eon, Teralina came before Mother Rhiate and Father Telches, announcing that she had found her consort. The two Creators of the Universe looked at each other in dismay.

"Who is this being?" demanded Father Telches with enough energy to cause a supernova nearby.

"It is I," said a voice, and a male being appeared before them. He looked vast enough, but Mother Rhiate and Father Telches were not impressed. The being draped one huge arm about Teralina, and introducing himself as Gravitos, informed them that he adored their daughter and had asked her to be his mate.

"Not so fast," thundered Father Telches, "what makes you think we would recognize such a puny power as yours as worthy of our daughter?"

Gravitos did not reply; he merely vanished. Rather than being alarmed, however, Teralina merely shrugged her exquisite shoulders, waiting patiently. Suddenly Mother Rhiate looked about, realizing that the universe was in trouble. Planets were beginning to leave their paths and move out of control. She immediately called the pattern back into order and Gravitos appeared before them.

"I may not be what you expected," he said quietly, "but my energy does have its purpose. I love Teralina and she loves me. Worth cannot be determined by power or recognition alone. Please give us your blessing."

Mother Rhiate and Father Telches realized they had been too hasty in their dismissal of Gravitos, and finally gave their consent to the union. Teralina and Gravitos were wed, remaining very happy together.

A few millennia later Delaphina came to her parents and informed them of her desire to marry as well.

"Who is he?" Father Telches demanded, pausing in his creation of a new galaxy.

As he spoke a brilliant light shone on them and a voice said, "I am Helios, the largest sun of the Androneocles galaxy. I love Delaphina with all the brightness of my being, as she loves me from the depths of hers. Please give us your consent to wed." Before them appeared a being whose radiance reflected Delaphina's depth and wisdom.

"Now this is ridiculous!" exploded Father Telches. Mother Rhiate tried to calm him, turning to Delaphina who stood smiling at her beloved Helios. "But how will he keep up with you, dear?" she protested. "He's really such a minor sun."

"I may be minor in the entirety of the universe," agreed Helios, "but my light is not without impact for the beings who depend upon me. I love Delaphina and she loves me, and that in itself proves worthiness, for your daughter is much too wise to choose one who is less than she deserves."

Mother Rhiate and Father Telches could not argue with that, for Delaphina's wisdom was well known throughout the entire universe. The two were married almost immediately and lived contentedly ever after.

Niaphani was bored. Her two sisters were wed and off inhabiting their own corners of the universe. She had completed her greening duties on the appropriate planets and had no intentions of making a fool of herself over some male being. With nothing new to do she decided to shrink herself down to visit one of her favorite planets. Donning a radiant sapphire gown, she grew smaller and smaller, finally appearing in a meadow by the side of a river.

Niaphani walked over to the river on bare feet, enjoying the feel of grass under her toes. She sat down, dangled her feet in the water, and let the cool liquid flow up to her ankles. All at once she felt a queer tickling feeling. She pulled her feet from the river, but saw nothing in the water. Again she dipped in her feet and felt the tickling. She pulled her feet out again, and leaned over to look more closely.

"Psst! Over here," she heard a voice say. Looking up she saw a young fellow dressed in tattered weed clothing floating on top of the river. He was completely barefoot. He sailed along downstream balancing on one foot, momentarily disappeared from view, and then popped out of the water again right back where he'd started.

Niaphani stood up, hands on hips, and demanded, "Who do you think you are, tickling me that way!"

"I know who I am," replied the being, with great good humor, "who do you think you are? Or don't you know?"

"I," said Niaphani, with an imperious nod of her head, "am Niaphani, Princess of the Universe, Daughter to Mother Rhiate and Father Telches, Creators of the Universe."

"Whew, what a title," said the being jauntily. "I am Heric, Sprite of the Water and Chief Enjoyer of Life. Would you care to join me?"

"I do not have the time for such frivolous activities," replied Niaphani shortly.

"Too bad," said Heric. He waved at her briefly before disappearing under water again, this time completely. Niaphani waited until she was sure he was gone and waded in to ride the waves herself. It was more difficult than it looked. She found herself swept along down the river, which had an exceedingly swift current. She fell in over and over until finally, completely soaked, she slapped the water in frustration.

"Easy there," said a voice, as two powerful hands clasped her about the waist and lifted her atop the water. "Balance with your mind first; your feet will follow," Heric said gently into her ear, not lessening his hold about her middle.

Niaphani found herself standing gently on the current. Heric let go. She was swept along laughing joyfully, until she remembered that a mere water sprite had dared to touch her royal person. Down she went under the water, later surfacing downstream. She swam quickly to the side of the bank and climbed out. Heric followed her, sitting down by her side.

"How can you bear always being this small?" Niaphani asked him, gesturing to her earthly body.

"I never feel small," Heric said. He grinned. "Kind of hard to balance upon one's dignity isn't it?"

Niaphani couldn't help but smile. "Perhaps, just a little. I really shouldn't bother spending much time talking to you though. You aren't worthy of my attention."

"How do you figure that?" asked Heric curiously, idly chewing a blade of grass.

"Well, you're only a water sprite, and I am me and you are you. It would be unfair of me to encourage your attentions. No female sprite could possibly compare to a Princess of the Universe."

"Don't worry, you haven't been encouraging at all," commented Heric. "But you do have some charm, despite your lack of manners, and your beauty, of course, is undeniable. Why don't you retire your pomp for a while, ride the waves with me? There's a lot you can learn from the water. I promise that once you leave this planet you won't have to waste time on such an unworthy fellow as myself."

Niaphani thought for a moment. Truly she had nothing better to do for a few millennia. Sometimes being the youngest was a bore.

"Very well," she agreed. "But I don't want to ruin your life, you know, by having you compare all other sprites to me. You would wind up alone and brokenhearted."

"Don't worry," said Heric cheerfully, "I won't let your beauty and brilliance blind me to your utter lack of humility. As to my heart, it will doubtless be shared with one who thinks the universe expands and contracts in my sea green eyes."

Niaphani looked at him doubtfully. It was true he was handsome in an earthly sort of way, and his good humor made him imperturbable. Her plain speaking had often overset her sisters, who'd explained that tact was a part of wisdom she would do well to cultivate. However, most of her cultivating skills had to do with plants and trees, for it was true that where she walked, plants blossomed.

"Enough concern for my all too loving heart," said Heric, reaching for Niaphani's hands to pull her to her feet. "Let us walk on water and ride the currents downstream."

Niaphani spent the next few centuries with Heric learning the depths and properties of water. At last she realized it was time to return to her regular duties. She bade Heric farewell rather regretfully, to her own surprise.

"Thank you for spending this time with me," she said sincerely, as she could not remember being so happily engaged since she had last blossomed a planet. She sighed a bit. She had grown fond of Heric and his humorous patience.

"The honor has been partly mine," Heric replied, bowing low before her until his head nearly touched the ground. "That your Gracefulness has honored me with your Divine Presence will be one of my notable memories, a tale I shall pass along to my grandchildren some day."

"Perhaps one day I will meet them myself," suggested Niaphani a bit wistfully. She would actually miss the irrepressible water sprite, unlikely though it seemed.

"I doubt it. You'll probably be too busy with your royal duties. And I did promise you that you would not be burdened with the presence of such an unworthy sort when we finally parted. Therefore, oh beauteous one, loveliest of Rhiate's daughters, blossomer of planets, and tolerator of my lowly self, farewell." He bowed again, and taking her hands in his, he kissed each palm with a resounding smack.

Niaphani trembled with the strangeness of her own response. "I do wish you'd be serious for once," she said crossly to Heric as he stood smiling, still holding her hands. Heric squeezed her hands gently and let them go, shaking his head ruefully.

"I don't think you're quite ready for that, Niaphani," he said, his green eyes no longer smiling. "Therefore, let us part on a joyous note. May your existence be full of discovery and many blossomings." Heric bowed once more. He waded into the river, turning briefly for a final wave before vanishing completely.

Niaphani felt curiously bereft and promptly berated herself for feeling so. It was definitely time to resume her work when leaving such a small planet caused such sadness. She expanded back out to her normal size, marveling that for so many centuries she had forgotten to feel small and constricted. She checked in with her parents, found a new group of planets to cultivate, and set to work. She concentrated fiercely, trying to work out her longing to see a pair of laughing green eyes and a ready grin. At last she finished her blossoming and found her mother waiting for her in the receiving room of the universe.

"Niaphani," said Mother Rhiate with approval, "there is a depth to your creativity that was hitherto absent. I am proud of your new maturity, daughter. Your Father and I think you are ready for more responsibilities. We have been discussing a new kind of being with the capability of greater awareness and have decided to give you the task of creation. Because our vision is a complex one, we have invited Life Force to assist you, he who has imbued water with its life-giving qualities. Please work with him in establishing these new beings we call humans."

"Very well, Mother," said Niaphani somewhat impatiently, "but there is something I need to do first. I'm afraid I am following in the path of my sisters. I seem to have developed a fondness for a being of questionable magnitude. I really must return to a certain planet before I begin a new course of creation."

"I'm sorry, dear," said Mother Rhiate firmly, " but you may not treat an honored guest with such little courtesy. Life Force is already here and even now awaits your arrival. Come and meet him before you gallivant off again."

Mother Rhiate gestured to Niaphani to acknowledge their approaching guest, who bowed low before her and smiled, his green eyes twinkling at her stunned expression. For the first time in her existence, Niaphani blushed like a startled sunset and immediately disappeared.

Mother Rhiate stared after her in confusion. Heric explained, "I forgot to mention that we have already met under less formal circumstances." Mother Rhiate nodded in dawning understanding as he added, "I'll go after her. I think I know where she's gone."

Sure enough, Heric found Niaphani sitting by the river on a small planet he knew quite well, staring disconsolately at the water. Heric sat down beside her, dangling his feet in the flowing green. They sat in silence for a while. Niaphani sighed. "So that is why I never felt small around you."

Heric nodded. "The size of one's form is no indication of the magnitude of one's being, or the depth of one's humility." He raised a hand to her chin and gently turned her face until he met her eyes.

"Niaphani," he said quietly, "I knew who you were before you arrived here. The entire universe knows of you and your sisters. I did not set out to deceive you, I merely allowed you to jump to your own conclusions. Technically, I am a water sprite, or more accurately, the spirit of water. I wanted to know if you could enjoy being with me in a less lofty incarnation. Once you let go of your own importance you were a most delightful companion.

When your mother and father asked for my help, I did not hesitate. I have looked forward to working with you, as joyfully as we once played. I think you have not been indifferent to me. In fact, I would guess that I made as much of an impression on you as you have on me. It must have been quite a blow to your dignity to find yourself attracted to a mere water sprite." He grinned mischievously. Niaphani smiled weakly in response, leaned over, and dipping her hand in the water, splashed him quite thoroughly.

"What was that for?" he asked, smiling through the drops that ran down his face.

"That was for tricking me," she said simply. She leaned forward and kissed him.

"And what was that for?" he asked, his green eyes wide.

"That was an apology for my arrogance," Niaphani confessed.

"Apologize some more," he demanded, taking Niaphani into his arms.

"I know that look," said Father Telches resignedly. Niaphani had stepped into his presence with a wondrous glow about her.

"Who is he?" he asked cautiously, knowing any protests he made would probably be futile.

"Don't worry, Father," said Niaphani, slipping her arms about him and kissing him on the brow. Father Telches wondered to himself how it was that he could easily let go of whole solar systems, but had such trouble when it came to his daughters. At that moment Heric stepped forward and Father Telches breathed a sigh of relief. "Thank the Great Pattern itself!"

So Niaphani and Heric were wed, and set about creating new beings called humans. They filled our world with the abundance and wonder that we share today, and acknowledged the worth of every living thing, which is all of creation. That is why we celebrate the miracle of life in each and every one of us."

## Chapter 3

As Imanayon stopped speaking, Rebecca glanced around and noticed that the sky outside was quite dark, though the stars still shed enough light to see by.

"That was really interesting," she said, mentally comparing it to creation stories back home. It seemed more real somehow, because the Princesses were like people, only bigger and more powerful. "I like how everyone is valuable, not just the princesses and their parents."

Imanayon stood up slowly, his joints creaking slightly, and nodded in agreement. "Yes," he said, "the value of all creation seems to have been forgotten on your world. That is partly why you are here. It is time to bring the memory of what was lost back to your people, so that they may remember their own worth, and the purpose for all things. You have many gifts that will help our world and yours, but you have not learned of them yet. It is difficult to use abilities you cannot even imagine, and so you are here to learn who you are. No one can know another's life path completely, but here we honor each other's knowing from birth. There are many things that you can do that we cannot, simply because of who you are, an Elemental Master.

In our world we have Folk attuned to each of the four elements, The Fire Folk, The Earthen Folk, The Air Folk, and The Water Folk. Once in a great while there are born those that may call all of the elements to them and through them. It has been a difficult responsibility for most of them, and I will not tell you that you have chosen a simple road. You may call upon us to assist you, in addition to all the elements of creation and the beings aligned with each."

Rebecca sat listening, and although some of it made sense in a strange kind of way, most of her felt like she'd just stumbled into a science fantasy novel and was unsure of the plot. Torin leaned over, nudging her shoulder. "Rebecca, it's really not as strange as you think. Imagine being born here and trying to handle a week in downtown New York. I thought the creator had disassembled my mind completely, although I did become fond of those yellow vehicles that move so quickly. The loud, honking machines, taxis, you call them."

Rebecca laughed, trying to picture Torin in a taxicab in the middle of the city. She suddenly realized what else was so different here. Missing were the background noises, of cars and airplanes, people shouting, foul air. Even the texture of the air felt different. Her lungs were able take more in; her breath had naturally fallen into a rhythm of ease. She noticed that her breathing had taken on the cadence of the pulse in her feet, and far from being alarmed, she was curiously relieved. Her posture had also changed, as if she'd grown taller, more upright.

"Even if I could understand what you're talking about," Rebecca said, hunching her shoulders in dismay, "I still don't understand. Why me? I mean; there are tons of kids who are smarter than me. I'm not like the kids in the science fiction or fantasy books, because they have something special about them. I mean, I might be a little odd, but this is all a bit much, don't you think?"

Torin immediately burst out laughing, tried to control himself, and ended up falling over onto the mossy ground. Rebecca stared at him in consternation.

"Please pay no attention to my grandson's lack of manners," Imanayon said. He moved over to sit next to Rebecca, while Torin tried to pull himself together. "But you seem to have no idea who you are and what you are able to do. Most children on Thianely know their lineage of lifetimes, the skills and tasks previously undertaken, and abilities already established. In present time we are all discovering our current paths, but we do have some idea of who we are, the magnitude of our full natures.

Torin is laughing at the idea that you are not capable of fulfilling your own destiny. Every being here is unique, and therefore special, though none more worthy than another. For now, you will have to accept that since you are here, there is much about yourself you do not remember. Many times, over the centuries, people from your place have been called here for training in our ways. They return to your world with such wisdom as they may share.

I promise you, Rebecca Bloom, that your self-knowledge will return. For now, you must trust the Creator and the Great Pattern that has brought you here, and also, despite his deplorable manners, my grandson and his strong ability to travel between worlds and time."

Torin rose to his feet shakily and bowed low before Rebecca. "I am sorry," he said somewhat sheepishly, his green eyes twinkling, "but it sounded humorous that you know yourself so little. I do apologize for mocking your world's ways. I was not trying to offend you. May Rhiate forgive me and may you as well."

Rebecca felt as if she'd wandered into a video game and someone else was at the controls. She sighed. "I'm not mad or anything, but I am confused. What exactly happened when I was sick? How did I get here and not remember? I feel like my brain isn't working properly."

"About six weeks ago, your time," Torin said, "I was cleaning the herb-drying room. Or you might say that I was asking it to clean itself."

Rebecca thought that self-cleaning rooms had to be one of the best things yet. Imagine not having to make your bed, dust, or vacuum at all! She could picture it, a completely transformed Earth, no pollution, no chores, no effort.

"The wall crystal began to glow," Torin continued, pulling Rebecca away from her dirtless musings. "Usually this happens only when someone is traveling through the spatial gate to our world. It means the portal is opening. All I could see was a vague shape, as if someone was visiting with only one of his or her bodies. You may not remember this, but we have other bodies in addition to our physical one. One of these bodies carries our emotions, another our mental activity, and so on. I could make out that this was a young woman's astral body, like when you're in the dream state.

I recognized that you were trying to access your previously acquired knowledge, but had no one to guide you there, so you'd come to us. We could see that you had developed a fever in order to separate your bodies enough to travel here. Grandfather decided that if you needed help so urgently for you to risk yourself this way, I ought to reach through time and space to bring you here. It wouldn't have worked if you weren't so gifted, but luckily your telepathic imaging is very keen. You saw me clearly, didn't you?"

Rebecca nodded, though what Torin had said made little sense to her except in a vague way. It was the same experience she'd had in her Algebra II class. Her brain was trying, but couldn't quite grasp the concepts.

"Your astral body has spent the last six weeks with us, mostly preparing yourself for your arrival here. That's why you have felt so divided from yourself. In addition, Grandfather and other Centerians have asked for help here on Thianely. Your arrival seems to have a twofold purpose, to assist us, and to remember your training for the benefit of your own world. Because our worlds are connected, the damage done on either planet always has some effect on the other. So it is with all things."

"I'm afraid I don't understand most of what you've said," Rebecca admitted. "I didn't know there are crystal gates and extra bodies that float around when we dream or get sick. No wonder I've been so strange the last few weeks, if part of me was here. I've been in two places at once! It makes sense, but only if I don't try to think normally. When I do I get a headache."

"It can be a stretch for your mind to take in all of this new information so quickly," Torin said. "Soon it will feel more like remembering and less like learning. Then your head will not ache so much. I had difficulties when I went to your planet; the sheer mind noise there is deafening."

"But what is the problem here on Thianely?" Rebecca asked in confusion. "It seems from the way you live that you don't have problems like pollution and overcrowding and violence. You don't even have window panes to keep out bugs."

Imanayon shook his head sadly. "It is true we do not have the same difficulties that your world does, but when Nature is upset, all things are upset. The very fabric of our reality is unraveling, and those of us who are of the Fire Folk, for instance, are finding that our abilities to work with the elements are being affected. For example, when Torin cooks our food he does so with the intention of heating it to the highest possible benefit to our bodies, where the nutrients are digestible and still potent. Lately, however, his ability to manifest this intention is being thwarted by something."

"Yes," interjected Torin ruefully, "I burnt not only the wood pulp toast, but also my own tunic. If I hadn't seen it with my own eyes, I would've said it was impossible. I mean, how can the embodiment of fire burn itself? Some strange separation must be occurring, and if we don't stop it, we here may all end up like most Folk on your world. They are so apart from the elements in which they live, they do not even remember themselves."

As Rebecca tried to decide if she should feel insulted or not, Torin placed his hands palm up towards her. He hummed quietly. His palms began to glow first red, then orange, then yellow and blue. Fire began to circle the centers in a series of raised rings, one inside the other, until he had two hands full of spiraling flames. Before Rebecca could even gasp, Torin made a high note in his throat and the fire died out instantly.

"See," Torin said casually, "here on Thianely we Fire Folk have the knack of fire-making. We rely on this ability to cook our food, travel, and protect ourselves, but somehow this expertise is being obscured. There is a gap between intention and manifestation that has simply never existed before. Something alters and obstructs purpose, working against the natural laws of our world.

Grandfather has proposed that we contact the other Folk and discuss this wide spread occurrence. With the help of the Air, Earthen, and Water Folk, we must find the center of Creation itself and recover the Great Balance. Unfortunately, no one here knows how to restore balance for an entire planet, so we asked for the Creators to send one who does know. That, Rebecca, must be you. Now you may understand better why I laughed to think of you feeling unworthy."

Rebecca sat stunned. Not a sound would come from her throat. She had seen magic so casually displayed she could not quite believe her eyes. She was too overwhelmed to comprehend what Torin had said.

"But I don't know where the center of anything is," she said finally, her voice trembling. "I don't understand most of what you're saying and sometimes it sounds like you're not even speaking English."

Torin put his arm around her shoulders. "I'm sorry," he said kindly. "I got a little carried away with our problems and I forgot you really just arrived. By the way, we aren't speaking English; your language is missing some of the concepts we need. We are actually communicating in the Old Tongue, the original language of all Star Folk. As soon as you arrived your mind switched to this speech. It is the language people on your world spoke as well, until the speech splintered during the Great Separation. But we can go into that another time."

"Yes," agreed Imanayon, noticing Rebecca's complete bewilderment. "Perhaps it is time to rest for the night. Torin, show Rebecca the way to her room again, while I clean up here. I may be up quite late conferring with the Devas, so please do not rouse me before dawn. Rest well."

Torin led Rebecca out of the eating room down the hall to her room. "Here you are," he said, motioning toward the open doorway.

Rebecca stared wearily at the clear crystal imbedded in the far wall.

"You're exhausted," Torin said suddenly, noting Rebecca's glazed look. "I have bombarded you with too much information, haven't I?"

"It's not so much that," Rebecca protested, sitting down on the bed, and holding her head in her hands. "It's that I've never seen anyone make fire come out of their hands before, and it scared me a little. I mean, you seem to think it's no big deal, but how am I supposed to get used to things like that?"

Torin sat down next to Rebecca and gently pulled her hands away from her head. "Look," he said, placing one hand palm up over hers. "See, a normal hand, nothing that will hurt you. I have spiral lines on my palm and fingers and my palm is cool. Now, look at your palm. It's like mine only without the spirals and with different lines. Now before you decide I'm some sort of dangerous fellow, let me show you something. I'm going to warm my hand with yours."

Torin put his left hand palm to palm with Rebecca's and began to hum. Rebecca could feel the middle of her palm begin to tingle.

"Now," Torin said, humming more strongly, "notice what happens next." His hand had begun to grow uncomfortably hot when Rebecca felt something very odd beginning to happen. A feeling like flowing water traveled down her head and up her legs, meeting Torin's palm through her own palm. Immediately, the heat between their hands began to subside. Rebecca looked at Torin questioningly.

"Now you've just experienced a gift inherent in Water Folk," Torin said, "that of cooling extreme heat. It isn't something you have to work at, it simply occurs naturally. So you know I can't possibly hurt you, Rebecca."

Rebecca sat staring at her palm for a while until the tingly sensation faded. "Torin, how long did it take you to become accustomed to my world? I mean, I've only been here for part of a day and it feels like a few months. Already I'm doing things and experiencing things I didn't even know were possible. How did you stand the rush and noise, the whole mess of Earth?"

Torin shrugged. "I didn't the first couple of times. I became ill from feeling the utter loneliness of most of the people there. I had to learn to shield and ground through the noise, through all the misery. Once I got so sick that I had to return home quickly, but I did find beauty there too. The song of your earth is still strong if you can listen. Mostly I felt the sorrow of so many that have separated from themselves and do acts and think thoughts that cause great pain. There was a man from your world who lived among us who said, "Forgive them, they know not what they do."

Rebecca gulped. "I think I know who you mean. In my world he was a great teacher, and some think even more than that. How did you know of him?"

"I met him a few times when I was very small. The gates allow Folk to visit other worlds and return with very little ripple effect. I remember he had luminous eyes and told wonderful stories, though he often seemed very sad. Everyone loved him here. He said that this was a peaceful place he would remember always. I often wondered what became of him, but Grandfather told me that no matter what happened to him in his world, he was always welcome wherever he went. I like to think he is still traveling somewhere, telling stories."

Rebecca sighed. "I'd like to think so too. Thank you for telling me this, Torin, and for showing me my watery hands. I'm still not sure what to do with any of this, but I suppose I'll figure it out."

"Surely you will, Rebecca," Torin said firmly, standing up and moving toward the door. "You're already doing very well. Sleep as long as you like, and feel free to explore the garden when you awaken. If you miss morning repast, there are always fruits and nuts outside. Ask the trees for what you need."

He waved briefly before he disappeared down the hallway to his own room. Rebecca quickly undressed, curling up on the bed. It was surprisingly comfortable. As she lay under the warm covers, she thought about everything that had happened so far.

"I wonder," she murmured, before sleep claimed her, "how Mom and Dad are handling all of this. I hope they don't worry too much. Maybe there's a way I can reach them to let them know I'm okay. This world is so extraordinary, but comforting too. What a fantastic place!"

## Chapter 4

Rebecca opened her eyes to soft daylight streaming in through the open windows. The light had a pink glow, and Rebecca sat up, feeling very refreshed. Although she still felt concerned for her parents, it was not a panicked kind of worry, only a quiet hope that they not be too upset. Somehow, the day seemed too promising for worries. She got up and dressed, absently wishing she'd packed a bag of clothes before she'd arrived. She wished for a toothbrush for a moment, mentally reminding herself to ask Torin for something to clean her teeth. She grabbed a piece of fruit, and bit into it, letting the turquoise juice run down her chin. It was delicious, tart and juicy, with a hint of mint.

Rebecca next used the waste room, wondering how she could read Thianelian books, yet not understand much of what she read. She wandered through the house stroking the smooth purple walls and feeling the gentle hum of the earth. It was quiet, without the ticking of clocks or the background hum of appliances. She didn't see Torin anywhere so she decided to head out to the garden for breakfast. When she asked the door to open, it did, causing her to smile in satisfaction as she stepped out into the fragrant beauty of the garden.

She walked round the path, smelling the flowers and soaking in the pink tinged sunshine, stopping now and then to touch a fuzzy stem or examine an unusual bloom. Torin had explained that the ground was dark purple due to high mineral deposits, which also colored the grass a lavender shade. Rebecca loved the contrast of the dark soil against the lighter lavender grass. After finishing the fruit she dropped the core onto the ground and watched it sink down into the soil and vanish. She shook her head in amazement.

"This place is something else!" she muttered aloud, stepping around a huge orange bush and continuing her stroll. "Here I am on a whole different planet, but I feel quite at home. I wonder if I actually died from my fever, and this is really heaven..."

"Ouch," interrupted a voice, "Why can't you look where you are going? Try getting your mind out of the sky and back into your feet while you're walking!"

Rebecca looked down and saw a very small, slender person wearing some sort of gauzy dress, standing on one foot and examining her other foot with considerable concern. The little woman couldn't have been more than a yard tall, but she seemed to have a much larger temper. Her naturally light blue skin was flushed red with anger, and her ears, long and pointed, quivered indignantly.

"I'm terribly sorry," Rebecca said, as she bent over to look at the little woman's foot. "Did I step on your foot? Is there anything I can do to help?"

"Well of course there is," the little person said disgustedly, "Put your hand on it and cool it off. You're of the Water Folk aren't you?"

Rebecca nodded, "So I've been told. I'm not quite sure what to do, but..."

"It's not something you do," said the little woman in exasperation, "It's who you are. Stick your hand right here and be yourself."

Rebecca placed her hand over the woman's sore foot, and again she felt the flowing of something rising from her feet and descending from the top of her head. The flowing met in her palms and coolness poured from them.

"Ah, that's better," the small woman said, pushing Rebecca's hand away and standing on both feet. She walked about experimentally, pronouncing herself satisfied.

"For an outworlder at least you have good manners. Here we hold ourselves responsible for alleviating any pain we cause. Too bad there aren't more like you on your planet. Give them time, I suppose. Now I must leave; it's time to call the rain."

She paused, as if trying to make up her mind about something. "I suppose you could come along and meet the others if you wanted. As one of the Water Folk you may even be of some help. Come along now."

Rebecca wasn't sure whether she should accept the invitation, but there was something about the woman's peremptory summons that made refusing difficult, and besides, she was just plain curious. So, she followed the little woman further down the path.

"What is your name?" she asked somewhat hesitantly, unsure of the politeness of her query.

The little woman stopped abruptly, her green-flecked eyes widening in surprise. "Bless Rhiate, I didn't even introduce myself! I am Rhianold, of the Devas. I am honored to meet you, Rebecca of the Water Folk, especially when you are not flattening my nether digits. I work with the other Devas to help create plant life here. Imanayon's garden is known well for its healing properties. Many members of the Devic kingdoms, The Water, Earth, Fire and Air Spirits, all live here together. Exquisite, isn't it?"

Rebecca looked about at the pink leafy stems, the lush blossoms of every color imaginable, took a deep breath of the scented air, and nodded. "It's the most beautiful place I've ever seen," she admitted. "I imagine this is what my world looked like when it was new."

Rhianold nodded, "Yes, and Thianely is full of such places. You should see the Threshold of the Tree Devas. Magnificent!"

She halted on the path and led Rebecca over to a thick bush of flowering shrubs, higher than Rebecca's head. "Follow me," she beckoned. Rebecca followed her into the wall of shrubbery, which seemed to part and make way for them. Inside the shrubbery walls it was cooler, as the high foliage blocked the sun. Just as Rebecca began to feel uncomfortably cool, Rhianold motioned her under a viny overhang, dotted here and there with multicolored flowers. Rebecca stepped under the arch and into an enormous meadow, where many of Rhianold's folk were clustered in small groups. Rhianold put a slender hand on Rebecca's wrist and drew her forward, onto the grassy field, a long lavender expanse with clumps of wildflowers.

"Sit here," Rhianold ordered, pushing Rebecca onto a soft hump of grassy earth. Rhianold clapped her hands together and to Rebecca's astonishment, unfolded a pair of gauzy wings from her back. She fluttered them quickly, like hummingbird wings, and flew about the meadow, exhorting her people to gather together. As Rebecca watched, Rhianold's folk, who ranged in skin color from blue-green to light brown and pale yellow, unfolded what Rebecca had thought were clothes into large wings that carried them to their places in an enormous circle, of which, Rebecca noticed with some dismay, she sat at the center. She was also the only one who appeared be wearing clothes of any kind.

First Rhianold made sure everyone was settled into his or her proper place. Then she approached Rebecca at her central location, bowing low before her. Rebecca sat, unsure whether she ought to stand and bow in return. Finally she merely nodded her head politely.

Rhianold smiled. Whirling around to face her people she cried, "It is time for the raining of the garden, and today we have one of the

Water Folk here. Let us honor her with our song. May Rhiate bless us and the purpose for which we create." Rhianold raised her arms into the air, signaling for the entire company of Devas to sing. They circled slowly around Rebecca in a winged dance.

"Circles of Rain dance round
Dance round the sun in radiant sound
Dance round, dance round...

We call them forth in springed song
To lush the leaves and wildflowers long
Dance round, dance round...

In ecstasy the earth gives birth
She loves us all and knows our worth
Dance round, dance round...

Bows of rain complete their bent
Fulfill themselves in circlement
Dance round, dance round...

Let us cherish this new ground
Dance round, dance round..."

Slowly the dancing circle stopped. The Devas began to move in the opposite direction, again chanting loudly with their wings outstretched. Now and then they would completely lift off of the ground so that the entire circle would be dancing in mid air, their wings outstretched like gauzy butterflies. Above them the sky grew deeper and deeper pink, until at last Rebecca felt drops of warm rain trickling down her face and arms and hair.

As she laughed in sheer delight, Rebecca tasted the raindrops, fragrant as flowers and sweet as nectar in her mouth. She giggled, to think that even the rain here had flavor. The water coursed down her face, her arms, and her legs, soaking her clothes until Rebecca could no longer separate herself from the drops of rain falling from the deep pink sky. She was the whole world, falling in liquid sweetness to the ground. She could have sat there forever, soaking in the sensation of being water, but Rhianold tugged her to her feet.

"You must not stay out here too long," she said, hovering in the air and using the force of her wings to propel Rebecca out of the meadow and under the viny arch. Rebecca noticed that all the other Devas had gone. She and Rhianold were the only ones left.

"You would have become drunk on all that rain if you'd stayed, and you'd be no good to anyone, including yourself." Rhianold grasped Rebecca firmly by the wrist, marching her back through the shrubbery and onto the path. Rebecca felt extremely happy, and quite as silly as she had when she'd tasted some of her parents' liquor.

"It was delicious," she protested, wishing she could return to the meadow and drink more rain. Out on the path it was quite dry. She would have noticed that the dampness of her clothing was uncomfortable, but by then she wasn't registering much of anything. She walked a bit unsteadily and would have fallen once or twice had Rhianold not had a strong grip on her arm.

Torin met them halfway back to the house. He looked at the state of Rebecca's clothes and at the huge smile on her face. "Rain dazzled," he grinned, as Rhianold shrugged. "Come back to the dwelling, Rebecca," he prompted, taking her arm from Rhianold and letting her slump against him. "We're expected to go to the council of Centerians since Grandfather has called a meeting for later today. I hope we can get you back on the ground before then."

"I have some root powder that should help," offered Rhianold. "I'll have one of the Devas bring it by shortly."

She bowed low before Rebecca and inclined her head to Torin. "Greetings to Imanayon. We will be waiting for word of the council's plans to assist Thianely. We will do as much as we are able to assist the Folk. Farewell for now." Rhianold waved her wings goodbye and floated off above the garden.

Torin put an arm around Rebecca, who was still unable to stand upright. "Come on, we'd better get you back to the house and let you lay down for a bit. We've still time before we're expected at the council."

Rebecca smiled, leaning her head on Torin's shoulder. "It was quite lovely," she murmured. "All the singing and dancing. The rain tasted of flowers, all the tastes you've ever smelled, all the smells you've ever tasted. Each drop was a separate flavor, and inside the flavors were colors of drops, and inside each drop was the whole world. Your world and my world and little raindrop worlds all falling down..."

"Yes, I know," Torin said, helping her in through the door to the house. He tugged her gently along the hall into her room. "Why don't you change into some dry clothes? Grandfather found these for you." Torin motioned to a neatly folded stack of clothes at the end of the bed. "I'll be right back. I'm going to see if the Devas have brought the root powder."

Rebecca lay on the bed, feeling totally and completely happy, with the taste of rain flowers in her mouth and visions of Devas dancing before her eyes. Torin returned shortly with an enormous purple flower petal cupped between his hands.

"Here, Rebecca, sip this." He poured the powder mixed with water into Rebecca's mouth as she closed her eyes dreamily. All at once the feeling of euphoria diminished, and Rebecca sat up.

"Did I dream that, or were there really little funny-colored people dancing naked round the garden?"

Torin sat down on the bed beside her. "No dream. Those were the garden Devas. You got completely rain dazzled from drinking too much. They might have guessed that it would affect one of the Water Folk more strongly than the rest of us. We usually feel quite refreshed and lively. I'd have to drink gallons to be as affected as you were after so little, Rebecca. We'll just have to be careful about what sorts of elemental food you try; you may react oddly to other edibles on Thianely."

"I didn't have any trouble with dinner," Rebecca said, swinging her legs over the edge of the bed, and gingerly trying to stand. Torin arose also, waiting by the bed for her to get her ground legs back.

"That's because dinner was cooked and pretty inert. The rain is straight from the Sky Source, and its potency is undiminished by interaction with fire or ground. The air helped infuse it with enough extra energy to completely inebriate you. But you look recovered enough to stand at council. Go on and change into some dry things. I'll get you some food to break the night's fast."

Torin paused for a moment and cocked his head as if listening. He nodded briefly, responding to someone Rebecca could not see. Turning to Rebecca he motioned for her to hurry. "We need to feed you now, since Grandfather says the council is convening soon. It's almost time for us to make an appearance."

"Can you hear your Grandfather in your mind?" asked Rebecca, wondering what else Torin could do.

"Oh yes, we can all hear each other when we wish to, although it's possible to block out another's thoughts when you wish to be undisturbed. I would never have survived in your world if I couldn't." He pushed open the door. "I'll wait for you outside."

Rebecca looked over the stack of clothes. There was a pink, short-sleeved tunic like the green one Torin wore, a soft skirt of deep green patterned with tiny pink flowers, that when closely examined proved to be real, and sewn so tightly into the fabric that they seemed to be part of the material. The garments were soft and comfortable, as were the undergarments made of some fleecy material in a sky blue color. There were also green socks and slippers, which seemed thin and weightless, but which gave a lot of support. Rebecca felt as if she were walking on firm clouds.

She finished dressing and asked open the door. Torin nodded approvingly, motioning for her to follow him. He led her through the hall, and into the eating space. As soon as Rebecca had eaten her fill of the roots, nuts, fruit and oatcakes, they stepped out the front door and back out into the pink sunshine.

# Chapter 5

Looking about, Rebecca could see that Imanayon's house was at the top of a hill. As they descended, she noticed more dwellings set into the base of the hill, appearing as if they grew right out of the landscape. She counted nearly fifty altogether, and like Imanayon's house, they too were round at the top, with flowery walls and grassy roofs. Torin led Rebecca along the packed earth road, occasionally waving at children of various ages playing in the grassy fields between houses. He explained that the roads too had been asked into place, and the earth compressed itself smooth in order to make walking easier. Rebecca thought about all of the road construction crews on Earth, and shook her head at the ease with which Thianelians lived.

"Why are the children playing without any adults nearby?" Rebecca asked.

"The older children often tend the younger, and of course, everyone is only a thought away. All adults among us keep their thoughts open for the benefit of the children. Fathers and mothers share a special physical bond with their own offspring, but everyone is connected by thought. One of the first things children are taught is to respect each other's mind space. Otherwise, no one would have a private moment.

And we are not a very crowded planet," Torin added. "Most of our villages hold no more than a few thousand Folk, which is very unlike one of your cities. Thianely as a whole has nowhere near even your country's population, and I include those beings other than human in form. We don't tend to reproduce in large numbers. The mind noise would be overwhelming, as it does take energy to block so many thoughts.

That is also why the council meeting happens only once or twice a year, because anyone can speak to the Centerians if they need to, if they are out of balance somehow or having a problem. Centerians are chosen for their strength of mind and their empathic abilities, and it doesn't hurt to have a high sensitivity for long-range telepathic communication. Like you, for instance."

"Like me?" Rebecca repeated, almost laughing. "I can't hear anyone's thoughts, I'm only a regular person."

Torin shook his head. "I'm not going to challenge your lack of self knowledge, Rebecca. You'll have to wait and see. Come along, we're almost there."

He led her off the main road and down a grassy path into a sheltered meadow. As Rebecca watched, perhaps fifty to sixty Fire Folk, including men, women and several children, came together in a large circle in the center of the meadow. Torin led her directly to the circle, and people made way for them until they had become part of the group. Everyone smiled and nodded to Rebecca, making her feel welcome. Most of the Folk were dressed in clothing similar to hers and Torin's, the women in skirts and the men in long tunics with trousers underneath. The colors were rich and warm, and the gathering of people made a bright ring in the meadow.

They stood waiting until Imanayon stepped forward into the center of the circle from his place in the ring. Although she heard no sound with her ears, it seemed to Rebecca that she heard him speak somewhere inside her head.

"I stand in council, Imanayon, Centerian of the Fire Folk. I ask permission to tel." Rebecca could feel a thought of assent from the group. It was a strange; she heard their thoughts in her mind, but it was if they were spoken aloud. Each person's thoughts were distinctly recognizable, as if thought and voice were inseparable. Her mind tingled a little, unfamiliar with the sensation of hearing thoughts directly.

"As you all know," Imanayon said, although Rebecca noticed that his lips did not move at all, "the Deva's and Sprites, as well as the Folk of the Four Elements, have noticed a huge rending in the fabric of universal law. Something is causing this unraveling in the natural laws, and we must discover how to heal this before we become separated from one another and even ourselves. Perhaps even, if this remains unchecked, from Thianely itself." Rebecca thought she could hear a huge gasp from the collective at this, but again it was soundless.

"You also know that the councils of Centerians have called to Rhiate for help. We shortly thereafter received a message from the gatekeepers that a young woman was attempting to answer our call, but was forced to disassociate in order to do so. At extreme danger to herself, she sent her astral body through the gate in order to offer her assistance. Torin pulled her here through the crystal gate in my home. The information we Centerians have received is that balance can only be reestablished by finding the center of Creation. None of us really knows what such a center might be. This being, called in her world, Rebecca Bloom, has answered our call. On her world however, children are not told of their previously acquired wisdom and lifetimes of learning. Innate abilities and inner knowledge are seldom encouraged.

We must assist her in remembering her true nature, and with the help of the Fire, Earthen, Air, and Water Folk, she may find her way to center. I am proposing that she travel to the Threshold of the Tree Devas to receive information from the Great Tree, thus she may know of her lives and gain some grasp of her abilities. My grandson, Torin, will accompany her. We have already consulted Meridwen of the Trees and she has offered her assistance in this matter as well. In the meantime, the more minds we can link in this matter, the better. I'm asking that all of those with any long range abilities be on call until we can shift the Great Balance back to center."

Imanayon stepped back into his place in the circle, and another man stepped into the center.

"I stand in council, Doronam of the Fire Folk. I ask permission to tel."

Again there was a thought of agreement that traveled among the Folk.

"I think we should put out a long range call to the other Folk immediately and have a Grand Council among us all. The Centerians have contacted each other, but what of the rest of us? We have a say in the decisions of our Folk. Who knows how long it will take for Rebecca of the Water Folk to recover her memory? Remember the world from which she comes! Those of us who have traveled there know some of the obstacles she faces. There may be others among the Air or Earthen Folk who have elemental mastery. The Great Tree would know." Again, there was a consensus of thoughts among the circle as Doronam regained his place.

This time a woman with long silver hair stepped from her place and entered the center.

"I stand in council, Keroni of the Fire Folk. I ask permission to tel." She bowed slightly to Rebecca, who was feeling uneasy at the thought of so many people debating her fate.

"You are aware that I am a wind watcher. I have followed the tides of Air, through our realm and those of the other Folk. I have spoken to the wind that blows clear across our Thianely and it brings such dreadful news! The Earthen Folk have lost their connection to the Gate of Time. Earth shifts are happening without warning, causing great devastation, and there has been no success in stopping them. The Air Folk have noticed strange currents that rip and gouge the fabric of the skies. You all know what has been happening with our own Fire abilities. Even such Water Folk as still dwell in our seas are struggling; some unbalanced force has laid waste deep beneath the waves. They spend much of their time clearing their watery home just to survive.

This rift in our world grows wider and the disastrous results become more apparent every moment. I say we send the young woman to Meridwen and the Great Tree right away. We cannot discount the fact that she has come so far. Nor can we discount the prophecy of the Old Ones. At the same time, I agree that we must come together with the other Folk and see what can be done. Perhaps there are other beings that have arrived among them to help us all. One never knows how the Creators will answer our prayers."

This time as Keroni stepped back into place, Rebecca could hear a huge wave of sound, a keening coming from the Folk around her. The sound grew louder and higher, pressing against her ears, her body, her mind, until her brain felt as if it would crack in half. She fell to the ground, clutching her head, trying to stop the piercing sharpness that sliced right through her. Torin immediately dropped down beside her. Clasping both of his hands over her ears, he began to rock her gently. The sound quieted, diminishing to a hum, and finally faded completely.

She heard the voice of Torin's thoughts softly in her mind. "Rebecca, you need to renew your mind shield; the power of our response has broken through. I'm holding it for now, but the force of our grief for Thianely is hurting your mind. I want you to imagine a shield, a strong colorful barrier, that increases in thickness whenever you need it to, but diminishes when you don't."

Rebecca sat up, sobbing. The whole thing was too much. She wanted to go home. At Torin's insistence she tried to picture a blob of color around herself, but had to shake her head at the idea that her imagination would be her only protection. Still, it seemed to help. But for a bunch of people who had learned about respecting one another's thoughts, she wasn't too impressed by the Thianelians so far. She pushed Torin's arms away and stood up, walking angrily out into the circle.

"I am Rebecca and I'm going to mindspeak whether you like it or not. I don't think you understand what it's like to show up in a place where people treat you like you're an idiot. Ever since I got here everyone has been telling me that I don't know myself, and I'm here to do some big job, and I'm not really only a teenager from planet Earth. I've been told that I can hear people's thoughts and travel through gates without my body and with my body and I'm of the Water Folk and my planet stinks and people there are lost from themselves.

Well, I guess I don't mind helping. And apparently I can hear other people's thoughts, because you people certainly gave me a headache! I don't know what an Elemental Master is, I don't know what most of you are talking about, and it turns out that I'm not even speaking my own language. I don't like you all discussing me as if I don't have any say in what happens to me. Right now I can't even think straight! On my planet I'm not old enough to have mastered anything, and I don't know much about the elements except what little I've studied in chemistry. Maybe they aren't even the right elements, because nothing seems to work here the way I'm used to. I've been here two days and already I've seen more strange things than most people I know have seen in their whole lives.

Maybe in books everyone quietly accepts that they're having a magical experience and they go along and save the world or whatever. But this is real life! I'm a real person with feelings and maybe this place does seem familiar, but I'd appreciate it if you would all give me a break, okay?" She ran quickly from the center, pushed through the ring of Fire Folk, and raced back up the grassy path out of the meadow.

Rebecca soon found herself back out on the dirt road. She strode angrily away from the direction of Imanayon's house, although that was mostly a guess. She realized she couldn't tell directions, although the pink sun was directly overhead.

"I bet the sun changes its course all of the time too, depending what it feels like," she muttered crossly, having to admit that she was a little lost without the reliability of east, west, north, and south. There were no more dwellings in sight, only rolling hills covered in lavender grass. Occasionally she saw clusters of trees with thick blue trunks and multicolored leaves on the tips of their twisting branches.

Finally, out of breath, she stopped by the side of the road and sat glumly down in the grass. She lay back with her eyes closed, feeling the warm sun on her face, the soft grass beneath her. All at once she felt a pang of homesickness. She missed the bright yellow sun that hurt her eyes, the comfort of her own room, and her parents' familiar faces. She wished she could see them, at least to let them know she was okay.

"At least, I think I'm okay. I wonder what they would think if they could see me now, stuck on a strange planet where everything is so different and familiar at the same time." As she lay there feeling homesick and not homesick at once, she felt soft tickles as if ants were trailing up her arms.

"Oh great," she thought, "now the ants are going to bug me too." She opened her eyes to see what sort they were, and found herself being sprinkled with flower petals. They had settled on her arms and all over her tunic and skirt. The little creatures that were sprinkling them fluttered gaily around her. They were no more than a few inches tall and wore flower petals wrapped around their middles. Their wings tickled her face as they flitted by. Then she heard them begin to sing in surprisingly clear voices:

"See the angry Child of Water,
Sullen faced Rhiate's daughter
Humor helps to heal the mood
That occurred in council, rude.
Here we sprinkle a flower petal
All to help her temper settle.
Tickle her skin and tickle her toes,
Scents of flowers up her nose.
Now we see she smiles at last,
The bitterness has all flown past."

Rebecca couldn't help but laugh. It seemed she would not be able to wallow in misery for very long. She smiled at the little sprites and sat up, scattering flower petals all over the grass. As she looked about at the rolling hills of grass, the beautiful, clear pink sky, she noticed a strange figure coming towards her.

There was nothing particularly menacing about the fellow, who wore richly colored clothes and a tall, multicolored hat perched high on his head, which made him look much taller than his normal height. He strode over the grass with a jaunty air, scattering the sprites from around Rebecca with a careless wave. Rebecca, who'd gotten to her feet, could have sworn that one of the little people tried to bite his hand. The man stood before her with twinkling brown eyes and a crooked grin. He doffed his hat with a flourishing bow.

"Darden Bollux, at my service. And you must be the one we've all been waiting for, Rebecca of the Water Folk. Delighted to make yourself known to me, and likewise I'm sure."

Rebecca stuck out her hand. "Nice to meet you. Where did you come from, anyway? I didn't see you a little while ago and there's really only grass around here. You weren't at the meeting, I don't think."

Privately Rebecca thought that there was certainly no way she could have missed him, with his swirling cloak and tall pointed hat. He looked completely unlike any of the others she'd seen, as he was a bit taller and thinner, almost prehensile looking, as if he could tie himself easily into knots. He had a long, narrow face and a small orange beard that matched his high-peaked orange hair. His tunic, bright crimson with blue swatches, hung over rust colored trousers. His whole outfit was curiously blowzy, swirling about him like a strong wind. He examined her hand as if it were a particularly disgusting rodent, so Rebecca dropped it back to her side, wondering if perhaps Thianelians frowned on handshaking.

"I came from here and there, mostly there and now and again and sometimes why," Darden replied casually. "You not being from here wouldn't understand my methods of transporting myself else and not elsewhere. But say, how do you like our little Thianely so far? Myself, I find it a bit dull now and later, with an occasional then and whom to liven things up."

Rebecca began to wonder if she'd met her first mentally ill person on Thianely, for certainly no one else could possibly talk so oddly. Part of the time she could make out what he meant, and she wondered if that meant she was a little sick in the head herself. She began to edge backwards towards the road again, wondering if Torin was within hailing distance. She tried to call to him mentally, but didn't hear anything in response. As a matter of fact, her mind seemed to be wandering, for she had a hard time following what Darden Bollux was saying.

"But unseriously now," Darden said, somehow moving in front of her retreat, "don't you find it a bit comical that you, of all people, should be stuck on a little planet like this when you could be off about your business some place more worthy of you? Certainly your world in itself would be more of a challenge, or at least not so stupidly simple. Oh my," he said suddenly, bending forward to peer into her confused face, "I forgot, you are stupidly simple! You have forgotten yourself completely. Ha! That's a great trial to the Folk I'm sure, but how lovely, how delightful for the rest of us."

He smiled gleefully and clapped his hands together, scattering more sprites that clung tenaciously to his sleeves. Rebecca turned to run, and found she could not move her legs. She stood frozen, completely terrified. Darden came closer and smiled again, displaying long narrow teeth.

"Don't worry, I only bite worthy opponents. In your current state you're no fun at all. Even I am not so heavy brained to harm one such as you, at least not till I have my delightfully vile brethren about. But don't think your fullness of memory will ever really protect you from us. There are those of us who like the seesaw side of things, you know. Oh, that's so right, you don't know! You don't even remember how to undo a simple still-rite. Oh bother, this is no sport at all. I'll see you again, Rebecca of Nothing, when you've become less mindless. Pity really, I must confess Thianely will be no trouble at all with you as the answer to the prophecy. Thank you for this moment's merriment, this instant's entertainment."

Again Darden bowed mockingly low, and then he spun about, disappearing right in front of Rebecca's astonished eyes. She struggled to move her legs, unsuccessfully. Again she mentally yelled to Torin, wishing he would hurry up and hear her. Suddenly the frozen feeling vanished, so quickly that she found herself sprawled on the ground. She lay there, shuddering for a moment. Being unable to move had been ghastly; she'd felt totally helpless, and she couldn't remember ever having being so completely insulted right to her face.

She finally picked herself up, listening to the sprites as they fluttered around her, murmuring soothingly.

"Darden Bollux cannot hurt you
Even if the powers desert you.
All the sprites your friends shall be,

Help will always come, you'll see!"

Rebecca hoped so. She started back down the road towards Imanayon's house, wishing she understood what was happening a little more. So far, nothing made much sense. She hadn't been walking for long when she heard Torin's voice like a whisper in her head.

"Rebecca, are you well? It's Torin, I ask permission to tel."

Rebecca shook her head. Then she realized Torin couldn't see her. "No, I'm not well!" she said furiously. She could almost hear Torin wince.

"Rebecca, your tel range is very far. I need to ask you to turn down the volume a bit. You're too loud."

"Sorry, Torin," she replied, "but I'm still mad. This creepy guy showed up, told me I wasn't worth biting, and scared the heck out of me. I thought you were supposed to be only a thought away. What took you so long?"

"Everyone was recovering from your outburst. You have high volume anger. We had to close our minds to recover, so I didn't hear your call until afterwards."

"So you have something like mental call waiting?" Rebecca asked interestedly, forgetting her temper for a moment.

"Something like that," Torin replied. "I'm sorry it has been so difficult for you, Rebecca. We've been so caught up in our own problems we didn't take into account how it must be for you. Also maybe we overestimated the influence of books in your world. You see; most of the fantasy stories written are an attempt to provide some truth. We assumed it would be somewhat adequate preparation for traveling here, because at least the ideas had been introduced. It appears that most of it isn't taken very seriously on your planet, but we hoped it would be enough. I truly am sorry."

"That's only part of why I'm upset," Rebecca said shortly. "Where are you anyway? I can't believe I'm talking to you in my head as if it's normal."

"I'm still standing council," Torin said, "and it looks like it may be a long one. Your leaving disturbed us, as well as the tenor of your mind. We have a certain tradition in making visitors welcome. We realized that we've not done a very good job so far."

"Bother all that," Rebecca said crossly, still making her way back along the road. She could see some of the houses they'd passed earlier and knew she was getting close to Imanayon's. "What I want to know is, who is Darden Bollux and why is he showing up out of thin air and threatening me? He mentioned some prophecy, thoroughly insulted me, and made it so my legs couldn't work!"

If someone's thoughts could suddenly stop, then that's what Rebecca felt Torin's do. All of a sudden it felt like a door closed. When the door opened again, Rebecca could hear Torin's thoughts, but without any feeling attached, like reading a book without any expression, or hearing a monotone voice.

"So, you met one of the Bolluxes?" Torin asked casually. "Tell me, what did he say exactly?"

"Why should I tell you?" Rebecca replied somewhat rudely. "You don't trust me enough to tell me what's really going on. I'm in danger here, aren't I? And it has something to do with a prophecy and that weird Bollux guy. I'm getting tired of being told how much I don't know, and you won't tell me what's going on."

Torin sighed. "Rebecca, I can't go into this right now, but I will, as soon as council ends. Why don't you go back to Grandfather's house and we'll meet you later. I'll tell you about the Bolluxes and the prophecy and all that I know about you. In the meantime, why don't you go sit in the garden for a while and rest? We'll probably be leaving for the Threshold of the Trees in a few days. It's quite a journey."

Rebecca heard Torin's voice switch off abruptly as she reached Imanayon's house. She decided to go straight to her room and lay down. The encounter with Darden had really shaken her up. It was like one of those dreams where she was falling and couldn't catch herself, finally waking before she hit the ground. She pinched her arm to make sure, but as she suspected, she didn't wake up and her arm hurt.

"It seems like everyone expects so much of me, and so little," she thought sadly, laying on the bed and closing her eyes. "At home I had chores and homework like all of my friends, but here I'm the answer to some prophecy, or at least," she reminded herself, "some of them think so. That Darden guy was so weird, and creepy in a familiar kind of way, as if his very friendliness was the worst part. Someone who would enjoy pulling wings off flies." She shivered. "I don't feel particularly masterful at anything, anyway," she reflected, "except maybe school. But I don't think good grades there count much for understanding this place. And what will I be like when I get home? God, I hope I'm not who they think I am; at home I'd be a total freak."

She closed her eyes, picturing her parents. "They're probably worried to death about me," she thought miserably, finally understanding that she probably couldn't go home any time soon. Here she was, missing school, and none of her friends knew where she was either. At least she was learning a lot, even though most of it wouldn't make much earth sense. The Threshold of the Trees sounded intimidating, although there was some consolation in the thought that if the Great Tree knew who she was, maybe she could go home sooner.

"They'll find out I'm merely a regular person and then I can go back. Earth may be full of violence and crime, but at least people don't fire up their hands and disappear right in front of your face or talk in your head when they need to reach you. Nobody there thinks kids are that great anyway." She tried to imagine a girl her age having a say in government, and had to laugh, considering she wouldn't even be able to vote until she was 18. She remembered the circle of people standing council and realized there had been children even younger than she and Torin.

She lay down for a while, but realized she felt better when her feet were on the ground. She went out into the garden and sat down by a small cluster of spiky flowers. She absently began to run her fingers through the purple earth, finding it strangely soothing having the warm soil spilling through her hands. She watched a Thianelian equivalent of an insect land on one open bloom and weave a sort of cocoony web, which was promptly inhabited by a plump sprite who pulled the web about her like a blanket and began to doze.

Rebecca lay back, watching the activity of the garden flow along in front of her, quite content all of a sudden. Water Devas sprinkled liquid mists over plants and trees to keep them hydrated, while Earth Devas smoothed the soil, harvesting the small tubers and roots that erupted periodically from the mounds of earth nearby. Air Devas created mild breezes to rustle the leaves, which allowed ripe fruit to drop gently into the Earth Deva's viny baskets. Fire Devas lit small bonfires and cooked, then cracked, the hardened cocoons of melworms. Once freed, the small, wriggling creatures burrowed deep underground to deliver nutrients to hungry roots.

As she lay back and observed, Rebecca realized that she could hear it all, the sounds of fruit ripening, melworms wriggling, leaves falling, even the quiver of the trees growing. It created a song, a gentle fullness of sound that steadied her, calmed and comforted her, like a lullaby. Some time later, Torin found her dozing in the garden, curled up on the ground as if Thianely itself were rocking her to sleep. He sat down beside her, letting the warmth of the garden soothe him as well, and watched the rise and fall of Rebecca's breath, the curling strands of her wavy hair, the flicker of her eyelids moving as she slept.

He sighed, wishing things were not so complicated, that they had weeks to spend relaxing and letting her acclimatize to Thianely. In the garden it was difficult to believe that Thianely was in trouble, and if he had not recently burnt himself making dinner, he wouldn't have been able to accept it at all. How much harder it must be for Rebecca, who had so much more to remember.

He sat in stillness for a time, until finally Rebecca began to stir and sit up. She stretched and opened her eyes, catching a brief glimpse of Torin sitting quietly with his eyes closed. He looked older somehow than she had first thought, as if he had carried more responsibility at a younger age than she.

"Hi, Torin," she said, as he opened his eyes slowly. "I'm not mad any more."

"The garden has a way of doing that," Torin replied, shifting to a more comfortable sitting position. He had asked the earth to form a kind of support behind him, and he settled back against it, prompting Rebecca to do the same.

"I ought to know," he added ruefully. "Anger is one of my most familiar emotional states."

Rebecca looked at him in surprise. "You? I thought you were perfect."

Torin made a face. "The belief in perfection as a goal does not exist here. It implies that the present is imperfect. Perfection then becomes a stagnant state that is not only unattainable, but creates lack of appreciation for the present. On Earth many of your folk feel ashamed about themselves. On Thianely everyone is aware of the changing nature of all in Creation. If you know and accept who you are in any moment, shame cannot live inside you. When I had to learn about shame before I traveled to your planet, it was a very difficult concept for me to grasp. We do not compare ourselves to others unfavorably here in the way that you do on Earth. We feel our feelings and grieve fully, by accepting what is. It's the first step in resolving difficulties. Unless you acknowledge what is occurring, you can do nothing to help.

I spent a great deal of time being angry as a child because I never knew my parents. Imanayon found me in an ash pit, in the aftermath of a great fire. Even the Great Tree could not tell me about my mother and father. I became frustrated over my loss and spent many hours in the garden. There is growth here, but death also. The plants and trees mature and grow old, then finally decay and pass away. Everything grows beyond and moves through seasons. I did too."

"I'm sorry," Rebecca said, unable to imagine not having her parents. "I've been thinking about my mom and dad too. Is there any way I can get word to them that I'm okay?"

"I think it's possible you could send a message through the crystal gate, but I'm not sure they would consider it anything other than a dream, as you did when you first started visiting us," Torin replied thoughtfully. "You might try it when you go to sleep tonight. Picture them and tell them whatever you wish. Then ask the crystal in the wall to send your message."

Rebecca sighed, relieved that at least there was a chance they might know that she was alive. "Torin, how old are you anyway?" she asked curiously.

Torin frowned and thought for a moment. "I think I'm about 17 or 18 of your years, but to tell the truth, I never could figure out your time translated to ours. It's not a consistent linear sort of time we have. How old do you think I am?"

Rebecca shrugged. "I thought you were younger, because it looks like you don't shave."

Torin nodded. "You mean the removal of the hair on one's face. I ask it not to grow there to save me the trouble. Few of the Folk bother to grow facial hair unless they are traveling in the northern region."

"So you do have north, south, east and west?" Rebecca asked.

"Well, sort of, at least for the purpose of overland maps. We have both elemental maps and overland maps. I will show you the difference before we set out on our journey. But the real word for northern is Rythen, which translates as the place where liquid becomes solid, fire cools, and movement slows. I will continue to use your direction words though, as will most of the Folk you meet. It is obvious that your thoughts are different than ours and it is polite to use concepts that make another feel comfortable."

"I'll be 17 in a month, at least in my time," Rebecca said wistfully. "It's almost fall at home and my birthday is coming soon. Do you think I'll be home for it?"

Torin reached over and draped an arm over her shoulders. "Actually, no. But even though we don't make a big occasion of our birth time here, I promise I will not forget."

Rebecca nodded and sighed, relaxing against the solid comfort of Torin's side. It was comfortable to be sitting next to him on the warm ground. She blushed as she realized that she hardly knew him. She pulled away and got to her feet. "Tell me about that weird Bollux guy," she said awkwardly as Torin quickly rose to his feet, looking at her questioningly.

He glanced down at the ground for a moment, as if trying to make up his mind about something, and then back at Rebecca. "We do not talk about the Bolluxes often," Torin finally said. "You know when you think about someone and they appear, or in your world, telephone you? Thoughts here are like connecting telephone lines. I will speak of the Bolluxes, but I have to disconnect something first." He paused for a moment, made a soft humming sound, and visibly relaxed.

"There. Now, a Bollux is a kind of being that thrives in chaotic situations. There is a saying here that where there's trouble, there's probably a Bollux close by. Luckily, according to our natural laws, every time they help create mayhem, they must soon experience the immediate consequences of their behavior. In a sense they are constantly punishing themselves; they know the results will be painful, but continue their malicious acts anyway. They are being true to their Bollux nature.

There is also a group of beings, the Griffin Folk, who act to uphold our natural laws. They keep the Bolluxes in check. Our laws of nature are somewhat different than yours, but still must be maintained. Lately a strange separation has been occurring and no one knows why or how to resolve it. There was an old prophecy that such a time would come to Thianely, and an outworlder would come to help, an Elemental Master, a Guardian. But if the Bolluxes know you are here and are already interfering, we must get to the Threshold of The Trees quickly. I have certain abilities that will keep you safe until you get you memory back. Some day you will remember how to protect yourself."

Rebecca trembled slightly. "I appreciate all of your help and everything, but I'm still having trouble with all of this. What happened with the council, anyway?"

"We're to leave as soon as possible, in the next couple of days. We'll have to travel overland and that takes time. In the meantime, Folk are communicating all over Thianely. The Great Council of all Folk plans to convene to decide what action to take next. We will gather supplies and give you a couple of days to relax in the garden. After that we must go."

"I guess I can handle that," Rebecca said somewhat doubtfully. "It doesn't seem like I have that much choice. What would happen if I refused to do anything and demanded to be sent home?"

Torin smiled broadly. "I think you'll have to ask yourself that question, since you wouldn't be here unless you'd called to us, and a part of you had come through the crystal in the first place. Why do you fight your own nature so much?"

"Because I'm not sure what I am any more. And I don't feel safe."

Torin grasped Rebecca by the hand and looked directly into her eyes. "I promise, by Rhiate herself, with all of the abilities and knowledge within me, that I will not let harm come to you. As your intention was to be here on Thianely, so my intention is to be here with you and assist you as much as I am able. That is a truth you may depend on."

Rebecca shook his hand somewhat solemnly. "Well, that makes me feel somewhat safer. I suppose you've got a deal."

They spent the next day packing up clothing, supplies, dried fruit, grains, roots and nuts for the journey. Torin explained that most Thianelians did not eat meat, not out of a sense of disgust, but simply because eating it was unnecessary for survival. For most of the Folk, feeling the pain of plants as they uprooted was difficult enough. All beings on Thianely had consciousness, not one of which was considered more valuable than the other, so all food was consumed with great appreciation and respect. No food was prohibited; it was how one ate it that was important. Food eaten without gratitude could not be digested properly and caused illness.

All fruits and nuts were asked from the trees on Thianely, rather than taken. Roots and plants uprooted themselves if they wished, or continued to grow if they were unwilling to be eaten. Torin spoke about Imanayon's years as a gardener, and a healer. He had learned much from his grandfather about what caused illness. Rebecca was interested to hear that healers on Thianely spent years learning how to cure themselves of injury and illness, not only with the help of flowers and plants, but also with great skill at listening to their own bodies. Rather than actually operating on anyone, they simply placed their hands upon the ill and reminded them, by remaining in an open state of awareness, of how to heal themselves.

A healer was only considered so if he had a high integration of the physical, emotional, and mental self. Most healers were born with the gift, although Torin commented that illness tended to be fairly rare on Thianely since most of the Folk had a pretty high awareness of their bodies anyway. Torin said that the word "healer" on Thianely was really "alhathra", which meant "reminder". All healers did was remind people that there was nothing intrinsically wrong with them, that perhaps they were holding some pain or forgetfulness in their body.

On Thianely, all beings were encouraged to feel their emotions and let them move out of their bodies, although learning not to throw them at one another was an important step. Rebecca thought about all of the disease and violence on Earth, and wondered if possibly a whole planet could be "reminded" at once.

They met Imanayon for dinner that evening, and he sat down upon the floor beside Rebecca. "Are you well, and ready for the journey to the Threshold of the Trees?" he asked kindly.

"I think so," Rebecca replied. "I've been helping Torin pack and learning more about Thianely and your healing abilities."

"Don't be surprised if such knowledge feels very familiar to you," Imanayon said. "You have some ability in that area yourself."

Rebecca shrugged and spent the rest of the evening looking at several strange old Thianelian maps that Torin had pulled off a shelf somewhere. The first few made little sense to her, for there were no directions posted upon them, nor were distances marked on any scale she could see. They were merely pictures of many places, drawn in great detail with rich colors. The ink was dew collected from garden flowers. Torin explained that the maps were elemental, illustrating destinations where one might wish to transport oneself.

The overland maps were even more ancient, and appeared much more like Earth maps in that they depicted roads and rivers, mountains and villages. Distance was marked in what Torin explained were travel days by walking. The Fire Folk lived in the central southern region, commonly called Bel-Warthen, while the Earthen Folk resided further south, Warthen and southwest, Bar-Warthen. The Threshold of the Trees was in the central region, or Belathgarin. The Air Folk lived high in the mountains in the western region, or Barden. The eastern region, or Methen, was home to Griffinkind; while the southeast region, Warth-Methen area, was inhabited by the Bollux clan. Not too many folk had traveled to the northern region, or Rythen. The weather there was unpredictable, seldom responding to the wishes of travelers, and there were many fierce creatures that had adapted to the cold, treacherous terrain. It was not a welcoming sort of place, and only those who had specific business there bothered to traverse the mountain ranges, deep frozen valleys, and icy rivers.

Rebecca forgot most of what Torin told her about who lived where, but she was interested to learn that Torin's name literally meant, "fire in the center." Many Thianelian names ended in the sound "in," "en," "an," or "on," because it was believed to denote balance. She also could not help but notice that Torin acted as if he had rarely studied maps. When she asked him about it, all he would say is that it was not his usual method of travel, but that circumstances made it necessary to travel overland.

Finally, she went to her room to sleep, but lay awake imagining what it would be like at the Threshold of the Trees. Torin had told her little, only that she would see when she arrived. She lay quietly for a time, appreciating Thianelian customs. Torin had shown her a small plant whose roots were used to brush one's teeth, and she'd rapidly decided that Earth toothbrushes were deficient. The root was soft, but had firm fibers that somehow, without much effort, cleaned ones mouth thoroughly. It left behind a wonderful aftertaste. Torin had mentioned that children chewed the root like Earth children ate candy, except that it prevented rather than caused tooth decay. Such roots were available everywhere, and Rebecca realized that she didn't miss grocery stores, or money, or modern conveniences as much as she might have. Thianelians were always singing, making the need for

CD's and stereos unnecessary. Recycling occurred naturally, and the air was always clear.

She noticed that Thianelians lived with an almost complete lack of fear. Although they considered the Bolluxes threatening, it was seldom that the creatures appeared, and Thianelians knew how to use the elements to protect themselves. There were no concerns about violence among the Folk, no busy streets to cross, no airplanes to crash. News happened through long distance mind communication rather than lurid stories written to sell papers. It was, on the whole, an ideal kind of place, except that it was somehow disintegrating. She contemplated what a disaster it would be for such a world to become like her own, and immediately felt sad at what a depressing place the Earth had become.

Rebecca's thoughts were interrupted by a strange humming noise coming from the wall. "Air conditioner," she thought automatically, before she remembered that they didn't have such things here. She glanced over at the crystal, which had begun to glow as it rocked back and forth. She sat up, wondering what was going on. The crystal shook harder, almost leaping out of the wall. Rebecca got up and ran over to it, worried that it was breaking.

"I would get the room with the exploding crystal," she said wryly, running her hands over the smooth surface as a strange pulling came from inside the stone. When she tried to remove her hands, she couldn't let go. Her palms were stuck to the crystal. As she stood tugging in frustration, the crystal began to dissolve in front of her eyes into a gray doorway with nothing visible beyond it.

"No way," she protested, as the doorway drew her in. "I'm not going through there!" But as she spoke she was pulled right inside the smoky grayness into the dark place beyond.

## Chapter 6

She floated in the middle of nowhere, in the middle of such emptiness that she wasn't even sure if she were alive, except that she could still think. She could feel nothing, hear nothing, and see nothing, except the image of her own thoughts. She could not feel her body at all, but nor could she feel alarmed. Being formless was simply a fact, like a thought without emotion. She wondered if she had fallen into the place her parents described once after they had meditated.

For the first time in her life, she saw her thoughts as separate from herself, and she pictured them as words on a huge blank screen. She played with them for a bit, making them move slowly in halting rows or speeding them up to lurch and gallop like wild animals. She gave them color and shape and form, then dissolved them completely. There was no effort involved, nor any particular pleasure at the results. She drifted in thought for a time that seemed no time at all. At once she knew there was something more than her own mind, because a flicker of light began to glow, off to the left. She found it interesting, although in this incredible emptiness of thoughtfulness, she had not felt bored at all, merely detached in a curious sort of way.

The light became brighter, and with a suddenness that was shocking, her body returned. As her feet touched ground, her eyes began to see more clearly. She was standing in a huge forest of trees, trees larger than any she could have imagined, even beyond redwoods. The ground was full of leaves, huge blue and purple and green ones. She bent down to pick one up, marveling at its starry shape. It had a leathery, soft texture, and despite her best efforts, was completely unbreakable.

"Tough little thing," she muttered to herself, absently stroking its furry underside. She stepped over to one of the trees and ran her hand up its smooth, blue-green bark. "What a beauty," she commented. "These are quite the most extraordinary trees I've ever seen."

As she stood there, resting her hand on the bark, she felt it move under her palm. "Excuse me, human child," said a deep voice. To Rebecca's complete astonishment, the tree moved three feet to the right. "I needed a bit more sun on this side," the voice explained kindly, "but you're welcome to rest against me now, as I'm going to doze a bit myself."

Rebecca sat down with a thump, resting her head against the tree's smooth trunk. Here she was, sitting by a talking tree, heaven only knew how, and she felt deeply happy. She imagined explaining to Torin that the wall crystal had sucked her directly to the Threshold of the Trees, for she assumed she could be nowhere else.

As she sat, trying to figure out what she ought to do next, she felt a gentle brushing against her hair. She looked up and saw a slender woman with long auburn hair and light green skin. The lady was absolutely radiant, and Rebecca quickly scrambled to her feet to make a spontaneous curtsy. The lady was the kind of person that one bowed to instinctively. The woman smiled, inclining her head gracefully. Everything about her was graceful, from her long flowing hair, reddish brown and golden, to the soft blue gown she wore that draped her figure so delicately. Her eyes were bright, a mesmerizing blue-green, and she wore a sparkling crystal medallion suspended on a green neckvine. For some reason, Rebecca could not take her eyes off of it. She felt embarrassed to be staring, but no matter how she tried to look away, her eyes stayed fixed upon the crystal.

"I am Meridwen, Rebecca," said the woman kindly. "As you can see, you were brought here more quickly than we expected. Actually the Crystal Folk have their own ways of communicating among themselves. They pulled you here in answer to a summons from the Great Tree. I am sorry if the crystal traveling alarmed you, but we have so little time and so much to tell you. You may feel strange for the next few hours as you return from the emptiness between spaces, but you are completely unharmed, though you may be a bit confused. Come with me to the Hall of Records in the Great Tree, and you may have some refreshment. Then we will speak more of all you need to know."

Rebecca still had trouble keeping her eyes from the medallion, until Meridwen passed a hand over it. When its luster dimmed, Rebecca could focus on Meridwen's words much more easily.

"Bless Rhiate," the woman exclaimed. "You are so sensitive to our ways! No wonder you were crystal called. I'm sure you've been one of the Crystal Folk before. Such sensitivity can be a blessing and at the same time create more difficulties for you as well. Come my dear, and follow me."

Rebecca trailed quietly after Meridwen, as she was the kind of person anyone would follow just about anywhere. She radiated calm and peace, and Rebecca felt better standing next to her. While they walked along the leaf-strewn ground, Rebecca felt the soft give of the strong leaves beneath her slippers. The trees bent and swayed at their progress, and occasionally the trees stepped, or rather, moved aside for them. There wasn't a particular path that Rebecca could see, only throngs of trees that reached upwards into the dusky rose sky.

At last Meridwen led her out of the forest into a clearing. There stood an old tree whose immense girth filled the entire meadow before them. It was so vast that Rebecca could not see around it. Its branches grew so high its purple leaves obscured the sun. Its bark was perfectly smooth, like emerald glass. As Rebecca watched, the surface of the bark wrinkled deeply, like the skin of an incredibly old person, then shifted back to a smooth expanse of green. Meridwen paused, bowing low, and indicated for Rebecca to bow as well. The tree, to Rebecca's surprise, actually bent its branches and leaned forward, paying homage in return.

Advancing gracefully, Meridwen gently patted the thick green bark. With a shiver, the great tree parted itself until a crack appeared. As it widened, Meridwen motioned for Rebecca to precede her, and Rebecca moved into the tree, closely followed by Meridwen.

At first it was dark, but soon the inner walls of the tree began to glow and illuminate the tunnel of wood in which they stood. The tree had closed its thick bark behind them, and Rebecca wondered for a moment how it was that she felt no claustrophobia, but rather a sense of safety. Meridwen moved in front of her, motioning for her to follow along inside the smooth tunnel. Rebecca felt incredibly comforted being in the Great Tree. Around them was a sense of extreme age, and if she'd had been asked to describe the tree, Rebecca would have used the term wise, for with its great knowledge came an extraordinary kind of compassion.

At last Meridwen led her into a large room, lit by four huge crystals that would have been in the corners of the room, except that the walls and ceiling were round. There was a curved wooden chair growing in the center of the room. Around it was a cluster of seats that all looked as if they had spontaneously sprouted from the floor of the Great Tree. Many of these were filled with others who looked like Meridwen, though none were quite so tall or with such an air of command. They ranged in skin color from light green to shades of blue, with long green or brown hair. They all moved with such grace that Rebecca began to feel very plain and awkward in comparison. She had no time to dwell on that for very long because Meridwen sat her in the small chair in the circle's center, where she received a leaf tray from one of the Tree Folk. Meridwen patted her shoulder gently and nodded for her to eat.

"This will sustain you for awhile, Rebecca. Eat now as we gather together. Even now the dwellers of the forest heed your arrival and come."

Rebecca wasn't sure if that was supposed to make her feel better or not, but the food was certainly delicious. As she nibbled some sort of nut cake, she realized that the Tree Folk weren't likely to tell her she was a regular earth kid that wound up in the wrong place and could go back to who she thought she was. She held the thick leaf tray on her lap, sampled two or three kinds of fruit, and drank a leaf full of juice that tasted like pomegranates.

Finally, when she was finished, one of the tall slender women came and took her tray. Many more people began to arrive, and Rebecca sat watching as all of the seats were filled. Soon the soft hum of voices became silent.

Meridwen approached Rebecca, bowed low, and turned to the rest of her people. "Listen well, my folk, for at last the prophecy shall come to pass, and that which is separate shall be whole and that which is forgotten shall be remembered. So it was, is and shall be. Thianely called, and this one has answered. As the prophecy says:

When the Gate of Time lies shattered, and life begins its death,
Then Balance is forgotten and separation draws first breath.
When elemental knowing is sundered each from each,
What mind no longer understands, intention cannot reach.
When gifts are disrespected, and love worth less than greed,
Then life becomes dishonored, and conflict plants its seed.
When Nature's laws are gone awry, and fallen from within
Then Thianely shall pass away, and so shall all her kin,
Unless a Woman Guardian, from some other place
Finds Elemental center through all time and space.
One who has forgotten, all that she has known,
And so will come in ignorance of true self, alone.
She may unite the elements, and hold the hope of peace,
Her very nature dancing joy, all sorrow to release,

And call to all companions, the Balance that they are
A universal oneness amongst the song of star,
Mind at last will matter, to heal and not to rend,
A pattern of intention, that wholeness soon may mend.

Rebecca listened in mounting dismay. She couldn't understand how someone might have mistaken her for this woman, whoever she was, since the prophecy didn't seem to have much to do with her at all. She'd never been a particularly dancing joy sort of person, at least not unless she was running through puddles. She had the fervent wish that the real Elemental Master would show up so that she could be Rebecca Bloom, sixteen-year-old teenager who happened to be visiting another world while recovering from a fever. She began to feel vaguely guilty, as if everyone she'd met were only being nice to her because they thought she was someone else. For some reason, the idea of Torin only liking her for that reason disturbed her.

As Meridwen finished speaking, many of the Tree Folk began murmuring. They began to hum, louder and louder until Rebecca felt the tones right through her feet. Her feet began to tap and finally she could no longer sit still. She stood up and to her astonishment, swayed back and forth in a dance to which she somehow knew the steps. Meridwen pulled her into the circle of Tree Folk, singing seasons into the Forest:

"Winter's wisdom is returning,
Summer's purpose gone to fall.
We sing the turning of the seasons,
Nature's rhythms in us all.

Birth and living, death renewing,
Winter's coming soon to us.
For every blaming there's forgiving,
For every fear there is a trust.

Sing the joy of all the seasons,
Past and present, future too.
Wind and rain and sun and snowfall,
All of nature inside you."

The Tree Folk gradually slowed and one by one broke away. They left the circular room, nodding kindly to Rebecca as they did so. Meridwen gestured for Rebecca to follow her again.

"How do you feel after hearing the old prophecy?" Meridwen asked her, as they made their way through another tree tunnel.

"To tell you the truth I keep hoping it will go away, and you'll realize I'm not who you think I am," Rebecca said. "Then you do things like sing songs that I could swear I know... It's confusing."

Meridwen nodded. "That's understandable, and that's also why you're here. I think the Great Tree may help you recognize more of yourself."

"I guess I hope so," Rebecca said, moving along another crystal lit corridor. "Though I'm not exactly who that is, me, I mean. It's weird thinking you know yourself and all of a sudden, you don't any more."

Meridwen stopped suddenly, almost causing Rebecca to bump into her.

"Wait a moment," she said, cocking her head as if to listen. Rebecca heard it too, the far off sound of someone shouting.

"It must be Torin of the Fire Folk," Meridwen said, smiling. "He cannot mindtel with you through the Great Tree, so he has chosen to throw his voice. It carries very well."

Rebecca laughed, partly at the thought of Torin having to shout to make himself heard, and also because she was glad he'd arrived. "Did he come the same way I did?" she asked.

Meridwen shook her head. "No, he has other ways of traveling. They're not the safest ways though, not as safe as being crystal called like you were. Here, walk through this tree parting here." She motioned to a side path in the tunnel. "I will go greet Torin. You will see him when you have spoken to the treeknown rings of yourself."

Rebecca looked at her questioningly, but Meridwen again shook her head. "I cannot explain it to you, you must go and remember for yourself. Go on, right through there."

Meridwen turned and hurried off, while Rebecca stood and waited for a moment. "Oh, well, I suppose if I must."

She walked slowly along the pathway, noting that the walls had dimmed a bit, and the path began to veer sharply downwards. All at once the path ended in a wall of thick, twisting tree roots. The roots branched out, almost completely blocking her view of where the path ought to have continued.

"There must be some way round this," she thought. "I don't think Meridwen would have sent me here as a joke." She reached out and gently pushed at one of the thick roots, but it stayed firmly in place. Then she remembered the doors at Imanayon's home.

"Excuse me, roots, I need to get by. Could you please move?"

The huge root bundle began to shift. One long thick root began to pull itself laboriously from the ground in a kind of snakelike movement. Instead of opening to let Rebecca pass by, the root bundle shifted itself into the shape of an enormous tree throne. As Rebecca watched this strange construction, the long root finished detaching itself from the soil, and nudged her gently toward the huge chair.

"But I don't have time to sit here," Rebecca said aloud, imagining Torin waiting for her impatiently outside. "I have to hurry up and talk to some tree thing. I have a friend waiting for me too." The root nudged her more firmly and Rebecca gave up. "Oh, all right," she said aloud, settling herself into the root chair, which was surprisingly comfortable.

She sat trying to be patient, while the long root twisted itself about until it lay directly across her lap. The very tip of the root lifted up as its layers began to peel themselves back. Finally Rebecca could see thousands of tiny rings, so close together they were barely distinguishable. "Well, you certainly must be older than you look," she said laughingly. "I've never seen so many rings even on one of our oldest trees on earth." She reached out gently to touch one of the rings and found it to be slightly raised, almost furry under her finger. Suddenly the chair shook. Rebecca felt the roots around her begin to blur.

She emerged into a vast symphony of darkness lit by thousands of night suns. She was born from the music of space and spheres, knowing herself star, only one of the many small dances, minuets of motion, radiating starlight. She became a burst of creation. Fire, air and rhythms of sound pushed and pressed and hurtled her spaceward, gradually expanding, increasing until she held millions of stars, millions of selves in spiraling arrays.

She shrank, dwindling into water, smaller and smaller until green waves pulled her, pushed her from her ocean father's pouch. She breathed deeply, taking the coolness into her lungs, feeling the waves lift and hold her, her buoyant fins already flowing her onward. The small mermaid, newly birthed, opened her gills and sang the joy of the depths, the underworld where she lived with her merkin, the brethren of fish and folk, all of the ocean born.

As she rested, gliding along the buoyancy of the sea, she trembled and shook, suddenly pressed and pushed down into a different shape. She slipped from the womb of her mother, out onto the soft lavender grass. Her mother bent down, licking away the afterbirth with a rasp of tongue, then gently prodded her to her feet with a spiraling horn. She stood awkwardly, four legs not quite steady.

She twisted, feeling her forelegs dissolve in a painful wrench that made her clench her eyes shut. Her body moved in sudden sharp jerks, driving the breath from her lungs, forcing her into contortions of change. When at last she opened her eyes, she was an old woman. Clothed in threadbare garments, she stood in a valley at the base of a tall mountain. Smoke poured from its heights as she stood trembling, balancing on weakened legs. She leaned on her walking stick, frightened but determined, as she visualized with her mind the cooling water, the soothing water that would prevent another volcanic disaster.

Rebecca returned to herself with a gasp, and sat for a moment, gripping the arms of the root chair to steady herself. The long root began to entwine itself up over her shoulders and around her head until she felt like she was wearing a tree helmet. She closed her eyes and hoped fervently that she wouldn't have to remember any more. Being a star, a mermaid, a unicorn, and an old woman had been enough for one day.

"Although," she thought rather resignedly, "being on another planet would be enough for most people for their entire lives. The strange part is that it feels so normal."

The root helmet began to tighten, and all at once she was sitting in a classroom with aliens from all dimensions.

"The topic for today, lesson holders," said the teacher, a white turbaned globular fellow sitting in the front of the group, "is cellular magnification and miniaturization. Can anyone tell me what purpose these serve?"

A many-armed elephant creature raised one arm. "It can come in very handy in terms of shape shifting and also for the amplification of energy in dense populations. I mean dense in terms of contracted consciousness rather than large numbers." Everyone laughed.

"That's fine," the teacher said. He noticed Rebecca sitting in the room. "Oh, here is a great example of what happens when one fraternizes too long with the natives. You can all see that our friend here," and the entire class swiveled around to stare at Rebecca, "has had to return for a refresher course, even after graduation, what was it, eons ago? Good luck, my dear, we all know you picked a tough assignment. Those unbalanced planets can be pivotal, but a real chore. Come back any time you need to see some friendly faces and hear evolved conversation. You know you're always welcome."

Rebecca watched the room swirl about in a disconcerting fashion and closed her eyes tightly. When she opened them she was sitting in the tree chair and the root had untwined itself from her shoulders and head. It looked as if it were trying to reroot itself into the ground. The roots beneath her began to move, twisting rapidly. She found herself once more standing in front of a root bundle wall. She turned to go back the way she had come, but the inner bark parted for her, creating a doorway into the fresh evening air. She took a deep breath, shaking her head in astonishment at her intergalactic classroom visit. As she walked out into the evening right onto the leaf-paved ground, she found Torin sitting down, sketching on a blue leaf pad. He smiled and stood up.

"So there you are," he said, and came over to give her a hug. Rebecca leaned into his arms, noticing how warm and safe he felt. She wasn't sure how long she'd been gone, but she'd missed him.

"I heard you arrived by crystal gate," he said teasingly, "wasn't the regular road good enough for you?"

"Look who's talking," Rebecca said, still holding his arm. "I don't know how you got here, but I doubt it was particularly safe."

"Traveling by fire seldom is lately," Torin said sheepishly, pointing to a singe mark on his tunic. "Nowadays we can't count on our elemental connections to be certain. That's why we were going to travel overland. I promised to stay with you though, and I didn't burn anything important. So, how are you?" He gestured towards the vastness of the Great Tree. "No one ever comes out quite the same as the way they went in."

"I'll say," Rebecca replied, letting go of Torin's arm to sit with him on the thick leaves. "I'm not sure I could explain it," she said. She lay down for a moment and closed her eyes. "It's like being someone I used to be a long time ago, but me in this time as well. I feel older, like

I know more than I thought, but I saw and felt things that don't even exist where I come from. It's weird being so much more than I've ever imagined myself to be, but at the same time it seems right. I guess I'm kind of stunned."

Torin smiled, and sat down next to her, idly flipping the pages of his leaf pad. "It's understandable. It's strange to think that every being born has a place on the inner bark of the tree that denotes his or her lives. The tree can actually tell how many lives you've had. That's billions of lifetimes when you consider that this tree holds the memories of universes. It's almost impossible to imagine so much knowledge in one place, and yet the tree is more than a place, it's a life gateway, a being in itself.

We usually travel here three times during our childhoods, once at three years, again at seven and finally at thirteen. Each time lasts a few weeks. Most of our schooling is completely informal except for these three trips to the Great Tree. I'm afraid you're going to get it all at once over the next few weeks."

Rebecca chuckled. "That's okay. Even if it is a little intense, do you have any idea how many years I've spent in school learning useless information?"

Torin looked at her curiously. "I have often wondered why your people have chosen to spend so much of their days at school or at work. It allows so little time for the joy of simply being. And life is not so long there."

"How long do Thianelians live?" Rebecca asked.

"As long as they choose to," Torin replied, "although accident and injury do cause occasional deaths. Most of us reach a certain age and feel that it is time to move on and so we do. It is simply another season."

"This is a whole different subject, but I wanted to ask you..." began Rebecca, looking somewhat sheepish. At Torin's look of expectancy she continued. "Where is Thianely, I mean in the star charts?"

Torin nodded. "It makes sense that you would wonder. Do you remember those books you have on Earth where there is one picture and another picture lays over that and so on, so that finally you have a complete picture?"

"Do you mean transparencies?" Rebecca asked, looking confused.

"That is the word," Torin said. "If you were to look at your planet Earth, and your solar system, and lay a transparency over it, Thianely, Torildian, and Hevald would overlap your solar system. We have only three planets in our system. Thianely is smaller in size than your planet, and has no moon. Our sun is about the same distance from Thianely as yours is from Earth. Torildian is much hotter and it is closer to our sun, while Hevald lies farther from our sun, though not so distant as your Mars. It would help if you thought of us as being in the same neighborhood, but in a different universe that overlaps yours."

Rebecca felt as if her brain needed a rest. Torin spoke about other universes as casually as if he were discussing what they would eat for dinner.

"What are you going to do every day while I'm learning in the Great Tree?" Rebecca asked.

"I've decided to make a leaf journal of our experiences. I know many of the Tree Folk from my earlier trips here. I can visit their trees or help them with harvesting. I'll be fine. When you're finished we'll consult with Meridwen about our next move. I don't think we'll be traveling elementally any time soon. And rarely are any of us crystal called."

"Have you been?" Rebecca asked, remembering the strange, in-between place she'd come through on her way to the Threshold of the Trees.

Torin shook his head. "No, but I've heard others say that it is very similar to the mindfulness of elemental travel, but without the sensation of being physical."

Rebecca looked at him quizzically. "I'd have to agree with the 'without sensation' part, but is becoming fire a physical experience? What is it like?"

"Very hot," he replied. "When you were drinking the rain and became water for a time, wasn't it thoroughly physical? Didn't you experience the sensations of flow in all of Creation?"

"I guess so," Rebecca said. "But on our planet being physical has a little different meaning. I'm not sure how you can turn into an element. It was odd being in my mind watching thoughts go by like little paper airplanes. What would have happened if I had gotten stuck in that place between crystals?"

"That is what the season of Yarwen is for, at least it was until everything became so separated. All beings that had difficulty moving in and out of form returned to a centered state during Yarwen. Though that was only necessary if friends and family members could not assist them in the first place. It happens much less often than you might think."

"Well, that's encouraging," Rebecca muttered, suddenly relieved that she hadn't known she was being crystal called until after it had happened. She relaxed next to Torin while he began an explanation of the difference between crystal, elemental, and space-time travel that soon had her mind wandering. She was beginning to feel very weary, which Torin informed her was one of the aftereffects of being close to the Great Tree.

Suddenly she was drifting, and Rebecca pictured the whole nightness of sky filled with the brightness of stars. She saw the greenness of waves, the face of her unicorn mother, the huge volcano she'd calmed, and the classroom of strange creatures. She let the pattern of universes wash over her, dissolving her separateness until she became shapeless and indistinct. She heard Torin calling her as if from a distance. Finally she felt hands shaking her shoulders and opened her eyes to see Torin's worried face.

"Rebecca, where did you go? I saw you float right up, almost completely out of your body. Maybe I shouldn't have mentioned traveling again so soon," he added humorously. "I guess I gave you the wrong suggestion."

Rebecca sat up, a little shakily. "I don't know what happened exactly, except that it was like being back in the tree, seeing all of those places. I started going there again."

Torin shook his head in chagrin. "I might have known you'd have the ability to travel inter dimensionally on your own as soon as you remembered how. Don't try it again until you've remembered how to take your body with you." He reached into a pocket in his tunic and handed her a bright red stone, mottled with shiny metallic specks. "Here," he said, dropping it into her palm. "Grandfather sent this along in case you had the tendency to bilocate indiscriminately. He must have known this would happen. It's a firestone, and keeps you in your body. Very handy at times."

Rebecca could feel the solidness of the stone in her palm and the ground humming beneath her. "Thanks, Torin, but what does bilocate mean?"

"It's how you got here in the first place," he replied. "It means to be able to be in more than one place at the same time. Some of the Old Ones could do it physically as well as subtly, but it can be helpful either way. It can allow you to be very efficient, but cause dangerous separation if you don't fully remember what you're doing. So for now, keep the stone in your pocket."

Rebecca leaned over, pointing to the leaf pad. "What are you drawing anyway?"

Torin flipped back to the first leaf page, and showed Rebecca the pictures he'd drawn. "Since I already had a bit of time to sit while you were being self-educated, I thought I'd start with your visit." He pointed to the first pictures, a series he'd done of Rebecca coming through the puddle gate, listening to Imanayon's storytelling, standing rain dazzled in the garden, and gesticulating fiercely in Council.

"Thanks a lot," Rebecca said, "these are really flattering. They show me at my absolute worst. This is how you're going to remember me?"

"Oh no," Torin said seriously, "This is only partly how I think of you. For example, you didn't look at a bit of inner tree bark in there." He indicated the Great Tree with a wave of his hand. "Did you?"

"No, actually," Rebecca mused, "it was more like a root came out of the ground and sort of opened itself up."

"I expected that," Torin said. "It means you were one of the beings that helped plant this tree. You are a Guardian, a being who originated in another universe entirely, and the essence of your being has helped maintain the life of this tree. I won't forget how much responsibility that is, nor how you earned it by right. Most beings don't ever see the roots of this tree. You are bound to recognize other tree bearers now that you have."

"Like you," Rebecca said, without even pausing to think.

"Like me," Torin acknowledged, and clapped a hand on her shoulder. "See how quickly you're remembering?"

"So, now what?" asked Rebecca, rising to her feet and stretching. "Where are you staying anyway? What about where I'm going to stay for the next few days? And I'm hungry again."

Torin laughed at the barrage of questions. "It's warm enough outside even during starshine," he replied. "We'll camp out beneath the trees here, unless you'd rather sleep inside the Great Tree.

Although, you may find it a bit much. I mean, even the Tree Devas go home at night to their own trees, because being in the Great Tree can become overwhelming with knowledge after a while. You learn all night in your sleep and don't get any rest. Some beings come to sit under its branches for months to learn and never even go inside. But if it rains in the Threshold, we'll be welcome inside any neighboring tree. Most Thianelians are known for their hospitality."

Torin rose to his feet, motioning to several large backsacks nearby. "I've plenty of leaf blankets for both of us, dried honey cakes, and other supplies. I came a bit better provisioned than you did. There are many fruit trees here as well. All you have to do is ask the trees which fruit is ready. Come on, I'll show you."

Torin spent hours taking Rebecca through the Threshold of the Trees. She saw many varieties of fruit and nut bearing trees, all containing plenty of food for thousands of people. Most of it was either eaten fresh, or dried for journeys. Torin explained that the Tree Folk, or Tree Devas, were what earth people called "dryads". They could not travel very far away from trees in general, although they weren't only tied to a particular tree. Each tree person had a tree home, but when traveling great distances they were always welcomed in any grove they came across. They had ground resonance so that any tree within a certain range could communicate with them, thus they were rarely caught without shelter.

That night, and many nights after, Torin and Rebecca slept under a huge plunerian tree, and ate pluners, a kind of thick, starchy fruit, for breakfast. They met hundreds of Tree Devas who'd come to chat, and for Torin it was a rekindling of old acquaintances he'd met during his mentoring journey, a kind of walkabout most Thianelians did when they arrived at puberty. Rebecca discovered that most of the Thianelians did their journeys directly after their final visit to the Great Tree, at age thirteen.

She tried to imagine being let loose at thirteen to travel the world, and couldn't picture it being very enjoyable, on Earth anyway. Torin explained that mentoring journeys reconnected all of the Folk, preventing any of them from becoming too isolated. It helped establish new friendships and also was the predominant way that ideas spread across their planet. Though long distance telers conveyed many new discoveries, those Folk achieving puberty were considered to be especially creative. Children on Thianely were treated with a great deal of respect, and often asked for their suggestions. It occurred to Rebecca that she would never have arrived on Thianely at all if Thianelians viewed teens the way Earth people did.

Over the next few weeks, they fell into a routine. Each morning Rebecca entered the Great Tree and learned more about her many lifetimes. In the afternoons she rested and later toward evening she shared a meal with Torin. Afterwards they strolled about the Threshold, visiting some of the Tree Folk in their homes, and keeping a diary of pictures in Torin's leaf journal.

Torin knew quite a few of the Tree Folk already, particularly one young woman named Leva. Torin had met her during one of his trips to the Great Tree. He mentioned that Leva's parents, Lenton and Morlina, were well known among Thianelians, partly because Lenton was of the Earthen Folk and Morlina was of the Tree Devas, and partly due to their accomplishments in seeding trees all over Thianely. They had met during their mentoring journeys and come to the Threshold of the Trees to live and raise their family. Although there were pairings between the different Folk, it wasn't all that common.

Leva had slanted brown eyes, light green skin, and dark turquoise hair that tumbled down her back in tangled waves. She lived with her parents, four sisters, and two brothers, in a cluster of dok trees, a thickly barked tree that bore soft-shelled nuts. She looked somewhere between Rebecca's and Torin's age, but was completely uninterested in her appearance, often showing up to visit with purple mud stains smeared across her face, or gaps in her leaf dress where she'd ripped it climbing a tree. Leva repeatedly asked Rebecca to tell Earth stories, as she was fascinated by the other world, although Rebecca omitted mentioning the practice of having Christmas trees. She figured that killing trees to decorate one's living room probably wouldn't be well received.

Rebecca learned that the relationship of a Deva to its tree was symbiotic. The Devas lived in the trees, needing them for shelter, dependent on them for the life force they emitted. In turn, the trees received nourishment of a physical nature, like water, bark care, and the harvesting of their fruit so that their branches would not snap. Devas also comforted the trees during the seasonal changes which brought the loss of their small leaf offspring. The Devas collected the fallen leaves for clothing and eating utensils. The trees were strengthened by the thought that their leaflings had merely changed form.

Rebecca could certainly understand honoring trees when she lay back and watched their beautiful limbs swaying above her or listened to them singing to their leaf children at night. Sometimes, long after Torin had fallen asleep, Rebecca would lie quietly, thinking about the memories of the day under the huge tree canopies and the night stars. At times she felt that not only her memory was returning, but also some large part of herself that felt at peace in each moment.

The days in the Great Tree were having another effect on her as well, for she appeared to be taking on a faint glow, both visible to herself and others. Torin smiled when she asked him about it and said that she was merely expanding into her true nature. The light of the star she was shined through no matter what form she took. Rebecca was also able to perceive this glow in others, and around the Great Tree itself. Her palms were tingling as well. Sometimes she could see colors coming from them and feel a gradually increasing warmth. Now if she stubbed her foot or bruised herself climbing, she only had to lay her palm across the sore place and the pain would disappear. When she asked Torin about it, he merely shrugged and said, "Alhathra," reminding her of what Imanayon had said about her healing abilities.

Rebecca, Torin, and Leva spent days climbing the huge trees, looking out over the forest and beyond into the next valley. Sometimes they chased the tree children about the Threshold, finding hiding places among the more gnarled trees, or burying themselves in piles of purple and blue leaves.

"You know," Rebecca said one day, while they were sprawled across a huge branch cracking nuts and dropping the shells down onto the ground below, "you never really told me what we're going to do next. I mean, wasn't I supposed to get all elementally balanced and centered? I hate to tell you this, but even if I am remembering lifetimes worth of stuff, I still don't feel particularly balanced."

"Considering you're having to learn at such a rapid rate, I wouldn't be so impatient with your progress," Torin commented. "Remember, what you've been doing all at once, we did over years. As to our next step, whatever it is, we'll have to walk from here, unless you remember how to water wave."

"Water wave? What's that?"

"Water waving means you become water and flow with a larger body of water to reach a place, like hitchhiking on your planet. Water people can also become water vapor and travel through the air, with the sky's permission, but that hasn't been safe lately either. There's been trouble with people remanifesting their bodies. Very unpleasant, losing parts of one's body. We get taught how to travel elementally at really young ages. I wouldn't expect you to try it even if you do remember how, since it takes so much practice. I was only teasing when I mentioned you water waving."

Rebecca cracked another nut in her teeth and munched loudly, then threw the shell at Torin.

"I don't suppose there's any way this could all be a mistake," she said casually. "I mean, yeah, I kind of glow and everything. I've had lots of lifetimes, but mistakes get made, don't they? I might be here kind of accidentally..."

It was Torin's turn to pelt her with shells. He shook his head in dismay. "Even after the last few weeks of remembering you still haven't accepted your place in the nature of things?"

"Well," said Rebecca, "considering that I never knew I had a place in the nature of things, yes, I'm having a tough time swallowing the whole idea. I suppose it seems silly to you, but I'm not sure I want this new me. How will I go home like this? I'm glowing all of the time now. People will think I'm some sort of phosphorescent freak. What will my parents say when they see me stick my hand over a cut and it stops hurting and heals so quickly?"

"I can understand your concern, I think," Torin replied. "But where is your trust in that which brought you here? You look much happier and more at peace than when you first arrived, and to heal pain is quite a good thing. Are you worried that your parents love you only when you do not remember who you are?"

"I don't know," said Rebecca sadly. "Maybe I am worried that they'll think I'm nuts or something. It's hard because I like knowing more of myself, yet I worry that I'll never be the same kid they knew. Maybe they'll be disappointed or something."

"It can be painful to release old ways of doing things to follow new ways," observed Torin shrewdly. "Do you grieve for your old self? There is a great deal more responsibility in acting from that which you truly are, rather than from a lack of self-awareness. I'm not going to pretend that you are completely safe from harm on Thianely either, but I will do everything in my power to help you. All of the other Folk are allies as well. You are not alone here, Rebecca."

Rebecca sighed. "Okay, Torin. You know, sometimes I can't believe that one minute you can be chasing me around the leaf paths, and the next be so old and wise."

Torin looked at her interestedly. "Do you not believe that one can be playful and wise at the same time? Are you allowed to experience only one state in each moment?"

"I don't know. Half of this stuff, okay, most of it, I don't think I've thought much about before. It wasn't really relevant at my age back home. You know what scares me the most? It's remembering all of the things I know how to do from those other lifetimes. Some of it is really exciting, but there seems to be so much responsibility that comes with it. I remember training in all kinds of healing arts and martial arts, learning about energy, force, and time, doing things that haven't even been invented yet on Earth. I learned all of this stuff, but I'm not sure I'll be able to do any of it when I really need it. Thianely will fall apart and I'll have let everyone down. I don't want to be the answer to some prophecy; I just want to be me."

"Maybe," Torin suggested, "being you is the answer. No one will think badly of you if disintegration occurs, Rebecca. It is already happening. It is our planet's responsibility, and that of every Thianelian, to become centered. There is, in the greater nature of Creation, no intrinsic good or bad associated with any particular state. It is only that we have chosen balance as the way in which we prefer to live. Somehow it is unraveling. Like our healers, once someone completely integrates, it reminds those of us who are willing to be reminded. That is all you can do.

In the most balanced state possible, if you were to place your palm over a Bollux and remind him of center, he would be very unlikely to respond. That is not your responsibility, but his. Either you find center or not, but few of us have your ability to do so, so why not make the attempt? It may actually bring you great joy. After all, it has brought you my wonderful company, hasn't it?"

Rebecca was extremely grateful that the nuts had soft shells, as they spent the next several minutes having a shell fight. Leva, who'd been looking for them, soon arrived with three of her siblings, and the shell skirmish continued. Finally, they called a halt and retired to Leva's parents' tree for the evening repast.

During the meal, Rebecca discovered that Devas lived in their parents' tree until they reached the age of thirteen. After their mentoring journey, they spent more time in their birth tree, the tree that was planted on the day they were born. Each birth tree was seeded from the parents' tree. When a Deva reached the age of seven, the tree and child participated in a tree bonding ceremony. Names were exchanged, and the child would become completely responsible for the nurturing of the tree. Tree names were considered sacred, and Devas were given the name of their particular birth tree. Most Devas could survive months in trees besides their own, particularly when traveling, but they didn't feel quite as healthy. After more than six months of absence, both tree and Deva would fade away, despite all the nurturing that others could provide.

When Devas mated, the two individual trees moved their roots together until the two became one tree. If one of the parents died, the former part of their tree withered. If a child died, so would his tree. If the child's tree died, often the child could live in the parental tree until a newly planted tree grew large enough.

Beyond the age of thirteen, the Devas and their trees were so closely bound, that if either died, both would perish. It was considered a great honor to be asked to nurture another's tree while they were journeying. A common parting phrase was, "May Rhiate bless the roots and the trunk. May she nurture and protect you. May all of creation cherish the leaves, harvest the fruit, and support the branches. And may Yarwen restore you to balance."

Lenton, Leva's father, explained that because he was born of the Earthen Folk, he had no tree to blend with Morlina's. Despite the perceived difficulties of such a match, Lenton had chosen to stay with the Devas at the Threshold of the Trees. He had moved into Morlina's tree, which had promptly doubled its girth to accommodate him. Rarer still, the tree had also bestowed upon him its name, thus ensuring Lenton's welcome.

Rebecca enjoyed Leva's large, somewhat noisy family, and remembered how many times she'd wished she weren't an only child. Morath, one of Leva's younger sisters, spent most of the evening sitting on Rebecca's lap, while Mornel, Leva's youngest brother, had become quite attached to Torin, often demanding that he fire up his hands so that he could see them glow. They stayed up quite late, and spent the night in the main living space of the huge dok tree, curled up comfortably on thick leaf mats.

The next morning Rebecca crept out to make her daily visit to the Great Tree, leaving Torin still half asleep. "I'll meet you in the usual spot," she whispered into his ear, as Torin mumbled something unintelligible. Rebecca smiled and made the dawn walk to the Great Tree, marveling at the bright pink sunrise. Leva's family trees were some distance from the clearing where the Great Tree stood, but she didn't mind the walk. She skipped in tune to the morning songs of awakening trees, feeling more at ease about being on Thianely, about being herself.

She bowed before the Great Tree, waited for its answering gesture, and entered the parting in its thick bark. She walked quickly through the tree tunnel, knowing her way by now. She took her usual place on the tree throne, but this time she did not visit other lifetimes. Instead, Rebecca spent the morning experiencing different emotions. If someone had asked her before to differentiate between sorrow, guilt, shame, anger, jealousy, and joy, and so on, she would have thought she could describe them well enough. But she realized after only moments that she had never really paid much attention.

Within the comforting presence of the old tree, she could perceive the subtle shifts that accompanied each emotional state. Her thoughts, body rhythms, the rate of her breathing, her temperature, even her muscle tension, all fluctuated wildly. She felt each emotion in her entire body, and for a moment, when she experienced the fullness of her own anger, she worried that she might explode.

For the next several hours she learned to tune into her equilibrium. She found herself increasing her temperature at will, adjusting her heart rate, and altering many other body systems. When she thought about it, she realized she'd always considered such things impossible. But now it felt perfectly natural and somewhat ordinary. It seemed ridiculous not to know her own body. And instead of feeling tired like after her usual sessions, she felt invigorated, cleansed, as if she'd unloaded old feelings she'd carried around for eons.

Late that afternoon, after a brief visit with Torin, Rebecca made her way back to the Great Tree. Although she'd already been there once that day, she felt an impulse to return. Torin had urged her to listen, for a summons from the Great Tree could not be ignored. He had offered to wait for her at their usual spot until evening repast, since they had promised they would visit with Leva's family again, mostly to satisfy everyone's curiosity. The Devas had many questions about Earth customs and the status of trees there.

"I'd better skip the whole topic of paper, and money, and building materials," Rebecca thought ruefully as she entered the clearing for her next session.

## Chapter 7

Rebecca made her way to the root room as usual, but found her way completely blocked by a huge branch that grew high on one wall of the tree tunnel. She could not see beyond it at all, and she wondered if she'd somehow taken a wrong turn to the tree throne. Then she realized that she'd never seen anything like it inside the Great Tree.

"How odd to see an ingrown branch," she thought. Testing gently with her intention to see if she could ask the branch to move, she felt a curious urge to sit upon it. There was no room at the top, and while she was wondering how she could possibly climb up, the branch slowly began to lower itself, as if kneeling down for her, so she scrambled up, holding onto the grooves in the bark for balance.

As soon as she was settled, the branch began to lower itself even more so that she was able to look over and see the enormous, tangled bunch of roots where she usually sat to remember. The branch kept descending, but instead of hitting the purple soil, the ground beneath opened up, spreading wide. The space grew larger and larger while the branch descended even further.

"Surely not right into the earth itself!" Rebecca said wonderingly, as the branch lowered itself down, down into the dark moistness. Rebecca held tightly to the branch, feeling as if she were on the back of some enormous earth serpent. It was so dark she could see little except packed earth, and the light from the tunnel room above became very faint as the branch made its downward progress. Finally the branch stopped and made a rippling movement as if to encourage Rebecca to climb down. She held still for a moment, hoping that there would be firm ground beneath her, and instantly felt ashamed at the thought that the tree would ever hurt her. She slid from the branch finally, finding her feet sinking into soft soil.

She was standing in complete darkness, glad she was not claustrophobic, when suddenly the ground began to shake, bucking beneath her so hard that she fell to her knees. She felt rather than saw the branch swiftly moving as it pulled back up into the tree, leaving her behind in the shaking, tumultuous hole. There was a terrible rending sound, and it sounded to Rebecca how the end of the world might, as she was tossed from her knees against one solid wall. She tried to sit up, but her knees were bruised and one arm ached. Again there was a rumbling, tearing sound and Rebecca felt the ground beneath her give way. She fell and fell. The last thing she heard was a loud splash, just before she hit water and banged her head hard.

She laid still, eyes closed, listening to the horrifying sound of the earth tearing and crashing. Gasping, she heard the pain sounds of trees, dying as their roots were pulled from the ground. With them came the mournful sounds of the Devas, perishing with their trees. She lay immobilized, stunned with the sheer weight of such pain and grief, her heart pounding too hard to bear.

Finally, when she thought she would be torn in two with the force of it all, she felt a soothing hand on her brow. Immediately, the pain in her head diminished; her panic subsided. As she opened her eyes, she saw kneeling beside her an old, old being, with a face so lined and wrinkled Rebecca could not tell if it was male or female. The being wore a dusty brown cloak and long dark tunic.

Rebecca slowly sat up and looked around. She was in some sort of underground cavern with a running stream. Three immense glowing crystals that looked at least six feet across took up a great deal of space on one side. From their light she could see that she had landed in a puddle of mud and water. The dampness had soaked through her clothes and one arm ached terribly. She felt severely bruised all over. As she finished her self-examination, the old being smiled at her, causing more wrinkles to blossom in the withered face.

"Come along, my dear, we haven't much time. Sit you up and bathe you in the stream to tend your wounds. Then to the crystals with you."

"I know you," Rebecca said, allowing herself to be pulled to her feet and assisted into the stream. Soon she felt the cool water seep past her barriers of clothing, clearing her head. The pain in her arm and body subsided. "Ah," she marveled, feeling completely refreshed, and amazingly, entirely dry.

"The waters of Life Force, himself," nodded the old one approvingly, handing her a small green flask. "Keep it with you on your journeys, and you'll know what to do with it when the time comes."

Rebecca took the flask and put it in her tunic pocket. "Thank you. You are Alphumerian, the essence being of the Great Tree, aren't you? I remember you from another place and a time long past. What happened up there, Esteemed Essence? I felt such anguish and sorrow I thought I would die from it."

The ancient one shook her head. "The Great Tree and those that marked its threshold have been sundered, Child, and with them knowledge and wisdom of ancient times has been severed from Thianely itself. I have little time to stay, for I could feel myself weakening as the great roots were ripped from the ground. Hurry now, come with me to the crystals."

Rebecca followed Alphumerian to the three enormous crystals, one pink, one clear, one purple. They were rough in places, many-faceted, and shaped like immense teardrops. Rebecca felt such shock she could barely take in the old one's words. Alphumerian sat Rebecca down in front of the pink crystal. "Now listen, my dear, listen carefully, for in case I die too quickly you must be able to complete the transfer yourself." At Rebecca's look of sorrow, Alphumerian spoke. "The time to grieve is later. Now listen well:

By air, by earth, by fire, and water,
Open to me, Niaphani's daughter.
Crystal wisdom, I desire
By water, air, earth and fire.
Let your records by me be held
That our beings together meld.
Stone of knowledge and rebirth
By fire, water, air, and earth,
With me your ancient lore now share
By earth and water, fire and air."

As Alphumerian finished intoning, Rebecca began to dissolve right into the crystal, as insubstantial as air. Suddenly she became solid, strong and knowing. Finally she felt emptied out, as if she had been completely taken out of herself and replaced again. Sitting outside the crystal once more, she could hear the earth itself speaking to her, murmuring her name. A sense of peace pervaded her, and she looked at Alphumerian's dying face with great compassion.

"Yes," Alphumerian nodded at her look, "I have only moments left. But you will be the keeper of the wisdom of these earth crystals. Take one of the golden roots from the Great Tree, my dear, and plant it in a place you know well. Now go and complete the transfer."

As she spoke the last words, the old one lay down upon the ground, breathing in shallow gasps. Rebecca bent over and kissed her face gently, waiting while the thin chest stopped its breathing. Lines and wrinkles smoothed out, leaving Alphumerian's face youthful and at peace. The young face began to fade. Soon nothing was left of the old one but a brown shawl and dark tunic.

Rebecca felt an overwhelming sadness at the loss of the Great Tree and the essence being who had lived among its roots. For a moment she paused, to honor the dead, but she felt a strong sense of certainty and purpose. She got to her feet, approaching the clear crystal. She sat down next to it, repeating Alphumerian's words. Again she experienced the sense of becoming crystal. She absorbed the records of the huge stone, finally reorienting herself back into her body, and repeated the procedure with the purple one. She sat for a moment, feeling full of knowledge, but somehow not weighed down at all. She tried to figure out how she could possibly regain the surface from so far underground.

Finally she stood, and the crystals began to dim, while the cavern walls slowly crumbled downward. She climbed to the top of the purple crystal, hoping to keep her head above the earth that was piling up, wishing all at once that the ground above her would simply open up and save her the trouble of having to find a way out. Immediately the ground above her split open and she could see daylight once more. She pulled herself out, pushing off from the crystal and making handholds in the collapsing earthen walls.

At last she lay outside once more, gasping from the climb and the sheer horror of what met her eyes. Nearly every tree within sight of the clearing was uprooted and dying, with great groups of Tree Folk huddling together in lamentation. There were still figures lying everywhere, both Devas and trees. Every few moments one of the survivors would start keening over bodies of family members and friends. The pink sky, which shone directly overhead, provided a kind of terrible comfort. Its warmth could be felt in a way that would not have been possible with the trees still standing. Rebecca stood up slowly with a mounting sense of dread. Torin always waited for her by the Great Tree. Where the Great Tree had once stood was only a dark chasm in the purple ground and a few piles of branches and shorn roots.

She made her way slowly over to the pile of branches, and recalling what Alphumerian had said, sifted through the torn and mangled piles until she found a small golden root, cleanly severed.

About four inches long, it fit nicely in her deep tunic pocket with the waters of life flask.

Rebecca walked from group to group, looking for Torin and Leva. She tried not to panic, but her stomach hurt, and her eyes watered constantly. The sheer numbers of dead trees and Devas was staggering. The surviving Tree Folk looked haggard, numbed by the deaths of so many.

Comforting a small tree child who'd lost both of his parents, Rebecca finally sat down to rest. Exhausted, they both fell asleep, and that is how Torin found them later, still huddled on the ground together. He sighed in relief, bending down to wake Rebecca. She opened her eyes when Torin plucked the sleeping child from her arms, depositing him with a grieving tree mother. He made his way back to Rebecca where she was sitting up, looking at him oddly. He said nothing, simply pulling her into his arms. She cried for the first time, for Alphumerian and all of the trees, for the Devas, but most of all because he wasn't dead.

Finally, Rebecca quieted and looked at Torin questioningly. "Where were you? I thought you'd be right here by the Great Tree. I'm so glad you weren't."

"Leva and I were looking down over the valley from the top of her parents' tree. Meridwen told me we'd need to journey to the Air Folk soon, so I was getting my bearings. Leva's fine, as are all her kin, but she grieves mightily for the rest of the Folk, and the Great Tree itself."

"I can feel your grief too," Rebecca said, putting a hand over his heart, "why is it that you don't cry?"

Torin shook his head. "The Fire Folk do not shed tears. I don't cry when I'm sad. Look." He opened his tunic above his heart. Rebecca could see a spiral of purple light coming off of him in waves.

"When I'm through grieving it will stop," he said. "When a close relative dies, we may even glow at night from our sorrow, and others may see it and respect our grief. In our culture grief is a sacred time. We are bound to give aid to those who are mourning. It is a celebration of life and death in everything that exists.

All the trees of Thianely will have felt the earth rending here at the Threshold through the root network that lies underground. There will be offerings of healing and food for all of these Folk. No one will do without. But Rebecca, Meridwen survived the earth shift and told me we must go soon to meet with Tehan of the Air Folk. The Air Folk live in the western region, or Barden. Meridwen sent word earlier that we would be traveling there for your elemental training at some point, so we will be expected. But tell me, how did you escape from the Great Tree intact? I felt you deep underground and worried you had fallen with it."

Rebecca told Torin of her adventures under the Great Tree and of Alphumerian's death. He shook his head sadly. "I hoped at least that the Essence Being had found a way to survive. Rebecca, you must not tell anyone of the crystal knowledge that you carry. Alphumerian has made it possible through you to plant another Great Tree, and there are those who would love to get their hands on that information. We must be even more careful to keep you safely away from the Bolluxes."

Torin squeezed her closer to him. "Besides protecting you for the good of the planet, I confess a more personal interest. Though I am only a teenager on your world, here I am of age. I don't think," he said slowly, watching Rebecca's eyes widen, "that I would have recovered very well if you had not lived." He stopped, anxiously searching her face for permission to continue. "I wanted you to know how I felt about you aside from fulfilling my responsibilities as Guardian."

Rebecca swallowed, trying not to blush. "I was worried about you too, and I felt ashamed that I was more concerned where you were than whether anyone else was okay. But, Torin, in the books there's never much point in dating someone from another world, because you always have to say goodbye at the end. I've been trying not to think about how much I like you, because there doesn't seem to be much point to it."

Torin tugged her even closer and grinned. "How do you suppose I was able to pull you here through a water puddle? As skilled as I am at space-time travel, water isn't my most accomplished element, you know. It had to be me because we are elementally connected. Perhaps you didn't get to that part of your memory yet, the part where you knew me before, and how many times, and how well you've known me."

Rebecca eyed him skeptically. "Okay," she said, turning an even deeper shade of pink, "I think I get the idea. But I still don't see how we can be dating between worlds. I mean I've heard of long distance relationships, but don't you think this is a little much?"

Torin nodded, "When you put it like that, I can understand your hesitation. But Rebecca, we'll come up with something. I've always known that I'm elementally bound to an offworlder. It's in my birth chart."

"Speaking of birth charts," said Rebecca, as Torin rested his chin comfortably on the top of her head, "how come so many people on my planet are born under different astrological signs that are different elements, but we all cry? Does that mean we're all water people?"

"Yes," Torin said, "you all share the connection to water, and the signs you are born under are your other elemental connections. Here on Thianely we have more land than water, and though many of the Folk require water to stay alive, only Water Folk weep tears. On the other hand, the elements are more confused on your planet, so it becomes very complicated." He sighed, and kissed the top of her head gently. "Come on, let's go see what we can do to help. Then we'd better find Leva. She lost many friends and she's still worried about you."

He helped Rebecca up. They walked past the groups of mourning Tree Folk and fallen trees into a large open space. Meridwen had set up a small nursery to take care of the injured and death shocked, those who had survived the rending, but lost their trees. Torin went to help bury the dead, while Rebecca lent a hand with the injured.

Many of the smallest children had lost one or both parents, and some had lost their trees. Many mated couples had lost their mates, including one Tree Deva who was carrying her first child. Rebecca spent the most time with her, reminding her of the child she still carried so that she could heal enough to comfort her ailing tree. Even the trees whose Devas had been spared were bereft, for the loss of the Great Tree hurt them beyond expression. Rebecca found that the healing arts worked just as well with the trees as with the Devas. Meridwen embraced her fiercely after taking a moment from directing the relief helpers.

"I knew the Great Tree would protect you," Meridwen said, patting Rebecca's back as she thanked her for her help. "Thank Rhiate, you've remembered so much of the healing arts! You must have saved at least three Folk already from death shock."

Rebecca looked at Meridwen sadly. "Meridwen, what caused such a great quake, and why didn't you know? Couldn't the Earthen Folk tell you in time?"

Meridwen closed her eyes briefly in anguish. "Rebecca, the Earthen Folk have lost contact with the deepest nature of Thianely. They simply did not know any sooner than we did. Something has interfered with the planet to the point that we have separated so much, I'm not sure how we can recover." She paused as a whole line of new volunteers appeared. "There now, the neighboring communities have sent more help. Why don't you go and make ready. You must leave here soon, for the Bolluxes tend to appear in times of distress and pain, and I would not want them to catch you off guard."

Rebecca nodded and gave Meridwen one last hug. She wandered past the injured Tree Folk and spied Torin standing with one arm about Leva and looking as if he were trying to be convincing. He glanced up as Rebecca neared them.

"See, Leva, here's Rebecca. I'm sure she'd agree with me that it's not a good idea for you to accompany us when you're still grieving so hard. Look, you have sap running constantly from your eyes and hands and feet, even after cleansing them."

Leva stiffened from under his arm and pushed him away. "I've lost my friends and the Great Tree, not my reason," she said shortly, even more disheveled than usual. Her clothes were sticky with sap and tree ichors from her dead friends, but to Rebecca she appeared to have a strange kind of dignity. "You need someone to rootspeak so that you'll have shelter during rainstorms. Besides, for balance sakes, you need someone who's tied to the ground. You are fire and Rebecca's water, but still, you have need of me, and my herbal plant lore."

She looked to Rebecca for confirmation, but Rebecca was staring at what looked to be a twirling wind heading right for them. Rebecca watched it approach with a sickening sense of dread. Torin quickly stepped in front of both her and Leva. The wind stopped and Darden Bollux stepped from it with jaunty bow. He was dressed much the same as Rebecca had last seen him, only his colors seemed even brighter. He surveyed the chaos about him with complete satisfaction, taking note of the dead trees and the sorrowing Tree Folk. He picked up a small twig from a fallen tree, idly chewing on one end.

"Greetings, one and not all, not any more with so many dead, don't you think? Say," he smiled at Torin's glare of anger, "it's the

Ash Boy. You know it's against the laws for you to harm any being, so keep some rain on your temper, you fiery fellow. Luckily I don't allow myself to be bound by such trivial conventions, now do I? Still have the little singe you got between elements, my little man? Nothing like a bit of fun between lower order and chaos, eh? Well, my, my, what a sappy little lady we have here, and what an utterly delicious event to have befallen the dear old trees, took them down a few roots, didn't we now!

I wonder where the old earth crystals have gone! All that lovely knowledge waiting to be gobbled up. Mind if I have a look about? There's a good chap, you can't throw the elements at me, my boy, this place is outside your jurisdiction."

"But it's not outside mine," Meridwen said, drawing near at the threat of danger. "By the Threshold of the Trees that yet remain, I charge you to leave, by your own name. By the balance of elements abiding here, I bid you, Darden Bollux, disappear."

"Oh blast," Darden said, as he began to vanish before their eyes, "just when things were getting interesting. Not to worry, I'm sure we'll meet again soon, now and later. Ta ta."

The swirling wind blew away, and Rebecca breathed a sigh of relief. Meridwen turned to the three of them. "It's time for you to go, now, before more of his kin arrive. I can fend them off here while you get away, but more will come looking for the crystal wisdom. Luckily they won't imagine that you received the transfer, Rebecca. Only Alphumerian was able to before. Get you gone. Yes, all three of you. Leva has the skills you will need, being of the Earthen Folk, and you know there is balance in elemental wholeness. I want you to visit the Air Folk and ask Tehan for an air companion. It will assist you in remembering your ties to the air element, Rebecca.

My dear, do not worry about your memory. Many of your skills will return when you need them. I have here a gift for your journey. It may be of some use, and when balance has been restored enough you may need it to crystal travel." Meridwen pulled her crystal necklace over her head, placing it over Rebecca's.

She turned to Leva and gave her a leaf, a bit tattered around the edges, but still a bright blue color. "Leva, this is a leaf from my own tree. No matter how far you travel, all trees will nurture you. You have a greater ability to be away from your tree than others because of your

Earthen blood, but remember to rest and nourish yourself. We will care for your tree while you are away. Be safe."

Finally she turned to Torin. She pulled a small clear piece of crystallized dew from her tunic. "Torin, you may have need of this when you least expect it. Keep it safely, and do not let it melt until it is time." Torin thanked her, as Rebecca stood hesitantly fingering her necklace.

"But what are we to do after we find an air companion? I mean, am I supposed to suddenly remember about the center of all things, simply because we have an elemental balance of companions? Isn't there some better plan?" She turned to Torin, "I know the council didn't agree on specifics, but didn't they say something about visiting the Earthen Folk and working with them?"

Torin nodded his head slowly, "We will go to the Earthen Folk, Rebecca, only not quite yet. We must reach the Air Folk's mountain range first. If we travel with an air companion, we may not have to walk any more. Until we reach the Earthen Folk, we'll rely on Leva's connection to the rooted folk for our earth expertise. And we're going to be in danger from more ground upheavals once the Bolluxes catch up to us. That's why we're going to stick close to water, the Salflow River to be more precise. Bolluxes hate water."

Meridwen put a hand on Rebecca's shoulder. "No more talking, my dear, you must all leave now. Farewell, and be safe."

As they turned to go, Torin bowed to her respectfully. "May Rhiate bless you, Meridwen. May your people recover and regain their strength."

They paused a few more moments to bid the Tree Folk and Leva's family farewell, then picked up their freshly stocked backsacks and set off. Torin led Rebecca and Leva through the fields of fallen trees. They stopped to murmur blessings for the dead, and occasionally gather fruit and nuts that lay scattered upon the ground. Rebecca put an arm around Leva, who continued to weep for her folk and friends as they began the journey west.

## Chapter 8

They walked steadily for several hours, dodging the huge trees that had toppled for miles around, sometimes even forced to climb over them. They found a few surviving Tree Folk, and after helping them as best they could, they sent them to Meridwen for care and healing. Finally, Torin called a halt and they sat down and ate fruit, nuts, and some dried seed cakes that Torin had brought. Rebecca felt tired, strained, and a bit peculiar from her experience with the crystals. She wondered where the information from them was stored inside her, and when she would find out.

After their snack Torin pulled a leaf map from his backsack and showed Rebecca and Leva the route they would travel to the Air Folk. He pointed out where they were in the Threshold of the Trees, in central Thianely. They would be traveling due west toward a long valley and a winding river that snaked along a mountain range. "We'll stick close to the Salflow River until we reach the mountain," Torin said, while Leva nodded.

They packed up the remaining food and began the long trek through the valley to the river. It seemed to Rebecca that the day had already lasted about a year, and she knew she would never forget the cries of the dying trees and their people. She tried not to think of how tired she was and concentrated on watching her feet. Torin kept an eye on both her and Leva, calling for frequent rests.

Finally, it began to grow dark, and Torin stopped. "That's far enough for one day," he said, looking expectantly at Leva. She stood quietly for a moment with her eyes closed.

"There's a tree just a few lengths ahead that offers us shelter. Follow me."

She led them along the valley floor to a small cluster of trees. They differed from the ones in the Threshold in both color and in girth, for they were much smaller, their trunks only eight to twelve feet in diameter. She approached one of the trees, a tall one with reddish brown bark, and tapped firmly on the rough surface. The tree parted its bark to let them through and they found themselves in a small chamber, big enough for them to stretch out comfortably.

The tree's occupant was away on a trip so the tree was quite thankful for their company. They told the tree all that had occurred at the Threshold, even though he'd been apprised of some of it through the root network. He grieved with them, his deep voice especially comforting to Leva. They all fell asleep to the sound of the tree singing leaf lullabies.

They set out again the next day. The tree had helped them plan their journey by communicating to its mates some distance away, therefore they had shelter ready for them when they stopped to rest without Leva having to expend any extra energy in asking. They traveled about fifteen to twenty miles per day, and Rebecca noticed that her slipper shoes showed no wear at all, staying comfortable and durable throughout their long hikes.

They had walked for several days when they reached a beautiful valley. The valley was covered in open meadowland, dotted with wild flowers and gigantic gray stones that lay haphazardly about, as if dropped from some great height. They followed a faint path etched out among the grass and stones that looked as if it hadn't been used in some time. It made for a very pleasant hike and Rebecca realized that she was more fit than she'd ever been in her life.

During the journey Leva's grief diminished somewhat, mostly for practical reasons, as the sap she exuded attracted insects. She tended to be a silent companion, though she did hum along with the trees when they passed a grove of them here and there. Torin, however, taught Rebecca some of the journeying songs he knew. What Rebecca remembered of the trek later was the lush lavender of the grass, the tall gray stones, and Torin singing in his melodious, deep voice.

One day, they were glad of a tree's sheltering bark when a particularly dense rainstorm caught them out in the open. The sky merely ignored their asking for drier weather and so they were all completely drenched by the time they located their latest rest stop. They huddled inside, waiting for the rain to subside. Rebecca was surprised at the fury of the storm, contrasting it with the gentle warmth of the rain she'd experienced at Imanayon's. She'd been longing to let the rain clean her hair, but they could hear the wind lashing tree limbs outside. She stood, damp and shaking, wishing for a hot bath, when Torin turned to her and hands aglow, dried her off in a matter of moments. Then he did the same for Leva and himself.

She smiled, feeling warm and dry and surprisingly clean as well. She noticed in the glow of her crystal necklace, which she'd found tended to radiate in the dark, that the grass stains on her skirt had disappeared, as had the dirt on her tunic. She glanced up in surprise at Torin's grin. "Water is not the only element that cleans and purifies," he said, "next time you want to take a bath in fire, let me know."

Rebecca thought it was a marvelous way to bathe, particularly when running water was unavailable. But she wondered what else Torin and Leva could do. As they waited out the storm she said, "One of these days you'll have to sit down and fill me in about your abilities, Torin, and you too, Leva. I know you both learned about your gifts at really young ages, but it's still so new to me. I remember so much about other lifetimes, but not yet what I'm able to do in this one. Tell me, what are the basic abilities with each element?"

Torin sat down comfortably on the earthen floor of the tree and Leva followed suit. Rebecca joined them as Torin began to draw a circle in the purple earth. He divided it into four equal sections.

"Let say this circle is the Great Balance," Torin said, motioning with his hand. "Each one of these quarters is an element, Fire, Water, Earth and Air. Each of the Folk on Thianely has the ability to contact all of the elements, but in the course of his or her many lifetimes, he or she has become more proficient in using one over the others. Once in a while there is born a being that has equal proficiency in all elements, and this being plays a large role in maintaining the balance of all things.

All are born in the month of their, what we call 'parent" element. I was born in a fire month for instance, and Leva was born in an earth month, while you were born in a water month. I think on your planet it isn't so clear sometimes, though, because you're on a water planet in general.

Thianely is an earth element planet, with much less water than your planet. Nearby us are Hevald and Torildian, two other planets of air and fire respectively. Hevaldians are much less dense beings than we are, as their planet has less gravity, while Torildian inhabitants all breathe fire. They exist in very high temperatures that even the Fire Folk here would find uncomfortable. I've had some contact with the beings there and they also are experiencing elemental difficulties. Rebecca, the important thing to remember is that you are one of those beings, who although you are aligned with water, also are equally adept in the other elements. It is through integration of the elements that your memory will return.

I can tell you of my gifts with fire, and Leva can tell you of her gifts of earth, though she has not yet received her full training from the Earthen Folk, but I cannot tell you all of your gifts of water and air, because I have only been lightly trained in those elements. One of the things that Grandfather has wished to put into practice is complete communication between all of the Folk, but some have wished to guard their knowledge, keeping it among those who are fully aligned.

But to get back to our gifts. Fire Folk are able, during balanced times, to become fire and travel in flame, and to create fire when needed. There are also mind abilities that most Folk have, to tel over various distances, to heal themselves, and so on."

"And Earthen Folk are able to nurture growing things, to speak to the ground, (at least we used to be able to all of the time), to mind and root tel, to use plant lore to heal, and to forecast earth events," Leva explained.

"I was taught perhaps more about the other elements because of Grandfather's efforts," Torin continued, "and I received my training early. No one knows who my parents are, not even Grandfather, who found me in a place of fire and ash. The Great Tree would not tell me of my family origins, so Grandfather trained me in as much as he could in order to be thorough, and also because I am a Guardian as well.

We need to find an air companion, Rebecca, partly to help you remember the qualities of air. Then you will be reminded in three elements. At some point you will meet the other Water Folk. Then you'll be more aware of all of the elements and may find the center. We can try at any rate."

Rebecca shivered, though she was warm. "Most of this is like walking in the dark and hoping we don't bump into anything terribly dangerous along the way. How do you live like this? I mean, most of the rules you follow are based on things you can't even see. I feel like we get only enough information to be able to handle what's happening right now, but there's not much planning for the future. We're going to find an air companion, go see the Earthen Folk, and hope I remember enough to know what we ought to do next?"

Torin and Leva exchanged a glance. "It may seem very strange to you, Rebecca," Leva said, "but most of our planning for the future involves making sure we all have enough to eat and that balance is being maintained. We do have foretelers like those who wrote the prophecy, but we do not know what to do or someone would already have done it. All we know is that the knowledge is inside you. You will remember when the time is right. The crystal information is in you as well, and it would not be unless you were the right person. We will know what to do when it is necessary to know. Much of life cannot be planned; it must be experienced in the moment. Stop doubting yourself so much; it leaves space for the Bolluxes to attack you."

Rebecca wondered how that was supposed to help her feel less doubtful, since now she had vague feelings of guilt that she'd been responsible for Darden showing up in the first place. She did recall that he'd first made her acquaintance after she'd gotten so angry during the council, and when the earthquake had caused such mayhem among the trees and their Folk.

Torin read her mind. "Look, Rebecca, the Bolluxes have been nuisances long before you arrived. What Leva is trying to say is that you will only give them more opportunity to disrupt matters if you continue to feel so unworthy. Any long held emotional upset or vulnerability is an invitation to them to make things messier. They love chaos of any kind, and to them there's a higher sort of order to it that they worship. Balance to them is abhorrent. So let's try to maintain some, okay?"

Rebecca nodded, leaning back against the tree for support. "I'm going to sleep now," she said. "I still feel a little odd from slurping up all of that crystal information. Sometimes I get dizzy. Lines of symbols kind of wander through my head."

Torin looked at her interestedly. "Can you understand any of it?"

"Not really," she said, yawning. "Most of it looks like numbers and letters and images mixed together. Familiar, but not enough to make much sense."

"It'll come," Torin said reassuringly, but Rebecca was already asleep against the inner wall of the tree. Meanwhile, Leva had stretched out on the ground and was quietly snoring. Torin moved closer to Rebecca and gently pulled her down until she lay fully stretched out. He lay next to her, speaking to the tree for a while, making sure the firewall of protection he'd placed about its circumference was still intact. Then he too slept.

Rebecca awoke to Torin tugging urgently at her shoulder. "Rebecca, wake up. The tree sent a warning a few minutes ago. A

Bollux is nearby, trying to block our route. They must have figured out that we'd travel as close to water as possible. This one, Varvane, is a master at creating obstacles. We've got to get out of here somehow and find an alternate path to the river."

Rebecca sat up, instantly awake as soon as she'd heard the word Bollux. She saw Leva hurriedly packing their food and supplies. Without thinking she said, "But why don't you use an obstacle block, you know, that creates obstacles for the obstacle maker?"

Torin stared at her in surprise. "What? You know how to send her spell reflex?"

"I guess so," Rebecca said wonderingly. "I mean I think I do. All of a sudden it came to me. I need to know what she's doing, draw a circle around us, and use the crystal Meridwen gave me. After that the spell returns to its maker."

Torin took her hand and pulled her to her feet. "I'll show you what she's doing," he said grimly. The tree parted for them as Leva hurried along behind.

Rebecca gasped when she saw the huge wall of stones completely ringing the valley. The thick stones were stacked up so high they could no longer see the valley beyond, and the distant purple of the Salflow River was completely swallowed up in gray. An imposingly tall woman with dark hair and a long, sharp face stood triumphantly before them. She wore a tattered black dress, prompting Rebecca's fleeting thought that the Bolluxes she'd met so far were lousy dressers.

"Might as well go home now, you elemental numbwits," the Bollux cackled in a harsh voice. "No point in sending a couple of girls to do a woman's job, or a little boy for that matter. Hurry along now, I'd hate to have one of these big stones fall down and crush you flat."

As she spoke one of the walls began to tremble alarmingly. Rebecca turned to Torin, demanding quickly, "Tell me, what's her name again?"

"Varvane," replied Torin without hesitation. Rebecca ignored the creaking tower of stones and concentrated fiercely. She created a large circle of blue light with her mind, imagining the three of them standing inside it, with Varvane excluded. She clasped Meridwen's crystal in her hand and called out,

"Varvane Bollux,
Like calls to like and mind to mind,
Crystal to stone and kind to kind,
Stone to earth and crystal to ground,
Spell in reflex and balance found."

Rebecca swept Meridwen's necklace out in front of her in a flourish. The walls of stone vanished. Still standing within the circle of light she'd created, Torin, Rebecca and Leva observed the angry Bollux's response. Varvane stomped her narrow feet, exposing the sharp talons on the end of each toe. Beneath her the ground sank down in dismay, trying to avoid her temper.

Varvane stepped closer, shaking in fury. Her dark dress swirled about her in tune with her mood. Her mouth was open, exposing long, pointed teeth, and she was so enraged that spittle flew from the sides of her mouth as she screamed, "So, the little vermin has found her powers, as well as lifted a few that didn't belong to you! Yes, you vile, waterous cretin, you've been crystal-marked, any fool could see that, except my bogwit of a brother. We have certain skills in separating idiots from information, so be careful not to make me too angry, or I'll tear you from knowing like a plant from its roots!"

She reached out a hand to slap Rebecca's face and encountered not only Torin's firewall of protection, but also Rebecca's blue light. Recoiling in pain, Varvane clutched her injured palm. Simultaneously burnt and shocked, it smoldered slightly, emitting a foul stench reminiscent of a manure pile. Varvane shook her damaged fist and abruptly faded away. Behind her she left a fleeting impression of a scowling face and a faint, noxious odor.

As Rebecca slumped to the ground, drained from the effort of repelling the Bollux, Torin put a hand on her head and began to hum loudly. Leva joined him in a song of renewal, and Rebecca could feel energy quickly returning to her body. Still holding Meridwen's crystal, she slowly rose to her feet.

"Nasty creature," she commented with a shudder. "And thank you," she said gratefully to both Torin and Leva. "I was exhausted until you hummed that tune for me. What was that?"

"It's a song for planting and sewing seeds," Leva explained. "We also sing it after great feats of strength. All Thianelians learn healing songs as part of their education. I can remind you of them if you'd like."

"I did remember the Autumn Song when I first visited the Great Tree," Rebecca said. "And the tune you hummed sounded familiar as well."

Torin eyed her thoughtfully. "Rebecca, you just successfully completed a spell reflex. Normally only highly trained spell spinners can do that. I think that if you can respond so well with only minor fatigue we'll certainly make it safely to the Air Folk."

Rebecca grimaced. "I don't prefer to work on that level, thank you, though I suppose it may be necessary. And I suppose I ought to know what a spell spinner is."

Torin smiled. "Obviously you are one. They are what on your world people call sorcerers."

"Great," Rebecca muttered. "Now I'm a sorcerer too."

"Not quite," replied Torin. "A spell spinner is more skilled. And as long as you use that level of ability only for defensive purposes, there are no negative consequences. Unfortunately, sometimes you do have to respond to beings at their level."

"Wait a moment," Leva interjected, cocking her head to one side and tapping her foot lightly against the ground. "Torin, there's been a ground breach here from all the spells spun. The earth is unsteady and the trees are nervous. Can you both stand with me to help me repair the breach? My Grandmother Imelina, of the Earthen Folk, taught me how during my training, but I'm not sure it will have any effect now that everything is so chaotic. Still, if we try we may be able to help. I couldn't bear another earth rending here."

Both Torin and Rebecca nodded. Leva motioned them close and they stood, hands clasped together, while Leva began to sing in a soft voice, which gradually became louder,

> "Purple earth, beneath our feet
> Let the will of mending meet
> To weave all time within this space
> And bring strength back to earthen place."

After a few rounds both Torin and Rebecca joined in and the song swirled through their bodies, creating a spiral of energy. The golden green light spun right in the center of their small circle. As their voices rose higher and higher, the energy spiraled faster and faster, finally plunging right down into the ground between the three of them. Leva motioned for them to stop singing and listened carefully. She smiled, unclasping Torin and Rebecca's hands.

"We did it, or as near as I can tell, we unbolluxed the earth here," Leva said in satisfaction. "The trees should be safe, at least for awhile. We've stitched time together here where it was torn."

Torin sighed. "I don't know about you both, but I've done enough mending for awhile. Let's continue on. I'll feel more at ease when we get to the river. Here you two, you might need something to eat after all of that."

Rebecca accepted the seed cake Torin handed her and ate it quickly. She was suddenly starving. Despite the nasty encounter with another Bollux, she felt curiously uplifted. It felt good to have helped heal the ground. Still, she had to agree it was time to move on, and the three companions continued on their way towards the Salflow River.

## Chapter 9

They walked throughout the rest of the day without interruptions, except for a few rest breaks. After sheltering overnight in a kind old tree that loved to tell stories, they reached the river early the next morning. Rebecca was fatigued, having remained awake late into the night listening to the tree describe the entire lineage of Tree Folk, from the beginning of Thianely to the present. She dragged a bit when they first started walking, but the exercise soon revived her.

The Salflow River was much wider and wilder than Rebecca had expected. A pale purple color, the water had the scent of wild blossoms, and tumbled along furiously. She was glad they were merely following along its banks rather than trying to cross it. After Torin assured them that the water was thoroughly drinkable, Leva immediately plunged in, completely immersing herself. Torin lay face down and dunked his head, while Rebecca approached the water more cautiously. She bent down and rinsed her hands, feeling the smooth purple water cascading about her fingers. Finally she cupped her hands to take a drink.

All at once Rebecca was the rushing river, forceful and flowing, gliding along the riverbanks, feeling the warm sun heating her, the wind playing along her surface, the creatures that lived and breathed and swam in her. She knew them all, every being that had ever sipped water. She felt formless, contained only by the feel of the ground beneath her, the sky above, the press of riverbank against her sides. As she felt the ripples of time slide past her, she remembered from the beginning, when Life Force called to her to help create the first people with his mate, Niaphani. Rebecca felt Torin's arm about her, his hands cupping her face, and she remembered him as well.

She opened her eyes, looking into Torin's as he stared down at her. "I have always known you," she said wonderingly.

Torin leaned over, kissing her softly. "Yes," he said, "I was wondering when you would recall that. I was feeling impatient to see you and wanted to pull you here sooner when you first started coming to Thianely, but Grandfather bade me wait. Also, you were ill with fever. But now, here you are, and here I am." He smiled. "Come on, Rebecca, let's keep moving. Do me a favor and don't get too close to the water for now. You'll lose any sense of being human if you remain in the water for long, like being extremely rain dazzled. You must experience water memories gradually to be able to stay in form."

He called to Leva to come out of the water, and she emerged dripping, refreshed from the purple current. They donned their packs and continued along the river, stopping occasionally to admire the view. Most of the trees that grew by the riverbanks were slender and short, offering little in the way of shelter. They decided to stop for the night along an offshoot of the river that had formed a deep pool. Rebecca watched curiously as small, orange, three-winged birds alighted on the water, dipping their beaks to drink.

"Milenna birds," Leva explained. "They can only fly after drinking water, so they tend to live by rivers and streams. Some live out in desert regions, but because they cannot fly without water, they become land birds and get their moisture from the bugs they eat."

When Rebecca asked about other wildlife in the area, Torin and Leva took turns describing the "animals" of Thianely. Rebecca learned that there were creatures with hooves called furpakas, many varieties of birds, nasty beings that lived in bogs, called bog sprites, and all sorts of insects. Torin tried to explain the Griffin Folk, but Rebecca had a difficult time understanding the difference between Folk and what would normally on Earth be considered animals. On Thianely the distinction didn't really exist. Most creatures communicated in the Old Tongue, able to think as well as speak. Few ate flesh, simply because other forms of food were so plentiful. The Griffin Folk, however, needed to eat meat in order to keep up their prodigious strength. The important thing, Torin said, was to eat all food with respect, whether it be plant life, fruit, or flesh.

Rebecca helped lay out the blankets for the night. Later, as she stretched out under the sky, well lit by stars and distant planets, she thought about her parents, imagining how she could possibly explain this whole world to them. She listened to the sounds of Torin and Leva breathing in their sleep. As she closed her eyes, trying to get some rest, she heard the sound of someone calling to her. It wasn't loud, but it was insistent, like the sound of water gently lapping shore. She lay quietly for a moment, listening, and heard the call again. Finally she rose to her feet and carefully made her way down to the river, where ripples of currents were gleaming under the stars.

When she came close to the water, she saw them, drifting slowly in the pool, women with long pale hair decorated with shells and flowers. As she approached them, one raised her hand and swam closer, singing hello. Rebecca saw the webbed fingers, the silver gills opening and closing along the sides of the woman's neck. Tails sparkling like metal in the moonlight, the women glided toward her. Rebecca waded in to her knees to greet them, these water women, her sisters. Each reached out a hand to clasp hers, one after another.

Finally, a very old woman swam close. Rebecca saw tears trickling down the wrinkled cheeks. She embraced the old one, whose flesh was surprisingly warm, her arms strongly comforting. The old one smiled.

"Do you remember me, your own grandmother? I am Niamiah, who sang your birth so long ago, five thousand lives past. Have you returned to us at last, though on the land you walk now, all water ways forgot?"

"I have not forgotten you, Grandmother," Rebecca said, recalling her many lives beneath the waves, the depths of oceans in the freedom of flowing currents. The old one sang proudly, head lifted high, reminding Rebecca of the sound of water in all its forms. Rebecca heard the syncopation of rain dropping from flower petals, the rush of rivers racing over rocks, the placid sound of pools and lakes, the pull of the tides in great ocean bodies.

Rebecca stood with her eyes closed, listening to her grandmother's song with great joy. With a suddenness that startled her, her legs twisted into tail beneath her, and the water embraced her fully. As she submerged, her clothes dissolved. She gave a strong push with her fins, exulting in the freedom of swimming with her sisters and diving down, down into the purple depths. She found without surprise that she was breathing steadily in and out through the sides of her neck, and she called to her grandmother in the language of the waves, "Niamiah, Grandmother, where do we fin?"

Her grandmother answered, "To the ocean, my dear, where you were once born, to help you remember our ways."

They were all moving quickly, allowing the pull of the current to hurry them along. The Merfolk soon led her to a fork in the river that diverted them from the Salflow. Rebecca breathed deeply, letting the motion flow into her veins until there was no difference between her and the movement. Farther and faster they swam, Rebecca enjoying the feel of her long tail pulsing her along, until finally the river emptied into the great vastness of warm seawater.

She surfaced, watching the reflection of the moon against the ebb and flow of the sea. She looked at her bare arms and laughed at the sensation of being without garments. Her sisters and grandmother surfaced as well.

"Welcome home, sea sister," they sang. Niamiah reached over and placed a shell comb in Rebecca's hair. She laid her webbed palm upon Rebecca's head for a moment.

"Do you know your mername, my granddaughter?" Niamiah asked.

Rebecca nodded. "I am Riamah, daughter of Ariah, granddaughter of Niamiah. I have lived beneath the seas of Thianely for many lives, but that has always been my name."

Throughout the Merfolk's long history, no matter how many lives one had, one was always recognized as the same being. The Merfolk lived for hundreds of years, eventually leaving their old bodies to be born anew.

Niamiah nodded, proud her Riamah had returned. Rebecca's sisters swam about, calling out their names so that she could greet them properly. Rebecca met lifetimes of relatives in the flick of a fin. Nearly overwhelmed by her reception, she found herself weeping salty tears of joy. She laughed, recognizing what she had always known, that merfolk, sensitive to tides of emotion, had helped create the sea with their own tears, of joy, of sorrow, of anger.

At first she looked about for the mermales, and then realized that they would be below, tending the young. Mermales kept newborns safe in their stomach pouches until they were old enough to leave. The mermales nurtured the young, fed the old, and kept the gardens. She longed suddenly to plunge down to the very bottom of the sea. There she could see the gardens of colorful sea foliage lit by phosphorescent shells left behind by sea creatures. She would feel the fluid movement of thousands of merfolk going about their watery duties. Most of all she would hear the songs, the rippling voices of mersingers, beautiful sounds of creation pouring from their lips. Rebecca wanted to go home, to the mercity where she'd spent so many lives.

Her grandmother heard her longing. "Riamah, now is not the time, but you will return. Soon you may come home beneath the waves. But for now, we have much to tell you, and little time. Listen."

Her sisters swirled around her, reminding her, in words and song, of all that water holds and releases. They demonstrated how to balance upon the surface no matter how rough the waves, how to dive so deeply that she felt as if she could never return, and how to be completely still. In order to rest, she had to relax and let the waves carry her. At last her sisters stopped and led her back to the mouth of the river.

"You must return on your own," her grandmother told her. "The way is more difficult because it is upstream, but it will allow you put into practice all that you have learned. Your tail will change once more when you are on land. Remember, we are always with you; merely call to us and let the watery nature of your own body hear our reply."

They bade her farewell, singing Rebecca an old mermaid song,

I see them smiling out at me
Sea sisters sighing, calling me
Under the waterfall.

Long hair green as seaweed fire,
Voices rising higher and higher,
Under the waterfall.

While human dancers turn and spin,
They breathe the air from skies grown dim
And so I shed my manworld skin,
Under the waterfall.

The deep, green world where I long to be
Homeward, sisters calling me
With silver fins and pearls for me
Under the waterfall.

Back in the depths where I am free
Safe with kin and home with thee,
Part of the song of the endless sea,
Under the waterfall,
Under the waterfall.

Rebecca waved at her folk and began the long task of swimming back. It was much more tiring, and sometimes she stayed as close to the bottom as she could, avoiding upper currents. At times she stayed at the surface breathing air through her mouth rather than her gills, but at no time was she able to simply rest. At last, exhausted, she reached the edge of the pool and dragged herself tiredly out onto the bank. She was much colder than she expected, and for some reason her tail and gills remained. She closed her eyes and lay panting in the air for a while, until suddenly warmth radiated along her spine. Her tail whipped about, dwindling into legs.

She opened her eyes to see Torin bending over her with his palms alight. Her clothing had returned and she was once again dry. Rebecca sat up gratefully, reached over, and pulled Torin down beside her. "I went home," she said simply.

He held her close while she began to tell him of her sisters and grandmother. He smiled into her hair. "I know," he said. "I wondered when this would happen. You have the look of the merfolk about you. They are the only Water Folk left on Thianely, besides the naiads of lakes and streams. So you are Riamah. I'm sure you will have many names before the end of this journey."

They stayed that way, curled up together by the bank of the river, and slept long and well. In the morning they picked up their backsacks and continued following the river. Leva appeared happier than Rebecca could remember since they'd left the Threshold of the Trees. She had bathed in the purple water frequently, because, as Torin explained, it helped to heal her grief.

"All water here on Thianely is sacred and healing. It adapts itself to what each being needs."

Rebecca smiled, remembering her mermaid kin, and the feeling of being so completely watery. She missed them already, but the mountains of the Air Folk no longer looked so far away. Each night they camped by the river without incident.

"No Bollux would approach you by the river," Torin said, "although Jierdan Bollux tends to accost people in swampy areas."

"Exactly how many Bolluxes are there?" asked Rebecca, as they stepped carefully around a patch of ground where the bank had given way.

"No one is precisely sure," replied Torin, after he disconnected his thought lines. He was extremely careful to do so before speaking of the Bolluxes. When Rebecca asked, he said that her talking about them didn't seem to have the same effect, perhaps because her thoughts and far tel weren't always aligned.

"The last thing we want to do is bring them to us by discussing them too energetically. But we do know there are at least these brothers and sisters: Varvane, Darden, Jierdan, Royden, Harlane, Haldar, and Mosten born to the Bollux leaders, Boleria and Etestian. None of us can decide who's worst, but we know they're all chaos born. Each of them has particular ways to cause destruction and mayhem. We've always hoped they'd get bored with the rest of us and take it out on each other, but so far, no luck."

"Aren't they worried that if Thianely is destroyed they'll all die too?" Rebecca wondered.

"I don't think logic is one of their strong points," Torin said. "Haven't you noticed that talking to a Bollux creates a kind of confusion in your mind? They actually feed on distortion and worry so they try to stir up as much of it as possible. At least the Griffin Folk have been able to keep them in check up to now. Rebecca, now that we're almost to the mountain path, we're going to have to be very careful. We'll have to leave the river soon."

"Can't we simply mindtel to Tehan and ask him to send us a companion?" she asked.

Leva shook her head. "Do you remember the storm we were in only a few days ago? That is highly unusual in this part of the western region. The trees are noticing disruptions in the air currents."

"Actually, I've already tried mindtel," Torin said. "I couldn't get through consistently. My thought reception kept going in and out, and I'm not sure I was able to send anything at all. Besides," he continued, "they'll want to meet you in person anyway. We'll need a volunteer to accompany us, and also you have some remembering to do at Tehan's mountain home. Tehan can remind you of air principles and abilities. He's also a Guardian."

They left the river that afternoon, walking across lightly forested terrain. It took several hours until they were out of sight of the Salflow. Soon they were following a steeply cut trail that led to the base of a huge mountain. It was the highest one in the enormous mountain range of the Air Folk. Torin said that their leader, Tehan, lived at its peak. Torin had placed a cone of fire about them, so Rebecca could only see where to put her feet, the backs of Torin and Leva, then a wall of flames in all directions. The fire was completely without heat when she touched it, but Torin explained that it would burn others fiercely if they attacked.

After a few hours of hiking it felt to Rebecca that she'd been climbing for years. She wondered how well she would do in school P.E. classes now that she had hiked for such long distances over difficult terrain. At least her swimming skills had improved. She spent time imagining what her friends would say if she grew a tail and gills in the swimming pool.

They continued walking until late evening, after which they made camp under the overhang of some large rocks. Because there was only sparse vegetation near the path they traveled, they were unable to shelter in a tree. As they slept close together under the night sky, Torin kept the protection of the fire about them, both to keep Bolluxes at bay and also to repel any curious insects.

The next morning they started out climbing strongly, but Rebecca's legs began to protest the uphill slope. The backsack of supplies she carried seemed to have doubled its weight. Her lungs began to ache due to the higher altitude. She felt stiff and sore, and although she would have liked to have rested often, she wasn't sure it would have helped much. They stopped to gather a strange looking root that Leva called Draxis, and resumed hiking. Finally, Torin called a halt and they sat down to eat lunch.

"Here," Leva said, pulling apart a bit of the root she'd gathered, "try a bite of this in your mouth, Rebecca. Suck on it for a while."

Rebecca bit off a piece of the tough root. It warmed her mouth. A curious, relaxed feeling came over her, and she felt her muscles begin to unwind and lengthen as breathing became easier.

They finished eating and continued to climb. Far below them they could see the winding purple river, and Rebecca realized they were very high up already. Torin had informed her that it would take them nearly eight more hours to reach the Air Folk's dwellings. They had to walk slowly in order to adjust to the altitude. Rebecca was relieved to think that it wouldn't be too much further, although Torin and Leva seemed to be doing fine. Up ahead was another sharp curve in the path. The view down the side of the mountain was beautiful, the purple expanse of earth dotted with occasional bursts of color from flowers and sparse trees far below.

She'd just glanced down at her feet when Torin stopped abruptly in front of her so that she nearly crashed into him. In an instant, the rim of fire that had protected them vanished, and Torin was hurrying forward to meet someone. Rebecca and Leva followed him. Rebecca was astonished to see Torin hugging a strange horse-footed person, who wore only a sort of dark loincloth over the shaggy golden fur covering most of his body.

"Tehy!" Torin cried, finally stepping back so that Rebecca and Leva could get a better look at his friend. "What are you doing here? I thought you were in Griffin Country."

Tehy replied in a deep gravelly voice, "Welcome, my friend. My father recalled me from my travels. Tehan says there is need for me here now, so I returned." He turned towards Rebecca, gazing at her with dark, penetrating eyes. "So, at last you have returned to Thianely," he said. "It has been many thousands of years since last we met. Do you remember?"

In that moment, Rebecca did, seeing his face shift into that of an old man with tremendously large wings and a wide, intelligent face. He had been her brother, and she recognized in him now the same patient wisdom that had been with him before. He was tall, this being, for she could not call him a man with his shaggy coat and hooves. He had a broad chest, heavily furred, a long torso and powerful arms. His two legs were somewhat horse-like, but straighter, and his ears, what she could see of them beneath his hair, were pointed at the tips. If she'd had to describe him using earth terms, she would've said that he resembled a cross between a Pegasus and a human, for he had large wings folded neatly upon his back, and a very human looking face.

"I remember you, Tehy," Rebecca said, stepping closer to give him a hug. "Are all of the Air Folk like you?" she asked curiously, wondering at his age, for his face, though mature, seemed ageless.

Torin laughed. "Tehy is somewhat unique, even among the Air Folk. His mother is the Griffin Queen, and his father Tehan, the leader of the Air Folk. That's why he has wings, hooves, and a tail." Tehy swung around so that Rebecca and Leva could see the long tail that he kept coiled like a snake above his loincloth.

"I thought griffins were part lion and eagle," Rebecca said, "But you look like a horse angel. Though your tail is more like a snake."

Tehy shrugged. "I am half of Air and half Griffin. Mother's face is as human as mine, though there are some Griffins who have the visages of birds or furpakas. It all depends. My kinfolk on both sides do not really resemble me, though some of them on my mother's side, the members of the Griffin Guard, have wings as well.

Torin, I am to accompany you all on the rest of your journey. Meridwen reached my father through the root network and he called me home from Griffin Country. Elemental air traveling is not always safe, now that the Bolluxes have provided so much interference, but my wings remain unaffected."

Torin clasped Tehy on the shoulder gratefully. "There could be none better as a companion, my friend. I am honored to have you with us."

"I am honored as well," Tehy replied. He turned to Leva and bowed. "Imelina of the Earthen Folk sent us a message after they lost control of the Time Gate. She said you would be coming soon; she'd seen it through a foreteling long ago. You are welcome among us. Father sent me down to meet you all after Meridwen alerted him. Follow me. I know a shorter route up the mountain."

He turned, leading them directly to the side of the mountain rather than along the path, and kicked the earth a few times. The side of the mountain began to crumble and when Rebecca would have jumped back in alarm, Tehy shook his head. He grasped Torin's hand, motioned for him to hold Rebecca's, and held Leva's hand as well. The falling of earth subsided, revealing a tall tunnel curving sharply uphill. Tehy led them into the wide tunnel where they could feel a breeze blowing through as they walked. Several times it gusted strongly enough to nearly knock them off of their feet, but holding one another's hands helped them stay upright.

"Our mountain range is the earth that accumulated on top of a sleeping troll," Tehy commented. "There are many such wind tunnels in the ground from when the troll first became covered, where he moved and created pockets of space. He isn't liable to awaken for another four billion years though," he added, noting Rebecca's look of alarm.

"But what about the earth rending?" Rebecca wondered.

"It would take more than a rending to wake this troll," Torin said, chuckling. "He's famous all over Thianely. He slept through the creation of the planet. Sometime I'll have Grandfather tell you all the story of how trolls arrived here."

They continued along until they came to another dirt wall, which again Tehy kicked to open. Rebecca wondered at his lack of courtesy, but figured she'd asked enough questions for a while.

Torin pulled her aside a little, whispering, "Troll earth is notoriously stubborn. You have to move it yourself, because asking only makes it think you're not worth moving for. It's strange I know, but you get used to it."

Rebecca soon noticed that she was again feeling the effects of the high altitude so they stopped to rest for a bit. After she ate more of the Draxis root she was able to go on. Moments later, Tehy stepped out of the tunnel on to the edge of a vast plateau, where they could look down a dizzying long way. Rebecca realized they'd knocked several hours off of their traveling time, and she wasn't even feeling the altitude any more.

They stood on a huge open field that was covered with lavender grass, flowering bushes, and hundreds of three-sided, triangular shaped buildings arranged in clusters of six. The buildings looked like they were made of stone. Rebecca wondered aloud if they were made from the huge gray stones in the valley.

Tehy turned to her with a nod. "Air Folk are gifted builders in that we are able to transport objects from several miles away. The gray stones were lifted from the valley and asked to assume the forms you see here. We Air Folk find the shape of the triple triangle to be especially pleasing. You will notice that the very tops of the buildings are flat rather than pointed. The tip where the triangles meet is reshaped flat to remain open, reminding us to keep our minds open as well. Many of the smaller stones may also revolve in the walls to act as airways. You only need touch a stone to ask it to create an opening for you. During storms we protect the top of the buildings with leaf nets that are kept in the roof. They automatically inflate up through the building tops before storms. Come now, let us see if we may find Father."

As they made their way across the wide plateau, people strolled by, smiling at them in a friendly manner. Torin and Leva recognized several of them from the large yearly gatherings to which all Folk were invited. The gatherings took place in the central region of Thianely, usually after Yarwen. They were often the only times that large groups of the different Folk met. The Folk traveled mostly during mentoring journeys or elementally for individual visits, usually content to stay at home. They stopped to chat, getting reacquainted with old friends, when Rebecca noticed quite a few children playing nearby. She tapped Leva on the shoulder.

"Leva, are those kids floating off of the ground or is it my imagination?"

"I'm sorry, Rebecca," Tehy responded, drawing her away from where Torin and Leva stood talking to old acquaintances. "I forgot that you might recognize us, but not our ways. Yes, you did see children "airing" themselves as we call it. They are children from the neighboring mountains, sent here to study the ways of our Folk. This mountain is the educational center for all of us. Those children do not yet have control of themselves in gravity, so they tend to drift up at odd moments..." He broke off as Rebecca shook her head in dismay.

"Tell me, Rebecca, what troubles you so much?"

"You know what?" she confessed. "Of all the things I've experienced since I arrived here, the things I have the hardest time with are Torin making fire come out of his hands and kids floating up in the air. I mean, I've traveled through a crystal, remembered other lives, met people who live in trees, and even swum with mermaids. I can't understand why this kind of stuff scares me so much."

Tehy scratched his head thoughtfully as his tail slowly untwined itself from behind and reached for the ground. "I think better with my tail touching earth," he explained, noting her surprised look. He paused for a moment. "I think perhaps your planet's laws of nature are difficult to let go of. On Earth your gravity keeps you firmly on the ground, and fire is created through mechanical means. Perhaps our laws here remind you that you will no longer be bound by the elemental rules of your planet, and therefore, what makes you human there no longer applies."

Rebecca validated his theory by promptly bursting into tears, bringing Torin immediately to her side and Leva not far behind. Tehy observed the expression on Torin's face as he held Rebecca, and smiled. He was pleased that Torin had found his mate, but realized that much difficulty lay ahead for his friend. Torin glanced up, caught Tehy's look of commiseration, and nodded ruefully. Rebecca soon stopped sobbing and stood rubbing her eyes.

"Well, sorry about that," she said shortly, as the others looked at her in surprise.

"Why would you be sorry? Anyone would experience such difficulties if the natural laws of their world changed," Tehy said slowly. "You are handling this very well." The others nodded in agreement.

"Some day I will tell you my adventures on your planet," Torin said, holding Rebecca's hand, "and you will realize that it is never simple having to adjust to such huge shifts in reality."

Leva added, "Look at us Thianelians, our elemental laws are collapsing and we are all upset. If we were not, you would not even be here."

Rebecca had to admit that she had a point, and felt better after her cry. Tehy soon led them behind one of the tallest buildings into a small stone courtyard. Lavender grass sprouted up between the stones, while green and blue vines clung to the stone walls, creating a beautiful garden effect.

"This is where we live," Tehy said, "or at least where Father lives most of the time. I spend time here and in Griffin Country with Mother's Folk. Ah, there he is."

Tehy led them over to a man of middle years who sat on the stone ground examining something intently.

"Father," said Tehy respectfully, placing a hand on the man's shoulder, "I've brought Torin, Leva, and the one Meridwen spoke of, Rebecca."

## Chapter 10

Tehan slowly rose to his feet and bowed. He had a smooth, unlined face, wide set golden eyes, and a serious smile. He was tall like his son, but his hair was close cropped and very dark, which made his eyes glow even more noticeably. He, like many of the Air Folk, wore blue trousers made of some fibrous material, and a long sleeved top that looked more like a t-shirt than a tunic. Most of the Air Folk wore belts or pouches, because they often flew off without much notice and therefore kept necessities with them at all times.

"Welcome," Tehan said, clasping each of their hands in turn. When he looked at Rebecca she could see an even stronger resemblance to his son, for Tehy, too, had very penetrating eyes. Despite the fact that Tehan looked completely human, he was unmistakably Tehy's father.

"I have been scrying," Tehan explained, pointing down to the intricate pattern of leaves he'd been so intently studying. "I had one of our air messengers, Vinian, bring them from your mother's nest, Tehy. They came from all around the world, and I was hoping they would give me a clearer picture of what steps we should take. It may be time to wake the Troll after all, and send out a general alarm for all beings to leave Thianely. There are planets in other dimensions that would welcome us."

Torin put up a hand in protest. "High One, we cannot give up so easily as that. There are many powerful Guardians among us, many allies among the elementals. Is it not worth a try to keep our planet from such gross separation and despair?"

Tehan laid one hand on Torin's shoulder, holding him firmly. "Peace, Son of Fire. I hold to the prophecy myself; I am merely emphasizing the serious nature of our situation. I do not know exactly what you will be faced with, or how you," and here he indicated Rebecca, "will accomplish finding the center of the Great Balance. I know you mean to try and I will lend assistance, including sending along my son."

Torin nodded, "I apologize for my temper, Tehan. I am grateful Tehy is to accompany us. I know he has duties among both the Air Folk and the Griffin Folk that he will be unable to fulfill while he journeys with us."

Tehan nodded, somewhat grimly, "And his Mother's people have more to do with this whole situation than you might think. Kerithan has informed me herself that the Queen egg has been stolen by the Bolluxes. They have promised to destroy it if the Griffins try to interfere with their plans. Kerithan knows that it is more important to look at the future of the entire planet, but some among her folk are more concerned with the future of their race in particular, and you know the lineage will die out if the Queen egg is destroyed. If you could manage to rescue the Queen egg, I think the Griffins would not hesitate to retaliate against the Bolluxes."

At Rebecca's bewildered look, Torin explained, "The Griffins are not bound by the law against taking of life, as they act as protectors of the planet. They are allowed under provocation to eradicate threats to Thianely. The Bolluxes have lost many of their ancestors to Griffins, and they have finally found a way to divide the Griffin Folk amongst themselves by stealing the Queen egg. A Queen egg is born only once every few hundred years. The lineage remains intact through her offspring, because only the Griffin Queen may give birth to another Queen. How did the Bolluxes manage to take such a heavily guarded egg, Tehan?"

Tehan sighed heavily. "The shifting of the ground itself, and the alteration in our planet's orbit have thrown everything off, even the birth cycles. Kerithan gave birth to the egg before reaching the nesting ground. She had to land in an open field to deliver. The Bollux twins, Harlane and Haldar, and their whole entourage of rage sprites attacked Kerithan and her guards. Kerithan tried to escape, but Queens are most vulnerable after a birth, weakened in both body and spirit. They took the egg from her as her guards were fighting off the sprites. I am grateful that Kerithan was able to protect herself enough to survive the attack. Unfortunately when the Griffin guards finally caught up to the Bolluxes, Haldar and Harlane threatened to smash the egg, so the guards were forced to retreat.

I promised Kerithan that Tehy would not use force against the Bollux clan while the egg is still in their possession. But I said nothing about you finding the egg and bringing it back. Kerithan would love to help all of the Folk, but she needs the egg back to do so. I cannot tell you what to do to complete the prophecy, but I can suggest that you try to recover the egg without engaging the Bolluxes."

Tehan, Torin, Tehy and Leva all turned and looked at Rebecca expectantly.

"Perhaps," Leva suggested, "you know something about becoming invisible?"

Rebecca gulped. "I remember something like that from another lifetime, and I suppose I could try. But it's been a long time since I've done anything like that."

Tehan bent down and picked up one of the leaves he'd been reading, placing it in the pouch he carried around his waist. "Come, sit down, and relax for awhile. Tell me of your journey so far and of the Threshold of the Trees. Meridwen said the death toll was very high." He looked at Leva with great compassion. "I know you must feel the loss of the Great Tree strongly, as do we all."

They entered the large triangular building through the courtyard and were soon sitting in a small dining area. The chairs were made of some thick mossy plant that grew from between the stones of the floor. The walls were covered in colorful viny tapestries, hand woven by young air weavers.

Tehan explained that the Air Folk had to pass several initiations before going on their mentoring journeys. In order to pass the elemental air test, they had to remain in the air at constant heights to insure fine quality of weaving. After a successful completion of a tapestry, the Folk were given harder tasks that included more responsibility. There were many air skills that the Folk had to master, including the study of wind and air currents, weather altering, long distance teling, altitude flying, and map making. Many were then sent on their mentoring journeys to put to use all the skills that they had learned.

Several wall stones had opened to the daylight and a clear, warm breeze wafted through the room. They sat eating nut cakes and drinking leaf tea, speaking of their experiences thus far. Rebecca liked to look up occasionally at the towering walls leading up to the small opening at the top. She noticed that though the walls were high, the home was only a single story. In fact, so far she had not seen multilevel homes on Thianely. Torin told her when she asked that there was plenty of space due to low population, which made multistoried buildings rare.

After they'd finished eating, Tehan gave them a tour of his home. His living space, complete with books and vivid tapestries, was the largest room. There were several sleeping chambers, smaller rooms with leafnest beds set on sunken stone platforms. Tehan said that Air Folk tended to sleep below ground level to keep from floating around too high during sleep. Between each room were stone partitions, but no real ceilings to obscure the high view. The overall effect reminded Rebecca of a cathedral. Tehan mentioned that most Air Folk were accomplished singers, and the acoustics of the triangular homes provided greater resonance.

Children still learning to manage themselves elementally were especially soothed by the kindness of the gray stones. The stones were treated as honored guests, and in return they provided shelter and taught the Air Folk about stillness and patience. Rebecca tried to imagine learning from a wall on Earth, or even talking to one, and was grateful that she'd probably never have to explain it to anyone back home. Tehan motioned to Rebecca and Leva to occupy one room, while Torin and Tehy were to share Tehy's usual bedroom.

"I'll leave you two to get settled," Tehan said. "Tomorrow I'll take Rebecca over to the Air Center for a time. I think it will assist her in remembering. Torin and Tehy, why don't you two follow me. I have some overland maps of Bollux Country that you may need if you're going to make a rescue attempt of the egg."

As Tehy and Torin followed Tehan out the stone doorway, Torin looked back and smiled. Rebecca heard his voice in her mind. "I'll see you later at evening repast, heartling," he said. "Rest well."

Leva dropped her backsack with a sigh and immediately lay down on one of the leaf beds. Rebecca put down her provisions as well, and tested the leafnest mat.

"This is really soft and comfortable," she commented.

Leva yawned. "I don't know about you, Rebecca," she said, "but I feel like I've walked to the end of Thianely and back. Also, being this high in the air feels strange."

Leva pulled out the blue leaf that Meridwen had given her, laying it on her chest. She took several deep breaths, relaxing more deeply into the bed, her tangled hair almost completely obscuring her face.

"That's better," she said, pushing aside her unruly locks. "I was getting separation sickness from lack of rooting. Did you notice there were only a few trees growing this high up? It's not the most tree friendly space. But don't worry," she added, responding to Rebecca's look of alarm, "I won't fade away this fast. I couldn't live here long term, but I will survive a visit. Luckily I'm half of the Earthen Folk, so tree sickness doesn't affect me as much as one of the full Tree Folk."

"What do I do for you if you start feeling really bad?" Rebecca asked.

"If the blue leaf doesn't work, you can think of trees and put your hands on me. You're alhathra, remember? As a healer you will be able to remind me of my roots. Besides, you've been a tree before. How are you feeling, here at the top of the mountain?"

Rebecca lay back, contemplating a tapestry that hung on one wall. It depicted several fire-colored birds flying through a huge blue flame. "Well, the altitude isn't bothering me any more. I'm okay as long as I don't think about everything too much. Luckily we've been so busy that I haven't had time to really absorb everything. I feel like I've known you and Torin forever, in a deeper way than I thought possible. I miss my parents, but I'm not so sure I miss being on Earth that much. It feels disloyal, but that's how it is. Sometimes when I sleep at night I can feel the crystal wisdom moving around inside me like it's trying to make a place for itself. I feel bigger than any idea I ever had of myself. Sometimes it scares me."

"It is a lot to understand," Leva said. "Sometimes I try to imagine myself in your world, but I'm not sure I'd survive even one of your days, from what Torin has told me. It takes great courage to allow your own ideas of yourself to fall away. And especially for your physical body to adjust. You are becoming lighter every day, you know."

Rebecca nodded. "Sometimes I look at myself glowing and wonder where it all comes from, but then I notice you're all the same way, and I don't mind so much. As long as I don't compare myself to the old me, I feel better than I could ever have imagined. Kind of free."

Leva nodded, yawning again. "I'm going to rest now, Rebecca. I'll see you later."

Leva turned over and fell instantly asleep. Rebecca lay down and tried to rest, but too many thoughts kept flowing through her mind. Finally, restless, she got up, walked over to one wall and gently asked the stone to move for her. It shifted silently, creating a doorway into the main passage of the house. Suddenly, Rebecca heard whispers of sound all around her. When she stopped to listen, she realized the stones were speaking to her. She placed a hand on one cool stone and the sounds became one voice.

The voice spoke softly, “Sit quietly, stop your thoughts, and let yourself become as stone.”

At once Rebecca sat down, letting her hand slide along the wall as the voice continued. “Feel the strength of your outer skin solidify. Let all of your feelings, thoughts, worries become the fine dust of the ground. Patience in time, in place, in being, is the only movement in this stillness.”

As Rebecca sat, she experienced the movement in stillness that can only be perceived when the mind stops. She perceived the stillness inside that movement and the movement inside that stillness, and so on, until she felt herself shaking with laughter without moving at all. When at last she opened her eyes, she felt completely rested in a humorous way. After thanking the wall for its generosity of mindlessness, she went to find the others.

They spent the next few hours trying to make sense of the Bollux map. Like the Bolluxes themselves, Bollux Country seemed to be depicted somewhat haphazardly. It was quite far away, on the other side of the Threshold of the Trees, southeast. There were several gaps in the drawing simply because no one had ever returned from the Bollux Stronghold alive, except for some Griffin warriors who’d merely flown around it.

“Basically,” said Tehan, “You’ll be flying blindly into dangerous territory. We know the main enclave of Bolluxes is located in the center of some extremely toxic swamps. Other Air Folk have perished simply by flying too low above the vapors. Each of the Bollux offspring has his or her own quarters, mostly because they can’t stand one another unless they’re destroying something and need each other’s help. Both Haldar and Harlane took the egg. Given how greedy the Bollux clan is, I would imagine they are probably fighting over who gets to keep it. If it had already broken, Kerithan would know.”

“One thing that may help, Father,” Tehy said, “is that I can locate the egg by bloodtel, because we are kin. I will be able to find it no matter where it is hidden.”

Tehan threw up his hands. “Of course, I should have known that. You knew the egg had been taken before I did. But remember that even bloodtel does not work as well below the clarity of this mountain, at least lately. Even up here there have been disturbing winds of interference in mindtel."

Rebecca had to nod. She was able to hear Torin's thoughts much more easily on the Air Mountain than down in the valley, but sometimes his thoughts would fade like a poor radio signal.

They discussed possible routes into Bollux Country until Leva awoke and they met for evening repast. After the meal they all congregated outside to watch the sun set deep in the valley, its pink rays casting a final glow. Soon stars lit the night sky with a special brilliance as a large number of Air Folk crowded into Tehan's home to sing. Their voices lifted high in traditional air songs and soft tree lullabies sung in honor of the Great Tree's passing.

Leva wept many tears of sap. The others couldn't help but join her grief as the mournful swelling sounds swept through them all. They finally fell asleep to the murmuring of sleepy voices calling goodnight as the Air Folk all went home to rest.

The next morning Tehan left Tehy and Torin still poring over the Bollux maps, while Leva went on a walk to visit the only nearby trees. After Rebecca received a good luck hug from Torin, Tehan led her outside. He motioned to a small building with a particularly low roof, indicating that it was the Initiation Center. She followed him through a thin stone door, which led to a very large empty room, carpeted in soft blue woven leaves that looked as if they'd come from the Threshold of the Trees.

Tehan led her over to the center of the room, indicating that she should sit on the carpet. Rebecca sat down cross-legged, Tehan sitting in front of her cross-legged as well, when she noticed that the room was no longer empty. Rows and rows of green garbed beings sat around them, intoning something in a soft hum. Tehan smiled at her look of surprise.

"These are the Sky-keepers of Wisdom for our people. Only those Air born may see them, my dear. Already the prophecy is coming to pass, that one born of water may sit with the air, the earth and the fire, each with each."

Rebecca closed her eyes at his words, shrinking from so much responsibility. Calming her thoughts, she leaned forward to better listen to Tehan. He reached over, touching her forehead gently with his palm.

"Look, Daughter of the Stars," he said, and placed in front of her a leaf he'd taken from a pouch around his waist. As Rebecca opened her eyes, the leaf veins began to glow and twist, merging into familiar symbols and patterns. She reached down and traced the symbols with her finger. She felt a quickening inside, shaking her slightly with the force of it. She began to chant:

"By air, by earth, by fire and water,
Return the memory of Rhiate's daughter,
The creative wisdom of my sire,
By water, air, earth, and fire,
The secrets gifted at my birth,
By fire, water, air, and earth
Let me accept that which I share,
With earth and water, fire and air."

Rebecca's body shook slightly, each atom in her body vibrating to some silent song. She flew through air and space to a time before she held any form at all, when there was no separation between herself and all that exists, for there was no self. She laughed at the thought of even having thought. Suddenly she felt the carpet beneath her. Tehan reached over, touching her forehead again. She sat quietly for a moment, and sighed.

"Tehan, sometimes I feel like the Rebecca of Earth and the Rebecca on Thianely are no more real than the thoughts that flicker through me. Then I remember everything that's happened is real. If I try to think too much I get a headache, because my mind feels so tiny compared to the vastness of everything. So much space exists even between thoughts and feelings. Sometimes I feel like I'm only playing. But the more I think, the more I keep forgetting to play and I start taking myself too seriously. You all believe I'm the answer to some prophecy, but in the middle of space, I don't even exist as me. How am I supposed to handle all of this at once? Until I know how, I'm not sure I can do anything useful."

"That must be your task, Rebecca," Tehan said, his eyes twinkling. "It sounds to me as if you are well on your way if you are aware of so many levels at once. Somewhere in the midst of confusion is the center you seek. But you will only remember as much as your conscious mind can tolerate at once, so have trust that your soul knows what you are doing."

"If my soul knows, do you think I could simply sit here and go inside myself and find balance then?" she asked, smiling. "I think it would save a lot of wear and tear on everyone else."

Tehan laughed. "Somehow I think that what you do here on Thianely has a bearing on what you find inside yourself, otherwise you wouldn't be here. Some abilities may be found only through experience. External events have an impact on internal ones and so too the other way round. I cannot answer for you exactly, but I think if you act according to what feels true you will discover what you need to know. Come now, Rebecca, let us join the others."

They left the hall and were heading toward Tehan's home when they experienced a violent shaking beneath their feet. The ground heaved, rolling alarmingly. Tehan grabbed Rebecca's hand before she could fall into a fissure that had developed right in front of them.

"Hang on," he cried. Rebecca felt herself lifted right up into the sky above the entire city of triangular buildings. Around them she saw others take to the sky as well, and soon the entire population was airborne. Rebecca could see that Tehan's mountain was not the only one affected, for the neighboring mountains were also in great upheaval. Whole sections of mountainsides were collapsing. The noise was tremendous. Rebecca tried to shield her ears while holding fast to Tehan, as he organized his people amid sky. The people formed a triangular shape for flight, leaving their cities in a matter of moments, as the great mountains shook and rumbled and collapsed in upon themselves.

Rebecca felt the wind in her face, the sheer freedom of flight, and thought that under any other circumstances it would have been exhilarating. She glanced back to see, rising out of the collapsed mountains of earth, an immense creature. Even by craning her neck she could barely see up to its knees. She shivered at the thought of ever having to confront such a being, and turned her attention back to Tehan.

"Do not doubt for a moment that all the Folk made it out safely," he said reassuringly. "We have been prepared for such an event for eons."

Finally, after less than an hour of flying time, they landed by the banks of the Salflow River, followed by the rest of the Air Folk. They congregated in large groups and spent the next several moments catching up on neighboring mountain news. For a Folk who had watched their homes of generations crumble before them, they appeared to Rebecca to be remarkably upbeat.

Relieved to see the comforting river of purple so near, Rebecca was even more comforted when Tehy arrived with Torin and Leva. He coasted downward, his great wings outstretched, but quickly took to the sky again with Tehan to survey the damage. Torin immediately drew Rebecca near, and kissed her firmly.

"That, my heartling, was too close once more. Thank Rhiate you're safe! That's two earth rendings since you arrived on Thianely. Would it help if I told you that they are usually much more rare than this? It's certainly hard to believe the old troll's awake after so many millions of years. I wonder what has finally woken him."

Leva stood nearby, mourning the deaths of the trees that had been root shorn in the mountain collapse. She finally went over and huddled in the river to comfort herself. Rebecca went over to help console her while Torin waited for Tehan and Tehy to arrive. They soon returned with odd expressions on their faces.

"Torin," Tehan said, motioning for him to come closer, "you are probably aware that we all have been prepared for this day for some time." At Torin's nod, he continued. "We have made other living arrangements. Kerithan has often offered sanctuary for those Air Folk who wish it. The rest of us will go to the Well of Springs for safety, for we have known that if the troll ever woke up, it would be due to a disaster. Thianely would be entering her troubled times, and we would all be on alert."

"Yes," Torin said, "I have known of this. Tehy told me during my mentoring journey years ago."

"Just now," Tehan said, looking somewhat puzzled, "when Tehy and I flew over the mountain craters, the troll called to us. He said Rebecca woke him up, and he must speak with her. We could barely understand him, he spoke the Old Tongue so badly."

"What!" Torin said in astonishment. "I don't think Rebecca did anything at all; she seems to know as little about the cause of his awakening as we do. Let me go ask her." He went down to the riverbank to speak with Rebecca. Leva, meanwhile, had fully immersed herself in the river to clean the sap off of her clothing.

Rebecca looked at Torin's face. "What is it?" she asked, rising to her feet. "You look a little weird. Is something wrong?"

Torin reached over, grasping her hand. "This is very, how you would say 'weird.' The troll that no longer slumbers says that you woke him and he must speak with you. Tehy will give you a lift up to the highest level he can fly, so the troll may talk to you there."

Rebecca shivered. She didn't want to chat with a creature that could disturb a whole mountain range merely by standing up. "How did I wake him?" she protested. "I've barely said anything since we got here. I certainly wasn't trying to reach him by thought."

"I don't know," Torin admitted. "We were wondering that very thing. I suppose the only way to find out is to speak with him."

They made their way back to Tehy, who told Rebecca to hold onto his neck. He wrapped both arms around her securely, and promised to take good care of her. He slowly flapped his enormous wings and soon they were aloft. At first Rebecca closed her eyes, but she realized she was as safe with Tehy as she'd been with Tehan. His wingspan was at least ten feet across, and Rebecca had to giggle a little when his hairy chest tickled her neck.

Tehy soared upwards, skimming over the valley and the fallen mountains, until at last they could see the gigantic troll. He was sitting in the middle of a pile of purple earth, trying to make himself shorter for their convenience. Tehy flew as high as was safe for their breathing, since the atmosphere was thinner up there, and they hovered right next to the giant troll's elbows. As he saw them nearing his arm, the troll reached out a hand the size of a lake, giving Tehy a place to land.

In a rumbling voice like thick sand, so loud it almost knocked them off his palm, the troll told Tehy to leave, saying that what he had to say was for Rebecca only. Rebecca could barely understand his speech, for he had a strange accent and his booming voice was only intelligible if she plugged her ears. Tehy smiled at her anxious face, reassuring her that he would not be too far away.

"It's best not to argue with mountain trolls," he advised her. "Unlike other trolls, they are the most stubborn creatures ever created and always outlast everyone else. Be safe, and I will return soon."

Tehy glided off, leaving Rebecca standing alone on the troll's enormous palm. As she stood trembling with fear, wondering how one conversed with such an immense creature, the troll's entire body began to shake. Rebecca immediately tipped over. After she got back to her feet, she realized that he was laughing. In a mind speech that she had not heard for ages, the troll began to tel. His thoughts were like gravel on stone, rasping but clear, and Rebecca recognized him at once.

"Of course," she said, tumbling her own stone thoughts his way. "I remember you, you old travel troll, Gomfrey Risco! How have you been?"

"I was sleeping like a black hole until you woke me up," he said, lowering his face down so that she could catch a glimpse of his huge, earthen colored eyes and bulbous nose. "Decided I'd provide ground for the Air Folk until it was time to arise. Doesn't an eon pass like an eye blink when you're having a good rest? I dreamed I saw you here and suddenly, there you were! Thank Rhiate, you haven't forgotten Trollspeak, though you do sound a little cracked."

Without even trying, Rebecca made a smoother, rock-shaped thought of assent. She heard the huge troll sigh.

"Ah, isn't that a relief? I'm a bit crusty with the Old Tongue, but Trollspeak never leaves me. Funny little human form you picked this time, my friend. You know it's the troll in you that allows you to contain the wisdom of those crystals. Once a troll, always stone-held. I had a dream that my friend had returned. What do I find when I awake? There she is, packaged small and tiny."

The troll chuckled at her next thought. "Having memory problems, you say? Nonsense, your memory is intact, you simply don't want the responsibility of being yourself. Worried about messing up? But you couldn't possibly mess things up here more than they are already, why this tiny little planet is disintegrating. Thank Rhiate you woke me up right out of my dream before I wound up in some stardust-covered corner of the universe!

I'm going to leave soon to find another planet to nap on. I still have four billion years until my next time on duty. I tell you, you should give yourself more time off between jobs; I think the responsibility is beginning to get to you. Have you remembered this is supposed to be an adventure? Relax, enjoy, and don't be afraid to take charge and finish up. Don't let that puny little body fool you. Anyone can tell it's you. Except maybe on that silly little speck of earth you've been hiding on. No one there recognizes anything, including their own selves."

Rebecca let her thoughts tumble like stones down a hill. She pictured herself at the top of a huge embankment of rocks, sliding down and down. Her vision was interrupted by Gomfrey guffawing in a crescendo of sound reminiscent of crashing boulders. Rebecca winced.

"Sorry," said the troll apologetically, "I forgot that you chose such small hearing appendages. But really, you're trying to tell me that you are worried about incurring physical harm. Not only because you wouldn't be able to finish the job, but also because you don't want to get hurt or die. How do you hold this view with the knowledge that there is no such thing as death since you've changed forms so many times, eh? I'll have to try this humanness, it sounds very complicated. Tell me, do you remember your troll name?"

Rebecca thought for a moment, and then nodded. "Sohar, Sohar Anala. It means Adventurer of the Stars. I've been a star troll."

"Are a star troll," Gomfrey corrected. "Everything you've ever been you still are. Now where do star trolls go to rekindle old memories?"

"The Well of Stars," replied Rebecca, without even stopping to think. She could picture it, a huge spiraling star well, with the creative energy of universes filling it endlessly.

Gomfrey shook his head. "Closest thing in this neighborhood is the Well of Springs, but since you're from a water planet this time, it should work fine in rekindling old knowledge. Now, that's all I have to say. Remember how you reminded me of myself during that lifetime with the Gitsnarch galaxy? Got me out of a tight little consciousness there. I owed you one; so don't bother to thank me. You know we trolls hate being thanked.

Sohar, it's been pure crystal speaking with you again. Let me know when I next see you, in about four billion years or so, how this particular lifetime turned out. Amusing bit about the prophecy too, you know?"

The massive troll calmly reached across the valley to the Salflow River and gently dropped Rebecca nearby. He stood up slowly, so as not to cause further earth rendings, and made a graceful bow. As the Air Folk waved, Gomfrey Risco turned to walk some distance away. Still visible like some giant monolith between earth and sky, the great troll shimmered and shook and shifted himself into a huge constellation of stars. It twinkled for a moment against the pink sky, and disappeared so quickly that Rebecca wasn't sure she'd really seen it happen.

By this time Tehy had returned from the sky vigil he'd kept by the troll. He landed, shaking his head in awe. "I never realized he could reach out a hand and return you to us," he told Rebecca, "but I'm grateful I stayed nearby. I watched him change to star form right before me. It was magnificent!"

Torin squeezed Rebecca's shoulder softly and smiled. "Trust you to know the old troll, Rebecca. You can still Trollspeak. I should've known. What did he say?"

Rebecca told them of her experience, including Gomfrey's mention of the Well of Springs to help her remember.

"That makes sense," Torin said. "And it's the safest space to be during earth shifts and elemental collapse. It's more a state of mind than a place," he added, noting Rebecca's puzzled look. "I mean, it is a physical place, but it does not exist on Thianely exactly. The Well of Springs is full of what you would call hot springs, but each pool is a gate to a different state of awareness or even universe. The Guardians of the Well of Springs are the old Elvinkind. On your planet they are portrayed as small flighty little creatures, but the Gatekeeper Elves that guard the gates between worlds are very tall and regal. They're warriors of a sort. They have a great deal of responsibility, and at the same time are not allowed to interfere in the worlds, only guard the gates. Entrance to the Well of Springs is denied to any who seek to manipulate or harm, so it is one of the only places of safety left."

"But you're not coming with me, are you?" Rebecca said.

Torin shook his head. Tehy broke in before Torin could explain. "I asked him to help me get the Queen Egg as soon as possible. The two of us have worked out a fair plan, but I would not have the strength to fly all of us there. We may not depend upon elemental travel, so we thought you could stay with my father's people. Now with the suggestion of the Well of Springs, we feel more at ease about parting from you."

At Leva's look of protest, Tehy said, "Leva, I know we thought to remain together for this entire journey, but we truly need the help of my mother's Folk. Without their support against the Bollux clan, no course we take will have as much success. You have been to the Well of Springs. Rebecca will need your assistance in finding the entrance. Once we have restored the egg to my mother, we may continue our journey together."

Leva and Rebecca had to admit that it made sense, but were still concerned about Torin and Tehy entering Bollux country by themselves.

"Tehy will know where the egg is; he's Griffin born," Torin reassured them. "The Bolluxes would have a hard time harming me since I'm impervious physically, and I can fire shield Tehy. You know we've studied the Bollux maps and we have a general idea of the layout. We've talked it over with Tehan. He thinks we have a good chance in getting there safely. Yes, we know it's like flying into a nest of rage sprites, but what choice do we have? The Griffin Folk must not endanger the egg by attacking and the Bolluxes would never expect anyone to go there anyway. No one ever has."

Rebecca shook her head. "That's not exactly comforting, but I understand that you need to go. I only wish I'd remember how to spin invisibility spells so I could be of some help to you. So far though, I don't."

Just as Leva opened her mouth to speak, Tehan floated above the Air Folk, beckoning them to gather. They formed a large circle around him, some sitting, some standing, as he raised his arm for quiet.

"You all know," he said, "that a large part of our history has crumbled today, our old way of life. The ancient earth dwellers are awakening, and in preparation for this day, we have two alternatives. One, Kerithan of the Griffins has offered us sanctuary in Griffin Country, only a few days flight from here. The Griffin Folk also seek our help against the Bolluxes, once the Queen egg is returned. The most advanced Air Folk among us may be of some service during these times of turmoil.

Two, we can journey to the Well of Springs. You know by now that no place on Thianely is truly safe from the enormous changes that are happening, but the Well of Springs is still a sanctuary for those who are admitted. Perhaps we all have little time left here on Thianely. No one truly knows. But these four," and he indicated Torin, Leva, Rebecca, and Tehy, "are doing all they can in regard to the prophecy. So now we must determine which among us will aid the Griffin Folk, and which will journey to the Well of Springs. I call the Folk to council."

Tehy drew Torin, Rebecca, and Leva away from the circle. "We should leave them now and be on our way," he suggested. "Father must focus on what needs to be done for his Folk. Rebecca, you must go to the Well of Springs quickly, as Gomfrey suggested. But first, have you recalled any abilities in becoming invisible, anything at all?"

Rebecca shook her head, "It's as if I'm forgetting something as simple as the alphabet, and I still can't figure out why I can't read. Maybe it will come to me later, since so much keeps happening that seems to be trying to remind me. I feel foolish."

Torin held her hand reassuringly. "None of us has had any luck either, heartling, so don't waste time being embarrassed. For those of us who travel elementally, it is theoretically possible to slow the shift from one element to another to be invisible. I don't think we'd be able to reclaim all of our body parts afterwards, not to mention our consciousness. Remember, I had a bit of trouble following you to the Threshold of the Trees? I traveled very fast, but I still got singed along the way. We'll have to get the egg by more physical means, like stealing it back."

Rebecca eyed him suspiciously. "You're really looking forward to this," she said.

Torin and Tehy grinned at each other. "There is a certain satisfaction in foiling the Bolluxes," Torin admitted. "They have plagued all the Folk for such a long time. But we will think carefully before we act."

Leva and Rebecca stood quietly for a moment, then Leva said, "Torin, remember Meridwen's dew when you need it. The air, I've heard, is very foul over Bollux Country."

"I would never have agreed to do this without it," he acknowledged.

Rebecca sighed, took the crystal necklace from around her neck, and gave it to Tehy. "Here, I think you should have this. Torin already has the dew," she insisted, when Tehy would have protested. "Torin, I think you and Tehy are right. We need all of the help we can get, and it will set the Bolluxes back a bit to lose that egg, as well as allow the Griffins freedom to retaliate. Leva and I will go to the Well of Springs. I understand why you think it will work best with only the two of you, but, like Leva, I'd rather be going along."

"We know," said Torin and Tehy simultaneously, laughing. Tehy and Leva left to prepare for the journeys, enlisting the help of some of the Air children who'd grown bored at the council. They loaded their backsacks with supplies, and Leva soaked in the river one last time.

"Where and when shall we meet?" Rebecca asked Torin when they had a private moment. "And how will each of us we know where the other is if mindtel is unreliable?"

Torin pulled Rebecca close, hugging her fiercely. "I'm going to try something. It may not work, but we can try anyway." Torin leaned his forehead against Rebecca's and began the parting ritual of life mates.

"Let your eyes be my eyes, let mine be yours," he said, and rested his forehead against hers. He raised his head, looking into her eyes. "Let our breath be one breath and our hearts be one heart. Let my ears hear that which you speak and let yours in turn hear mine. In all days and nights let us know each other as self." He kissed her slowly, and smiled. "Now we may be to communicate with each other, beyond telepathically. It's supposed to be much more sensory, but I've never done it before so I don't know for sure."

Rebecca shifted awkwardly. "I feel like we got married or something."

Torin nodded. "Yes, I suppose you could say that. Wait, I almost forgot. I wanted to celebrate your day of birth, heartling. I'm not sure when it is on your planet, but today feels appropriate. I have something for you."

As Rebecca stood in surprise, realizing that she had just celebrated her 17th birthday by watching a mountain range collapse, not to mention talking to a troll, Torin handed her his leaf pad and a small neckvine.

"Here," he said, "I want you to keep these. I recently finished some sketches of the Air Folk's mountains, Tehan's home, and a few others. I'll keep adding to the leaf pad and someday you'll have many journals to show our grandchildren. The neckvine was wrapped around my wrist when Grandfather found me in the ashes. The blue stones are benrickle, for courage, and the red ones are ruthard, for passion."

Rebecca threw her arms around him, unwilling to say goodbye yet. "I'll keep them safe," she promised, honored that he would give her such sacred possessions.

"Keep yourself safe," Torin replied. They stood holding each other for a time. "Rebecca," Torin reminded her, "keep a close eye on Leva. She's been away from trees for a long while now, and needs to be close to her Folk or she'll start getting irritable and weak. She's still grieving. Take care of yourself, and happy remembering. We'll meet you in Griffin Country, when we've found the egg and you're finished at the Well of Springs. Either Tehy will come get you two or Tehan will send someone to show you the way. In the meantime, we'll communicate with each other through our bodies. Be well and watch out for Leva."

Rebecca agreed. After she gave him one last hug, Torin made his farewells to Leva and Tehan. Tehy finally took to the air with Torin holding fast to one of his brawny arms. Rebecca and Leva stood watching them go, while Tehan turned to supervise the first group of Air Folk to leave. Soon the air was filled with many figures flying toward the Country of the Griffins.

Tehan, one of the last to leave, stood waiting for the rest of his people, including Rebecca and Leva, to make the shift to the Well of Springs. He clasped Rebecca's hand, squeezed Leva's shoulder, and said goodbye.

"We will meet in Griffin Country, after you have immersed yourself in the Springs. Do not worry about your mate and my son, they have many resources even they are unaware of as yet."

"Thank you for everything," Rebecca replied, and then turned expectantly toward Leva to show her the way. Around them she could see the other Folk shimmer, disappearing right in front of them. "How do we do it? How do we get to the Well of Springs?" she asked.

Leva thought for a moment, reached over to take Rebecca's hand, and held it firmly. "I have never been there, but my parents have. I remember what they told me, but I do not have words so much as images. Close your eyes and open your mind to me, Rebecca. I will see if I can send you the pictures of what to do."

Rebecca nodded, closed her eyes, took a deep breath, and imagined her mind opening, like an expansive, spacious door. She waited to see what Leva would do, and was surprised to see Leva's image step right inside her head.

"Go ahead, close this door behind me," Leva prompted her. Rebecca not only closed it, she dissolved it completely, figuring if she needed it again she could always recreate it. She giggled to herself at the thought of not wanting to clutter up her mind with useless doors. Leva, meanwhile, stood quietly inside her mind, drawing something. At once Rebecca could see another door, thin, almost vaporous, but somehow well defined.

"Now walk through this door right after me," ordered Leva's voice inside her head, "and don't let go of my hand."

"Okay, but does this mean you're going to be stuck in my head?" Rebecca wondered. Leva just chuckled.

"Okay, here goes," Rebecca said, and followed Leva through the slender door in her mind.

## Chapter 11

Rebecca stepped through the door into a flowering landscape. She and Leva stood knee deep in blossoming plants. Some of the flowers sprouted from lavender bushes no higher than her ankles, while others nestled on tiny blue trees. Directly across from the flowering field was a forest of thick green trees and tall, slender trees with golden bark. The sky was the usual deep pink, but the air held a subtle hush of expectancy. Rebecca tried to grasp the elusive quality, but finally realized it was like trying to describe a flavor to someone without taste buds. Her senses seemed very keen, and as she bent to touch the nearest flower with one finger, she tasted the color vermillion on her tongue. At her look of surprise, Leva laughed.

"Yes," she said, "here all of your senses are intertwined. You can see sound and taste color and smell what you touch. It's very nourishing. You'll notice that the ability to mingle senses will stay with you after you leave. You'll be able to integrate them or separate them at will. I remember when I first smelled the sound of trees growing as a small tree child. It's so succulent."

"Leva," Rebecca began hesitantly, "are you inside my mind still, or did we both leave and go somewhere else?"

Leva smiled. "I took you through your own mind, but the Well of Springs is both inside and outside at once. That's why it's so hard to explain how to get here. But don't worry; you won't be stuck with me in your head. Check and see if I'm right."

Rebecca closed her eyes and felt about inside her mind. "Nope, nobody in there but me, and I can hear Torin kind of faintly. He's okay."

"Good," Leva said firmly. "Now Rebecca, we must walk through the path between the trees over there, and we'll reach the Springs. Go to those that call to you. Don't worry if you wind up in different ones than I do. It's like that for everyone. You will receive exactly what you need."

"Where do you want to meet?" Rebecca asked.

Leva paused. "We can meet over here by the gelbark trees, the ones with the golden bark."

Rebecca nodded, and followed Leva to a path that skirted the field of flowers and wound through the grove of trees. She noticed a bubbling sound coming from nearby. Leva led her out of the woods into a huge open area, ringed on all sides by grass-studded mountains of gray rock. There were Folk of all sorts both in and outside the natural springs, and some turned to look at the new arrivals. Rebecca recognized several of the Air Folk, particularly mothers and fathers with smaller children.

"Now what?" Rebecca asked.

"Wait, and you'll be called," Leva replied somewhat absently. Her attention appeared to be focused on a bubbling pool to their left. She patted Rebecca reassuringly on the arm, and bent down near the edge of the nearby pool.

"Look Rebecca, it's a water blossom," Leva said, and showed her the strange cuplike flower that she'd found.

"Ought you to have picked it?" Rebecca asked. Leva shrugged.

"No, of course not. It picked me. See the faery still inside?" Rebecca bent over to see the little faery in the flower staring at her with curious eyes. When Rebecca smiled, the faery scooped up a bit of nectar and held it out, making a small curtsy as she did so. Rebecca took it carefully on the end of her finger and tasted it on her tongue. In an instant she felt a buzzing in her ears as something inside her head opened. She heard the faery speak, in a voice like jingling bells,

"Inside time you'll find all slow,
Outside time we lightfast go,
Flow inside the Well of Springs
Within the worlds creation sings.
Remember all must make their choice
And you are lacking but a voice."

Rebecca stood quietly with her eyes closed. Leva carefully replaced the flower in its watery bed, waiting silently until Rebecca opened her eyes.

"Come on,“ Leva said, tugging Rebecca by the arm, "Now that you've heard the faery, let's go soak in the springs."

Rebecca followed where Leva led, but asked, "Who was that faery? She reminded me of someone."

"Everyone reminds you of someone," Leva teased. "That's because you've had so many lifetimes you know almost everyone. That faery is actually well known to many in your world. She travels between times a lot, lives in lakes mostly. Usually she's much larger, but faeries don't hold themselves to a specific size. Too constricting. Oh, here's where I'll be."

Leva pointed to a small, bluish green pool surrounded by all kinds of creatures, who looked to be right out of faery tales back home. Centaurs, unicorns, and strange beasts Rebecca couldn't even name all shared the meadows and pools together. The quiet surrounding the pool was almost like another being, whose silence remained unchallenged. Leva entered the water fully clothed, and as Rebecca watched, she saw her friend turn multicolored like a rainbow and begin to laugh with delight.

It seemed to Rebecca that Leva had forgotten she even existed, but for some reason the thought didn't particularly bother her. She noticed that the pools kept changing color and size before her, as if she were seeing them in many ways simultaneously. She began to walk past the pools, waiting for one to call to her. She saw the other creatures at home in the Springs, but although she found the pools beautiful and fulfilling to look at, she felt drawn to none of them. She headed to the far end of the open area and turning back, she could see the bubbling pools, now clear, now vague, as if obscured by their own vapor.

She looked beyond, at the tall stone mountains, and for the first time since she'd arrived at The Well of Springs, she knew what Leva meant by being called. She began to climb. There was no set path, and the way was difficult because she had to find her own hand and footholds. Despite the effort she felt curiously soothed, for the firm stone of the mountain felt reassuringly solid under her feet and hands. She paused to rest now and then, for once she'd started there was no real hurry. She could look down and see the pools, the forested area, and the flowery field where they'd first arrived. All the Folk below began to look like little grains of rice, and Rebecca exulted in the incredible view below.

As she climbed higher the air grew colder. The slope became even more steep, but she continued hiking with a curious sense of determination that came from somewhere inside her. She trudged on until the air became heavy and she felt slow, weighted down. She could taste the sky, see the sound of the wind as it pulsed by, and hear the stone beneath her feet reaching impossibly high. Still she kept climbing, wanting to reach the top, not even knowing why. Her hands clung to rock; her feet stepped to stone.

At last she could no longer move. Her body felt stiff, aged like the mountain, old and full and heavy, thick, solid. She waited, arms and legs leaden. She stood for a time, feeling her breath rise and fall, her heart beating slowly. She heard a shuffling sound, the drag of footsteps. Around her the sky grew darker. It was as if the pink sun touched the purple earth and turned dark, like background. She could see nothing. In a kind of purple blackness that even night does not bring, she waited, standing calmly in the thick pulse of stone, hearing something still shuffling, moving closer. The noise grew louder, until at last she could feel the breath of something lifting her hair from her neck. But still she could not move. A voice resonated through her as if she were empty, a thin human flute.

"You have passed the pools, the wells of knowledge, the water of lives, loves, and healing. You have passed the meadows where senses linger and delight in nature and being. You have walked past the grounds of attainment and power. Here you stand, blind of the sights that comfort a human soul. Only by the grace of she who guards this place can you hear. Your arms and legs are frozen. Every motion is lost to you. You feel nothing but this breath of mine; all senses have you willingly given up and you are voiceless. What manner of creature are you, that walks into such darkness despite fear, who does not remember your own nature and essence, and yet dares to go beyond that which is known?"

Rebecca could say nothing, indeed, she could not think; she could only stand in the darkness as the voice penetrated her body and her mind. She waited, unable to do anything else.

The voice asked, "Who are you, tiny creature? You follow no form of learning, no set path from which I could knock you like a tiny cell from the veins of life. You are nothing, yet you have an attachment to being, but within, you have no attachments at all. You exist in this place between everything, a place where there is no name for you, so I give you none. I give you nothing, and in this nothing may you receive all that you need."

In that moment when she heard the word "nothing", the meaning of it filled her completely. Rebecca began laughing, laughing in full voice, in a sound that came through her and to her from creation itself. She found herself beyond breath as the full measure of sound came up through her feet, her legs, into her chest and out the top of her head. With the laughter all her senses returned to her, and she quickly turned to see the being whose voice was so piercing. There was no one there. She was alone, standing on the top of the mountain under the pink Thianelian sky.

She shook her head, giggling. There was nothing there at all, because the darkness had vanished from her own mind. She grinned at the thought that all the fear she'd ever felt was a creation like any other. Suddenly curious, she quickly stepped over to the edge of the mountain peak. As Rebecca looked down she saw that on the other side of the mountain was just another mountain.

"There is nothing to accomplish unless I enjoy it," she said to herself. "Purpose is only an excuse to do that which makes us real to ourselves. If I have no ultimate purpose except to have none..." but she couldn't finish the thought because everything that she made definitive seemed so petty and small that she had to laugh. "I like being all of me!" she finished in conclusion. "If I have no definition of myself, I can never screw up, because I can't be me wrongly. Ha!"

Rebecca decided to do something for the sheer joy of it. She stood on top of the mountain and danced. First quietly, feeling the air moving past her face and arms, then more wildly, whirling about, leaping strongly. When she finally collapsed, breathless, she lay for a while watching the energy rush by in the sky. The tiny rivulets of streaming sound constantly shifted above her. She looked down, noticing details in the stone beneath her, as well as patterns in her own skin that she'd never paid much attention to before.

"I have a whole network of webs all over my skin," she announced. "I'm like a huge spider who wears a web for protection. How funny that I should get so caught up in it! How could I not have noticed?"

Finally, Rebecca sat up, said a last farewell to the top of the mountain, and made her way back down. "I suppose it makes sense that the downhill journey is always ten times faster than the uphill one," she commented wryly. "Though I guess since I had to go through my own mind to get here, this mountain is only a thought away."

She walked back to the meadows, the pools, the grass, the flowers, and the Folk. She could shift her perceptions and see or smell light, taste color and sound, feel the texture of thoughts. Depending upon how she looked, the Folk were motion, light, energy, or solid in form.

"This must be what people mean when they talk about being responsible for your own perceptions," she thought. "There are so many more levels than I ever could have imagined, and yet, I have. I can't wait to tell Torin! I hope he can feel how happy I am."

## Chapter 12

Torin and Tehy flew until Tehy needed to rest his wings. They landed on a grassy hill, somewhere west of the Threshold of the Trees.

"I have never been to the Country of the Bolluxes," Tehy admitted. "I don't know anyone else who has deliberately sought them out. Even the Warrior Griffins are careful to avoid their stronghold, although strictly speaking we are their closest neighbors."

"I have never been that far southeast either," Torin said, pulling some acorn cakes from his pouch. He handed one to Tehy. "I don't like the way the Bolluxes have been focusing on Rebecca and I'd really like to get that egg away safely. I suppose you could say that the Queen egg holds your sister."

"You could say that, though we do not share a father," Tehy agreed, biting into his acorn cake. "Mother did not have to mate with anyone in order to bear the Queen egg. The Griffin Queen always holds the next Queen egg within her until it is time. Just like the Warrior eggs, which could also be called my brothers, I suppose. Sometimes I feel very unusual among my clans, both Griffin and Air at once. It happens rarely, you know, that a Griffin Queen bothers to take a mate at all, and even more rare to take a mate outside the clan."

They munched in silence for a while. While they ate, Tehy took a stick from the ground and asked some grass to move aside so that he could draw.

"We're right about here," he sketched, drawing the line of mountains they'd recently flown over. "The land of the Bolluxes begins over two days of flight southeast of the Threshold of the Trees. In a few days we will reach the Bollux enclave. Father said the Bolluxes live dead center in the bogs. Can you imagine being surrounded by the foul stench of bogs on all sides?"

Torin shook his head. "I've never actually smelled a bog, but Imanayon has told me something of the noxious odor."

"We lost several Warriors who flew too close to Bollux Country," Tehy said solemnly. "I saw the state of their bodies when they were brought back from bog territory. It took several days to wash the stench from them. We'll attempt to fly over and find a place to land, but be aware of the foul air we may run into. Meridwen's dew will be helpful, but still, we don't know exactly what else we'll face."

"I've heard Jierdan Bollux is particularly likely to show up in bogs," Torin commented. "And Tehy, remember years ago I asked you to what extent your authority as a Griffin extended? You never did answer me."

Tehy smiled. "You're right. I didn't want to mention it in front of Father, but though I'm only half Griffin, by soul right I can defend myself even if it involves the taking of life. I did not wish to join Mother's Griffin Guard and actually attack anyone, but I do have the authority to do so. Father has always been against violence even in response to the Bolluxes, although he admits it may have been necessary in the past. You know that's why they do not live together, my parents. They visit each other often, but they are so different in their ways. It's amazing that they are mates. In any case, I did bring a weapon."

He reached into his waist pouch and pulled out a starber blade, a weapon forged from a fallen star. It was extremely sharp and therefore folded itself to prevent injury to its holder. It had the properties of causing immediate death of mind and body, with the added principle of sending the opponent straight back to the dust of stars. Torin had never actually seen such a weapon, and examined it curiously. It had a double blade forged together by the impact of colliding space particles and shaped by Barlus, Queen Kerithan's master weapons crafter.

"Have you ever had occasion to use it?" Torin asked, gingerly handing it back to his friend.

"Mother gave it to me when I told her I would answer Father's summons. She thought I might have need of it. I have practiced with it before, but no, my Father's ways are too deeply ingrained in me to have used it previously. I hope that it will never be necessary, but to save the Queen egg..."

Torin nodded. The two lay back to rest for a moment as they finished their slight meal. Tehy reached over and nudged Torin with his foot. "How does it feel to have an outworlder for a mate?" he asked teasingly.

Torin opened his eyes and looked at him. "Not so surprising. I have always known that I would love an otherworlder. On her planet she is not of age yet though, so I think she fears it a little. She does not fear me, of course, but love on her planet is not so simple. They have something called dating, remember I told you of this once before?"

Tehy shrugged. “Yes, but I did not understand it. Is it not based on the idea that Earth people do not recognize their mates and spend much time searching?”

“Something like that,” Torin said. “There are many strange rules for this dating, and mating becomes very complicated there.”

Tehy began to laugh. “How could it be, unless... Don’t tell me that they have different parts than we do?“

Torin reached over and cuffed him good-naturedly on the arm. “Not that I noticed, and it is very easy to notice there. They place a great deal of importance on appearance, particularly those who wear no clothes.”

Tehy scratched his head in bewilderment. “But what does that have to do with anything?”

“They use their appearances to attract their mates. Recognition of one’s soul is obscured there, so they spend much time trying to appear physically attractive. There are special paints and clothes that cover what they see as imperfections. I told you it was complicated. They experience shame about how they look and how they feel. So I must be patient. Rebecca does not know we are mated in the sense that we understand it. She is not ready yet. Mating physically there is separate from joining on all levels. There are even more complex rules there for the joining of bodies.”

Tehy shook his head. “I can imagine the difficulties ahead. If you are not mated fully yet, how will you know where she is and how she does? What about the longing to be one with your mate? I have heard it is very intense. You know that even though my Mother and Father do not often share the same living space, they must meet at certain times.”

Torin smiled ruefully. “Yes, I do feel it. Truthfully, I find it difficult to be close to Rebecca and not be able to speak of such things. But she does not experience the same pull yet; it is still overshadowed by her planet’s ways. I did do the ritual parting with her, and I can feel that she is well. It is not perhaps as strong as if we were full mates, but she is very powerful in communicating. Did I tell you what happened when she stood in council with us?”

Torin brought Tehy up to date with his and Rebecca’s adventures so far. They soon took to the sky again, reaching the Threshold of the Trees hours later. Hovering solemnly, they noted the terrible devastation below, particularly the ground upheaval where the

Great Tree had once stood. They continued on, finally descending after several hours, and spent the night in a thick copse of friendly trees. Refreshed, they set out again, flying continuously for hours until Tehy needed another rest break. They headed due east, flying until starshine. That night they slept nearby a running stream, and started again soon after sunrise.

Within a few hours they could see a dark mass in the air before them. It appeared almost solid, neither wavering in the high winds, nor moving like clouds of vapor. Torin motioned for Tehy to land so that they could discuss their next move.

"If you look far enough ahead," Torin said, "you can see that the dark patch extends all of the way to the ground. It's got to be the foul air above the Bollux bogs."

Tehy nodded somewhat dismally. "I'm not sure my wings are strong enough to make it through that stuff."

"Let's get closer and see how bad it is," Torin suggested. "Fly very slowly, and stop when I tell you, but at some point we may have to head right into it."

They took off again, slowly approaching the dense darkness. As they hovered nearby, Torin tried to peer through, unsuccessfully. Tehy shouted to Torin to hold his breath and they flew directly into the putrid vapor. As they emerged into a small patch of pink sky, they both exhaled, immediately taking deep breaths. Below them were bubbling pools of black bogs sending their poisonous vapors into the air. Torin and Tehy flew onwards, trying to find another clear space, only to choke and cough as the fetid air entered their lungs.

All around them was a thick, rotten smell in the heavy air. Tehy began to lose altitude as the lack of clear air took its toll. With Torin still grasping his arm, Tehy began to descend rapidly, finally landing on a small clump of ground between two boiling black pools of some viscous substance. Torin immediately wrapped part of his tunic over his face. They sheltered for a few moments under Tehy's huge wings.

"I can't stand much more of this," Tehy gasped, and Torin nodded shakily. He carefully drew from his pocket the small, crystallized dew that Meridwen had given him. He cupped it between his palms and heated his hands. As the dew began to melt, water vapor formed above them.

"Quick!" he motioned to Tehy. "Breathe this in."

Tehy bent over and took a deep breath. Torin did the same before the dew had completely vaporized. Immediately they felt the soothing dew coat their lungs with a kind of protective clarity.

"That's better now," Tehy said, "but it appears that we may have to walk. My wings are completely coated with this slimy stuff. It's times like these that I almost wish I wore more than my waistcloth. And hoof coverings would have been helpful."

Tehy made a face at the thick gooey substance that not only covered his wings, but also their hair and clothing. It felt like glue on their faces and had a tendency to itch, but at least they could breathe the foul-smelling stuff without asphyxiating.

Tehy folded his wings as well as he could while the two surveyed their surroundings. Torin shuddered in disgust. They were standing on a dank patch of ground in a field of thick boiling pools as far as they could see. Above them the air was heavy and thick with the black, clogging steam rising from the pools.

"Only a Bollux would want to live near here," commented Torin, as Tehy tried to scrape some of the junk from his wings. His entire body was covered with the stuff, and it matted his fur and clung to his tail. Torin was heartily glad he wore clothes and didn't have to feel the stuff all over his body.

"I would fire cleanse us," Torin said, "except that we'd probably ignite ourselves. This bog matter looks like it would only feed my flame."

Tehy gave on his efforts to clean himself. "Shall we walk?"

"I would suggest," said a voice from behind them, "that you swim instead. I can recommend the boiling hot bog nearest to you."

Torin and Tehy whirled around, already knowing whom to expect. Standing in front of them, floating above a bog, was a tall, slender man wearing clothes suited to a bog sprite. He was dressed head to foot in dark, drab gray splotched with brown and black patches. His hair was long, greasy and matted to his head, and his smile was full of gray stained teeth. He looked as if he'd never bathed, and Torin was sure that he probably smelled worse than his environment, but it was impossible to tell.

"Jierdan Bollux, master of Bogs and Boggets, the nasty little creatures that suck the life out of you before you boil to death, at my own service. Now, let me guess, this particular flying thing has the look of the Griffin Folk, and a bit of his father as well."

He eyed Tehy with disdain. "Half hatchling! You are neither Griffin nor Air Folk and a bad mix of both. And you," he turned to Torin, "Must be the ash brat of Imanayon's get. Where's the water wench?" he looked around suspiciously and then laughed. "Don't tell me, you came alone! How brave, how human, how elementally imbecilic of you."

Torin felt his hands begin to warm in anger, looked around at the bubbling gassy pools and thought better of it. Tehy attempted to spread his wings, but couldn't get them to move. Jierdan chortled gleefully at their helplessness.

"Let me see now, you wouldn't by all chance have come to retrieve a certain egg, have you? No, that couldn't be it, my horrid sister Haldar has been sitting on it very dutifully, and no one is stupid enough to come into our territory for something that wouldn't even make a substantial breakfast. I must conclude that your business is with my dear family. Therefore, much as I would like to poach you both, I'm afraid I will have to disappoint myself and the dear Boggets once again. Alas, it is so difficult to be a younger son. Father always lets Darden and Varvane have all of the fun."

He paused as the nearest pools began to boil furiously. Torin and Tehy watched as a bulbous slimy creature started to rise from one of the bogs. Jierdan waved it back with one grimy hand, "Not today dear, these two would barely give you enough life force for a paltry snack. Later I'll send something your way."

As the creature sank back down, Jierdan turned to Torin and Tehy once more. "Don't just stand there, you elemental ineptics, let's go pay my family a visit. You're going to make my father's digestive system very happy, you know, even though he doesn't know the meaning of the word. I'm a little disappointed that the fumes didn't kill you myself. I could have hung you on my nonexistent art wall, desiccated carcasses of air and fire, elements of extinction. Ah well, perhaps later."

Before Torin could even blink, he and Tehy were caught up in a foul smelling whirlwind of Bollux travel. It was like being wrenched into pieces, pressed, squeezed, and torn apart, then put back together again into a too-tight container. At last they collapsed, wheezing and coughing, onto a marble floor. Torin raised himself to his hands and knees, looking about at the huge marble hall in which they found themselves. Tehy, too, had caught his breath and he glanced over at Torin as they both got to their feet.

"This must be the stronghold of the Bolluxes," Tehy commented, still scratching at the now caked bog mud that stuck to his skin. "I'm amazed we made it this far, and without that overgrown bog sprite."

Torin shrugged. "I'm sure he'll turn up at the earliest inconvenience. I'm not sure what our chances are, but at least my fire will work here without blowing us up. That was the foulest place I've ever had the displeasure to smell. Let me give us both a fire bath so at least we'll be comfortable."

Tehy closed his eyes while Torin sent a warm splash of fire waves over his body. He sighed as the bog mud burned away, and experimentally flexed his wings. Torin gave himself the same treatment. Clean once more, they both turned to explore the huge room in which they stood.

The long hall, with rounded walls, ceiling and floor, was made of a milky white marble with dark veins. The room was completely empty, except for themselves. They couldn't see any openings at all. There was no trace of Jierdan Bollux, and when Torin attempted to burn a hole through the wall, the marble merely singed a little, quickly returning to its normal hue.

"Fireproof," Torin muttered. He tried asking the floor to move, but the marble merely laughed and refused. "Earth proof," he said.

"It's probably completely elementally stubborn," Tehy said, sitting back down on the floor. "I think it is Epless marble, you know the kind that comes from the Northern caves. I've heard that it isn't helpful unless you give it something first. Mother's Folk call it "bribery brick". I suppose it's likely to refuse entry to the Bolluxes as well, so I wonder why we ended up here. Perhaps Bollux travel doesn't work properly either."

"I'm amazed we're both intact," Torin commented. "That was not a method of travel I would willingly repeat. No wonder the Bolluxes all seem to be missing mind sense. They've probably lost parts of themselves en route. I have to say, though, that this isn't what I would have expected. This place is clean and doesn't stink at all. Not very Bolluxlike."

He pulled some flasks of water out of his backsack, along with some oatcakes and dried fruit. They sat in silence for a while, eating and drinking while they could, talking about possible ways to escape in order to locate the egg. Tehy tried to tune into the egg, but found that the marble prevented him from making contact.

Finally they both tried to get some rest, which proved difficult since they expected to be accosted by a horde of wild Bolluxes at any moment. When nothing happened to disturb the quiet, Torin suggested that they sleep in shifts, and offered to take the first watch. He tossed Tehy his cloak. Tehy gratefully wrapped himself up in it to soften the impact of the hard floor.

As his friend slept, Torin sat and quieted his mind in order to contact Rebecca. He wasn't sure if it would work with the limitations of the marble, but he felt the need to be close to her, even if only in his thoughts. He let his mind go still and reached out to her.

At first he felt blankness, but suddenly a sensation of warmth and comfort swept over him. He sighed, relieved that Rebecca was well and that they were still connected. He brought his awareness back to his own body and the marble floor. He stood up, wishing he could have heard Rebecca's thoughts or she his, but he simply could not connect mentally at all. Torin watched over his sleeping friend, aware of how worn out Tehy must be from all of the flying he'd done. He spent several minutes trying to decide what he could tempt the marble with so it would move for them. As he paced back and forth he heard a strange scraping sound and quickly shook Tehy awake.

"Get up," he ordered. "I think the walls are beginning to move."

Tehy came to full alertness and rose to his feet. The walls around them trembled and shook, and the floor began to sink. As they watched, their arms clasped together to maintain balance, the walls became translucent. The floor stopped sinking and began to rotate, making them both slightly dizzy. Suddenly the floor stopped turning, and a tall opening appeared in one wall. Torin and Tehy stood watchfully as a slender young woman stepped into the marble chamber. She was tall, red-haired, and slightly freckled with a warm, open expression on her pleasant face. She seemed to be surprised to see them, for her mouth parted in an expression of consternation.

"Oh no, not again," she said, surveying them quizzically. "I suppose one of my dreadful siblings put you in here and left you until Father could be bothered to deal with you. I imagine he'll find some extraordinarily vile way to dispose of you." She shook her head disgustedly. "I guess it was your misfortune to wander where you oughtened to have. Really, this is a terrible place to hang about. We Bolluxes are quite nasty in general."

She came closer, peering at Tehy interestedly. "Oh, it's you! You are the winged one Jierdan used to watch through his farview scope. He used to describe all the ways he could pluck the life out of you, but you probably don't want to hear about that. I'm sorry he caught you at last. What was your name?"

Tehy found himself responding as cordially as he would to a newly met acquaintance, simply because he couldn't imagine this woman being much of a threat. "I'm Tehy of the Air and Griffin Folk, and this is Torin of the Fire Folk. You're a Bollux?"

The young woman smiled at his tone of disbelief. "I'm an odd sort of Bollux to be sure. I have a strangeness about me. No matter how much my family insists, I will not cause harm. I am very adept at causing the weather to change and I have the ability to sing travel. I am also a singstress, though no one would ever know outside my family. I create with my voice rather than destroy. They're all quite disgusted with me really."

Tehy looked down into her freckled face, feeling strangely drawn to her wide set hazel eyes. "Your name," he prompted gently, as Torin stared at the absorbed expression on his friend's face in surprise.

"I'm Liliar Bollux," she replied, and her face as she looked at Tehy held the same rapt expression. Torin looked at both of them pityingly. "I thought I had it rough loving an otherworlder," he muttered, rubbing his hand across his eyes and wondering what could possibly happen next.

Somehow Tehy found himself clasping Liliar's hand in his while she explained that she'd sung the marble room into being as a present to Haldane, her youngest brother, who loved marbles in general, the larger the better. But the Epless marble had proved even more stubborn than Haldane, so he rarely spent time there. Instead, he played in an enormous destruction room, in which he could create and destroy to his heart's content.

"It's really his way of feeling that he runs the world," she said fondly, describing her younger brother as a lovable megalomaniac. Privately, Torin thought she must be a rare being if she could find anything redeemable about anyone in her clan. Apparently Tehy thought so too, for he seemed to hang on her every word. Torin clapped Tehy firmly across his shoulders to snap him out of it.

"And how many of you Bolluxes are there?" Torin asked Liliar. "We've met Jierdan, Darden, Varvane, and you. I've heard before that there were at least nine altogether. How many of you actually live here?"

"My parents, Etestian and Boleria, my sisters Haldar, Varvane, and myself, and my brothers Mosten, Haldane, Harlane, Darden and Jierdan all live here. Right now Haldane is off playing in the outermost regions of Bollux country. Father banished him there for a few days for creating a maelstrom in Father's living space and destroying his favorite death spiral."

At Tehy and Torin's looks of puzzlement she explained further. "It was a huge, dark vortex that separates Folk completely and spits their parts out all over Bollux Country. Father says it makes the bogs smell riper. I usually try to sing everyone away to safety, but sometimes I'm too late. Lucky for you Haldane destroyed the spiral, because that's where father usually tries to throw trespassers, if he doesn't eat them. We don't get too many visitors though, as you can imagine.

As for my other relatives, my oldest brother Royden rarely stays here since he spends most of his time off world. My mother's father Baldark is still living somewhere up in the Northern Country and my father's mother Vilerpia lives in the southernmost bogs. The bogs there are really no more than mud, but she's always felt best in them. Old Bolluxes have to spend time in bog ground to maintain their health.

Right now though, Mosten and Darden are off causing mischief somewhere else. None of them have a life mate yet, though my brothers have had some experience with mating. Some of the female rage sprites, you know the malevolent spirits that feed off emotional turmoil, appreciate their foul humor, but not enough to move in with any of them. We all have our own dwellings since otherwise no one gets any rest due to all of the fighting. Haldar bit Jierdan's ear off once when we were younger, so our father insisted that we build our own dwellings. I think it would be safer for you if I took you to my home. Before Father shows up."

"Can we trust a Bollux?" Torin asked bluntly, startling both Tehy and Liliar so that they dropped their hands. "We came to snatch back the Griffin's Queen egg which holds Tehy's sister. Would you take us to it?"

Liliar looked Torin straight in the eye.

"My sister Haldar is keeping it in her den. I can't take you there. She wouldn't hesitate to destroy it. But I could sing it back to where it belongs if you can give me an image of the place."

Torin and Tehy looked at her in amazement. "You can sing teleportation?" they both cried, while Liliar merely nodded.

"I would have sent it back before, but I needed a location. I didn't trust it to arrive safely without a clear picture in mind of where it must go. I have never been out of the Bollux compound, and even Bolluxportation has become more difficult since balance has shifted. But I meant to return the egg; it really doesn't belong to us Bolluxes anyway. "

"I don't think you belong here either, Liliar," Tehy gently insisted. "Would you come with us? If you help us and stay, won't you be in danger?"

Liliar shook her head. "I can't leave now. Haldane needs me, but I could sing you home. It's the safest way to travel now that everything is separating. Jierdan took quite a risk bringing you Bolluxportation in times like these; you could have imploded along the way. It's somewhat safer for us since we're drawn to the pattern of patternlessness anyway, but for you who work in balance...

Don't worry; my family cannot harm me. I'm sure they would have disposed of me long ago, but you see, the very property that makes me unable to harm anyone also makes me impervious to harm. I won't live forever, but I simply cannot be killed. Father will be angry for a while, but there's really not much he can do. I'm always safe wherever I am."

Tehy reached down and grasped her hand. "Torin has a similar gift, that of being difficult to kill. I have no such ability, but I carry a weapon and am able to fly anywhere my wings may travel. I would protect you with my life. I would like you to come with me, not only for your protection, but because I want you with me."

Liliar smiled up at him. "I know that, and I know we will someday be together. I have known ever since I saw you in Jierdan's farview scope. The scope could bring close the image of places very far away, but I shattered it with my voice one day so that he couldn't harm you. He watched you during your mentoring journey when he spied on your mother's Folk. I didn't expect you quite yet, and I'm not ready. I will come to you when I am. Now, let us go to my quarters so that I may sing your egg safely home. My voice carries further from my own rooms. Hold my hands, both of you, and we will go."

Torin grasped one of Liliar's hands while Tehy held the other. Liliar opened her mouth, letting out a trill of notes in a high, firm voice, and they were suddenly traveling. For Torin and Tehy, who had never journeyed by song before, it was like swimming without moving, through oceans of sound. The sound waves carried them effortlessly. There was no sensation of dissolving into individuating cells of matter as there was during elemental travel, or the sickening lurch of disintegration that occurred during Bolluxportation.

One moment they were flowing in sound, the next they were standing in a small, beautiful room, with peach-colored walls iridescent as shells, and a woven bed draped with curtains of gauzy net. There was very little furniture, but Torin was interested to see that Liliar had many books on a wall shelf. Liliar explained somewhat guiltily that because most Bolluxes don't read, she'd sung the books from other Folk's archives, then copied them musically and returned them to their owners. She had to be able to visualize something to either create it or sing it somewhere, and had made use of Jierdan's farview scope a time or two before it had shattered.

Liliar showed them around the four rooms that made up her quarters, all with the same peach-colored walls. She had a resting room, waste room, eating room, and her marble workshop, which housed all of the marbles she'd sung into being. There were shelves and tables piled with dark brown and black spheres created from low notes, lighter browns and yellows from slightly higher notes, and marbles of all colors corresponding to each note further up the scales.

Most of the marbles were made from marble slabs dug from beneath neighboring mountains. Those marbles had swirling patterns and whorls of color, but others were fashioned of hard packed purple earth fired to a glassy state by the power of her voice. The glassy marbles were more translucent and reflected a great deal of light, creating a sparkling effect in the room.

Liliar entertained them for a few moments by humming a few melodies to send the marbles rolling about the room, some on the tables, some dancing in the air. She kept the marbles from falling off the tables and onto the floor by singing stick notes, a series of staccato tones that halted any movement.

She told Torin and Tehy that they each might pick out a marble for themselves, and that the tone each carried might serve to protect them in the future. Tehy selected a dusky purple sphere that maintained its own warmth in his pouch. Torin placed a golden yellow marble with sparkles of red fire carefully in his back sack. After thanking her appreciatively, they followed Liliar to the eating room, where she offered them dried bog snacks and unfiltered bog water. When she saw the expressions on their faces, she laughed mischievously.

"I was only teasing," she assured them, and sang a lovely tone. The food changed before their eyes into oatcakes and fresh harfruit, a dark, blue skinned melon that tasted crisp and tart. The water became clear and inviting, lightly scented with malanblossoms. At Torin's look of inquiry, Liliar shook her head.

"No, such flowers do not grow on Bollux ground. Harlane plucks out any that attempt to survive and the stench of the bogs takes care of the rest. There is a lovely valley to the west of us that grows many wonderful things. I saw it once in the farview scope. You probably flew over it when you journeyed here. I did not think you would enjoy our diet of bog grits and dank bog water."

After they'd finished eating, Liliar asked, "Now, where would you like me to send the egg?"

"Let me describe for you my mother's nest, and you may return the egg to its home," Tehy said thankfully. He spoke of Griffin Country first, visually taking Liliar through the mountains and valleys to the Griffin's nesting ground. He spoke of his mother's cave, set apart from the others, and finally Liliar nodded.

"I can see it, not only through your words, but also through your mind."

She stood for a moment, drawing in deep breaths, then opened her mouth and sang. Afterwards, when he tried to describe it, Torin realized that there were no words eloquent enough. It was simply an experience that had to be felt. It was as if he was back in Imanayon's garden, and all of creation was singing at once. He could feel tonal waves pulsing up from the ground, rushing through the room and beyond.

As he watched, an enormous, bluish gray Griffin egg appeared in the center of the room. Liliar emitted a high, piercing note, and the egg vanished. Her voice hushed, though the soothing sweep of sound still lingered in the room.

Surprisingly, in the midst of Bollux country, Torin found himself filled with exaltation. He realized what an honor it was to have experienced Liliar's voice. Who would have thought they would discover such a wonderful Bollux? He glanced over at Tehy, who looked somewhat stunned, both at the incredible music of Liliar's mind, and that their task had been completed so quickly. They were both struck speechless by Liliar's profound range. She had created beauty in her marbles, changed bog food into edible delicacies, moved them through space on waves of sound, and now transported the egg over a considerable distance. Before they had time to thank her, they heard a discordant, crashing noise and Torin, Tehy and Liliar found themselves standing before an extremely irate Jierdan Bollux.

Now that they were out of the swamp, they could smell Jierdan's pungent body odor. He bared his dark gray teeth at Liliar, too hideously enraged to give her companions more than a hateful glance.

"How dare you steal my prisoners without my permission!" he shouted. "I could have fed them to my favorite bog sprite, but I saved them for Father to dispose of. You heart brained halfwit, you're probably going to do something...nice!" he finished, saying the word "nice" with such vehemence that dark green saliva shot off his tongue.

"Speaking of asking permission," returned Liliar, "I don't remember you asking me to enter my living space, and I certainly didn't invite you."

"Theft of property renders all rules of space prohibition null." Jierdan shot back furiously. "Now give them back or I'll drown them and this sickening room of yours in swamp swill."

Jierdan finished his tirade to no discernible effect, causing him to become literally enflamed. Sparks of rage spit from both nostrils, and he charged toward them with clawed hands outstretched. Liliar stood in stunned amazement at her sibling's stupidity. Here was her brother, not only entering her room without permission, which he knew was punishable by death, but he had the gall to threaten her in her own eating room. No Bollux had dared to attack her since she'd sung Mosten into one of the clear water pools and nearly killed him with purity, purely by accident, of course. They all knew she had a powerful voice, and an inability to be harmed. Before she could open her mouth to utter a disparaging note, Torin had fireshielded them all while Tehy surreptitiously drew his starber blade.

Jierdan laughed harshly, "Don't think your paltry fire will protect you from me, ash brat," he scoffed. "I can neutralize it before you can even move." And he swamped Torin's shield with a deluge of stinky bog water, rendering it inert. At this point, realizing that her brother's sparse wits must have deserted him completely, Liliar opened her mouth to sing Jierdan back to the nearest swamp, but it was too late. The berserk Bollux hurtled himself at Tehy, who just managed to unbend his blade in time. The starber blade struck home in the Bollux's skinny body and in a flash he completely disintegrated, leaving nothing but a few small particles on the floor.

Liliar looked down in horror. She had always considered Jierdan at least somewhat intelligent, even if he did use his brains to ruin everything in sight. But his actions had been incomprehensible, as if he had chosen death deliberately. Though he had always tormented her, he was still her brother.

Tehy stood, shaking from the aftermath of wielding a blade in order to kill. He carefully tucked the blade back into his pouch, and not even daring to glance at Liliar, he sank down to his knees to do the ritual blessing for the passing of life. His face was pale and had somehow aged in only moments. Liliar stared down at him in anguish, as Torin put one arm around her shoulders and one hand upon his friend's head. They stood silently, barely breathing, listening to the slow recitation of the death prayer from Tehy.

Finally Tehy shook Torin's hand loose and stood up to face Liliar. He opened his mouth to speak, but could get no words out. Liliar reached up to soothe him, then embraced him fiercely. She hummed a song of comfort under her breath as they stood clinging to one another. Torin quietly left the room, shaking his head in dismay. Here Tehy had found his mate, and promptly caused the death of one of her kin. Although, if he were to be strictly fair about it, Jierdan had certainly brought most of it upon himself. Still, he thought he'd had it rough loving an otherworlder, and that couldn't even compare to dealing with the whole Bollux clan.

He sat down in the hallway, reaching out for Rebecca to reassure himself that she was well. For a moment he could feel her, but then her energy wavered. He kept trying to focus on her more clearly, but the strange flickering continued. Finally he stood up, puzzled, and returned to the eating room. Tehy sat on one of the marble chairs with Liliar on his lap, holding her close. He looked up as Torin entered, nodding bleakly. They had to leave soon, before the rest of the Bollux clan arrived.

Liliar stood up at a gentle nudge from Tehy. She tried to smile, but couldn't quite manage it. "I think you'd better go now, before the rest of my family shows up." But at that moment there was a huff of stale air and the rest of the Bolluxes appeared.

Etestian Bollux, the head of the Bollux clan, was a tall, skinny, balding fellow with two remaining black tufts of hair, like horns. He was thin to the point of absurdity, and his fingers and toes were prehensile. He resembled a lizard both bodily and in temperament, since his tongue flicked out rapidly when he raged. He stomped up to Liliar, shaking his claws at her.

"This, freakish offspring, is going too far! Never mind that you keep singing visitors away from my appetite and sounding them to safety; it was bad enough that you called the water girl to Thianely in the first place. I let that go, I figured it would be more sport for the rest of us. But this! You stole an egg that didn't belong to you, filched it right out of Haldar's den. She and Harlane stole it especially for us all to have poached Queen to celebrate the end of Griffinkind.

Although we cannot personally tear you limb from limb as we ought, we can certainly make life for you unpleasant, and the deaths of these two more painful. We all know how you hate watching things suffer, don't we?"

Liliar stood pale but firm in the face of Etestian's wrath. "What about Jierdan?" she asked stoically. "Do you not fear his same fate?"

As Etestian stepped closer, Tehy clasped Liliar's hand and drew her closer to him, while Torin strengthened the fire shielding around them.

"Fear these two creatures? Phaugh! They're nothing to be alarmed about. They barely raise my bile. You're useless for harming anything at all. And who cares about Jierdan?" Etestian added dismissively. "Except maybe you. He wasn't good for much anyway, the bile-brained bogster."

"Definitely one of my more putrid offspring," agreed his mate, Boleria Bollux, a large puce-haired woman. "But at least he was never tainted by strange fits of kindness."

As epitaphs go, Torin could truthfully say that he'd never before heard any voiced with such complete disregard. Boleria, the matriarch of the Bollux clan, hated each of her children equally, except for Liliar, whom she ignored for the most part as a complete disappointment.

"Aren't you going to introduce us, you thieving bratling of a sister?" asked Haldar, a blond statuesque Bollux with a face that rarely changed expression. The sneer that was permanently fixed on her scowling face had actually been there at birth. Her mother Boleria used to recount with pride how Haldar had bitten and pummeled her way out of the womb. She had later been forcibly dropped several times in order to unclamp her teeth from her father's arm. It gave Haldar shudders of joy each time her mother recounted the story.

Harlane, a waspish-looking fellow with buckteeth and the lower body of a snake, spoke with a lisp.

"Mother, tell uth we can eat them for thupper. The wingy one looks like he'd have thome meaty bones. But Father can eat the fire one, he's too thpicy for me. And maybe we could do thomething bad to Liliar, like break her thtupid marbles."

Before Boleria could reply, Varvane Bollux stepped closer and threw a Bolluxbolt right at Tehy's face. Liliar sang one note, disintegrating it instantly.

Boleria eyed Liliar coldly. "Want to know what monster fathered a creature like you? Your father was a cloud of fire vapor, an immaterial wastrel who didn't even bother to become enformed. I would have cast you from my womb, but for your invulnerability to harm. You are no true daughter of ours!"

Etestian Bollux spat a green glob onto the floor. "Halfbollux! You're not pure blooded, anyone could tell just by that foul friendly expression on your face. Weakling! Can't even kill anything. And that wretched voice of yours swells my ears and stunts all our brains. You'll never destroy anything useful. Look at what you'll get for a mate--a halfgriffin monstrosity with hooves. Ha!"

Sighing loudly, Liliar Bollux opened her mouth and sang three loud notes. In an instant her family had disappeared. As Torin and Tehy looked at her questioningly, Liliar said, "It was far easier to send them elsewhere than to sing you out. I won't make the same mistake again and allow my family to stay near us. I should have sent Jierdan away immediately, but I couldn't believe that he would be that bogwitted. Now tell me quickly, before they all come back. Where do you want to go? And don't worry, I've heard it all before, though usually they're not all angry with me at once."

Tehy shook his head in admiration. "Your voice is a gift from Rhiate herself," he said firmly. "May Rhiate bless you for all of your help. Griffinkind will be very grateful. As are we. I sorrow that the life of your brother was taken."

Torin nodded in assent. "You have done a great service. I must admit I never expected to be thanking a Bollux, or finding one of the Old Guardians among them."

Liliar smiled somewhat sadly. "Remember never to thank other members of my family. It's not safe to even appear to be beholden to them."

"I know," Torin said. "It's one of the first things we learn. Ask for what you need, respect all of creation, and never thank a Bollux."

"Wait a moment," Liliar said. "Did you say Guardian?" At Torin's nod of assent she shook her head in disbelief. "I often wondered how I arrived in this family and for what purpose. A Guardian among Bolluxes... No wonder I never fit! I always hoped that there was some purpose for my presence here. Moments like these remind me that being a Bollux isn't all bad. Now tell me, where would you like to go?"

"Please send us after the egg," Tehy said. "I think Mother will need an explanation for its safe arrival."

He offered to take her with them again, but Liliar shook her head. "I cannot leave Haldane quite yet; he's young and has no one else to look after him. He'll be back soon from his punishment. He'll know of Jierdan's death and will want to hear what has happened. I can't leave him here with them."

If the family members they'd met thus far were any reflection of the Bollux method of child rearing, Torin and Tehy could understand her hesitation.

"You could bring him along," Tehy offered, while Torin wondered if his friend had temporarily lost his senses.

"Perhaps you ought to ask the other Griffin Folk first," Liliar replied. "You ought never to invite a Bollux into your dwelling space if you are ever desirous of having him leave. Bolluxes are not a clan in which it is safe to have manners."

"You seem to have respect for others," Tehy insisted loyally.

"Not with others of my clan," Liliar returned. "I learned to meet them where they are. Besides, Haldane is not an easy child. I may be a Guardian as you say, but I am also a Bollux and would prefer that your Folk know of my arrival beforehand. I find that preparation helps to avoid much awkwardness. No one likes Bolluxes."

"I wouldn't say that," Tehy said, looking at her as if he never wanted to leave.

Liliar reached up and stroked his face. "We will meet again soon," she promised.

Tehy leaned over and kissed her softly. "Soon," he repeated emphatically. He smiled, and bowing with great respect, stepped away.

Torin bowed as well. "Farewell, Guardian Liliar." He grasped Tehy's arm firmly as Liliar began to sing. Again the sound of her voice filled the room, and Torin felt it deep in his bones, as the room dissolved and the air became radiant white gold.

When the musical waves subsided, they stood knee deep between some thorny bushes. Around them it was dark, under a pale night sky, with only the light of the stars to see by. Torin followed Tehy carefully through the nesting grounds of the Country of the Griffins.

## Chapter 13

As Rebecca passed the many colored pools, shifting her perceptions at will, she noticed something odd. No one seemed to be paying any attention to her at all. When she smiled or acknowledged snippets of conversation, none of the Folk responded. Finally she reached the pool in which Leva sat, conversing with a furry creature whose small purple horn grew right between his eyes.

"Leva," Rebecca called, "I think I'm ready to go find Torin and Tehy now, and maybe travel to Griffin Country."

Leva kept talking as if she hadn't heard Rebecca at all. When Rebecca leaned over and tried to grasp Leva by the arm, she was surprised to find that her hand merely passed through. She pulled back her hand and studied it for a moment. Other than the fact that she was able to see colored light around it, her hand didn't look much different to her. She tried again, yelling Leva's name as loudly as she could, but not only did Leva ignore her, so did the other Folk in the Well of Pools. She glanced down at her hands and saw her fingers lengthen and stretch into long streams of light, only to shrink back again as she refocused her attention elsewhere.

"I wonder," she thought, "if all is changing because I'm perceiving differently, or if I am changed and that's why others perceive me differently." She realized that for some reason she wasn't particularly disturbed by this turn of events, but merely found it interesting. "Perhaps I'll be able to help Torin and Tehy now that others cannot see me. But I wonder how I shift to visible again. I'm not exactly trying to be invisible."

She spent a few moments trying to communicate with Leva again, asking her to get out of the pool so that she could talk to her, and was heartened by the fact that Leva did climb out of the pool. Unfortunately she climbed back in immediately afterwards, seemingly unaware of having stepped out in the first place. Over the next several hours Rebecca discovered that while none of the Folk could hear her physically, they actually responded to her requests even before she voiced them. It was almost as if she could talk to their unconscious minds, but since that didn't seem to be getting her anywhere, she finally sat down in the grass, somewhat at a loss.

"Now what?" she thought to herself, completely at a loss. She sighed, missing Torin quite a lot. She wished he were here to explain things. Time on Thianely felt so different, she mused. So much happened inside and outside oneself in such a short period of time that she couldn't quite reconcile the extreme changes she'd undergone. As she sat quietly waiting for inspiration, she noticed a tall slender shaft of light making its way toward her. It stopped in front of her and shifted into the form of an old woman with long pale hair and deep orange eyes. She wore a gown of kaleidoscoping colors that twirled around without any particular distinction between them. The woman spoke; or rather she sent thoughts in streams of energy that somehow Rebecca could understand.

"There you are! Are you enjoying your new state of awareness?" At Rebecca's nod, she continued, "I'm Wilowren, one of the Elvin Keepers here. I see you've remembered how to expand your perceptions to the point that your sense of matter has disintegrated. Are you able to contract your cells, to diminish the space between them, so that you still exist in the physical plane?"

"If you mean can I make myself seen and heard by all of these Folk, then no, I guess I haven't figured it out yet. Can you help?"

Rebecca stood up expectantly. Wilowren waved her back down on the grass and sat down beside her with great relish, rearranging her skirts comfortably. "I'm glad you showed up," she commented to Rebecca. "It's a relief to sit and relax for a bit. Now, do you understand what's happened?"

Rebecca shook her head. "Not really. I can change my perceptions, but I don't understand why that makes me invisible."

Wilowren patted her hand reassuringly. "You have changed the way you view the world, but in order to do so to such a great extent, you have also shifted your own cellular makeup. As you increased the space between each cell in your body so that more awareness could move through, you became lighter to the point of transparency. Now we need to practice having you consolidate yourself so that you have your complete range of abilities."

Rebecca looked at her in surprise. "But it wasn't hard at all. I mean, I didn't even realize what was going on; I did what came naturally."

"Yes," Wilowren said approvingly, "it is natural for you."

"But if I'm invisible, then why could Leva sort of hear me, but not enough to really make a difference?"

"You were talking directly to her essence, or what people in your world call "soul," and she responded from a very deep level. It was not clear enough to reach her conscious mind, however. Later she may remember thinking about you even if she does not recall hearing the images of your mind."

Rebecca smiled for a moment, thinking that once the phrase, "hearing the images of your mind" would have made no sense, but now she understood it from the inside out. "If I'm invisible to everyone, would they consider me dead?" she asked curiously.

Wilowren laughed. "Death is merely a state of lack of awareness among the living. On your planet there is much fear concerning states called death and life, with nothing in between except sleep. There are so many fine levels of awareness that are available to you that the words have little meaning here. We may grieve for our inability to reach our friends that have moved on to other levels, but we do not experience only one state of existence as "life".

Now we need to bring you back to a more solid state in order for you to be effective both on Thianely and your own planet. You must practice dissolving and resolving until you are able to move effortlessly from one level to the next. Try to remember what it felt like when you first arrived on Thianely."

For Rebecca it was like remembering being a completely different person. At first she thought she'd forgotten, but within moments she realized that earlier experiences were stored inside her like old archives in a library. She thought back to her first moments of arrival, the fear that she had lost her mind, the excitement of being in a new world, the strangeness of feeling so at home and so far away from home at once. As she recalled the memories, she could feel herself shifting into a heavier sense of self, somehow denser.

"That's it," Wilowren said. "You're becoming more solid. Oh, there you go, you expanded back out again. I think that old sense of self is no longer enough to keep you in form. Try something else."

Rebecca thought for a moment and pictured Torin trying to reach her. Instantly she materialized fully, but soon she lost it again.

"Love is a good anchor," Wilowren said, "but it does not work at your level to be dependent upon another being in order to manifest. You must accept full responsibility for your presence here. Try simply willing yourself to be physical."

"How about if I ask to solidify, or ask the ground to help me?"

"If you must ask something, ask the part of you that remembers all that exists," Wilowren said somewhat sternly. "Pure will is simply giving yourself permission to be all of yourself in any moment."

"Whew," Rebecca said. "For some reason that seems like a lot of responsibility. I think on my planet, everyone thinks God is in charge so you have to ask Him. It seems kind of arrogant to will stuff yourself."

Wilowren began to laugh. "Do you think you are given your gifts and abilities so that you won't use them? Must you ask for permission to be yourself? Why do you think you incarnated, merely in order to constantly refuse to be yourself?"

Rebecca's brain began to hurt and all of a sudden she found herself in solid form once again.

"For now, it looks like your own doubts will keep you in physical form," Wilowren chuckled. "I must say it is quite enjoyable to witness your mind at work."

Rebecca suspected that she was being thoroughly teased, but it didn't particularly bother her. "Now what?"

"Let go of your doubts. Imagine them like small flying creatures popping from your mind. There, you've expanded back out. I think that will do for now, although I must tell you that soon your doubts will not be enough to keep you physical. At some point, you must will yourself so."

Rebecca practiced expanding and contracting several times, noticing with each contraction that she got a pain in some part of her body. When she mentioned it to Wilowren, the old woman laughed again.

"If you could see how your doubts make you lopsided you would not be so surprised that you feel pain. Right now your left arm looks shrunken and shriveled."

Rebecca winced. "I keep expanding the part that feels pain, but it only moves somewhere else. How come I didn't have any trouble healing the parts of me that felt pain before, like at the Threshold of the Trees?"

"That was a different level of pain. This is deeper. You haven't cleared the original pain of forgetting yourself," Wilowren said gently. "Stop trying so hard and it will come when it's time. Now expand back out and give yourself a respite from the pain; you have some work to do at this level."

Rebecca let herself relax into her more spacious state. She had noticed that even though she had become visible again as she had practiced, none of the Folk had paid any attention. Wilowren explained that to them she was only a flicker of light, because her transformation in perception had actually speeded up her timing. Rebecca shook her head, wondering again how so much could change in so short a time, when it seemed that for the first sixteen years of her life, nothing much had happened at all.

"Still your mind a moment and listen," Wilowren said insistently. Rebecca heard it too, the voice familiar from her fever, calling to her strongly. She thanked Wilowren, who nodded agreeably when Rebecca explained that she had to leave.

"Safe journeys," Wilowren said. "You'll meet more of us Elvin Folk later, when we'll have more time to chat."

Rebecca waved goodbye. She followed the threads of song through space as thin and as flexible as ripples of time, merely by expanding and contracting to the rhythm of the voice. It was fulfilling in a very profound way. The music nurtured all of her senses at once.

She stepped through what looked like a rainbow of infinite colors and found herself in a lovely peach-colored room. A young woman slept quietly on a small bed in the corner. She lay asleep, sprawled on her bed in what looked like a state of utter exhaustion. The room felt strange to Rebecca, as if it were an oasis of peace in the middle of mayhem. She stood waiting, wondering whether she ought to awaken the woman, whose long red hair tumbled about her face, when the woman stirred and sat up.

"Hello," said the woman, and Rebecca realized that even as insubstantial as she was, the woman could still somehow see her. "I imagine you heard me singing earlier and followed the chords of song here. I would have stayed awake to greet you, but I've had quite a long day. I'm Liliar Bollux."

Rebecca smiled, made herself more corporeal, and immediately felt a twinge in her left knee. After she patted it for a moment, she reached over to clasp Liliar's hand. Liliar pressed hers gently in return and glanced down at Rebecca's knee. "We'll be able to take care of that soon," she said reassuringly.

Rebecca shrugged. "It doesn't really hurt that much. It never stays in one place very long. I have a movable pain that rotates around my body every time I try to show up completely. I'm kind of working on it, I guess. You know, you probably hear this a lot, but you don't much look like the rest of the Bolluxes I've seen. You certainly don't act like them. I remembered your voice from when I was sick, from all the way back on Earth. You did call me, didn't you?"

Liliar nodded. "Sometimes when I sing, songs spring through me from the very earliest times of Creation. Such songs travel far beyond our worlds. I do not know if they ever stop. But yes, I called to you. I dreamed that you would come if I sang. Sometimes I think Thianely herself sings through me. And I must tell you; I have met your mate Torin, and Tehy, my own mate. Come with me to my eating room and I will tell you about it."

Rebecca sat down, drank some clear water, and ate flower cakes while she listened in fascination. Liliar brought her up to date on what had transpired in Bollux Country while she and Leva were at the Well of Pools. Rebecca was relieved that both Torin and Tehy were fine and had successfully retrieved the egg, thanks to Liliar's voice. She smiled when she heard about Liliar's first meeting with Tehy. She hugged Liliar when she heard of Jierdan's death.

"There is not much to commend in my siblings or my parents," Liliar admitted sorrowfully. "But I still mourn him anyway. It was very strange, as if he had become totally mindless. Ordinarily he had a cunning shrewdness and would never risk his life. He'd always been something of a coward, really, so this was out of character. As much as my family loves to destroy things, they've always been particularly careful about protecting their own hides."

"Torin told me that the imbalance on the planet is being supported by your clan, even to the point of Thianely's destruction," Rebecca said, wondering if she ought to have mentioned it at all. "That's not exactly looking out for themselves."

Liliar shook her head. "It doesn't make any sense, unless the state of imbalance is so extreme it's affecting my already unstable relatives. I hope they don't all go withered-brained at once. I mean, I was planning to leave some day, particularly when I met my mate, but I may have to go sooner than I thought. Of course, it's already difficult when the urge to mate is so strong. But you know how that is."

Rebecca raised her eyebrows. "I do?"

"You don't?" Liliar asked in surprise. "I would have thought that by now you and Torin would have mated, especially so that you could communicate during far travel."

Rebecca turned a bright shade of red. "What are you talking about?"

"I'm sorry," Liliar said, pouring Rebecca another cup of clear water. "I forgot your planet has different customs regarding mating. I only know a bit about your planet from books I've read. Here, once you meet your mate, the urge to bond is difficult to postpone. Even Bolluxes must mate when they meet their match. Do you not feel it at all?"

Rebecca turned an even brighter shade, if that was possible. "At my house we don't talk about this stuff so openly, although every family is different. Are you telling me that Torin would feel this sort of urgent mating thing?"

Liliar nodded, looking curiously at Rebecca's red face. "Did you know that your face changes color when you talk about mating?" she asked.

Rebecca laughed. "That's because I'm embarrassed by this whole conversation. In my country we actually have laws about when you're old enough to mate. Apparently no one here is ashamed of his or her feelings, but I'm not quite there yet. I'm glad you told me though. Torin didn't say anything."

"Doesn't he know the way of your world better than many Thianelians? Perhaps he realized you would not be comfortable with this topic."

"So on Thianely there is no shame associated with mating?" Rebecca asked.

Liliar looked at her in puzzlement. "Why would this bring shame? What do you mean by shame exactly? The words you use in the Old Tongue would mean Folk measure themselves against some idea of value. How could anyone be worth more or less than another? What does that have to do with mating?"

"I don't know how to explain it to you. Torin told me that it is a difficult concept for Thianelians to grasp. It's probably not something you'd want to experience anyway."

"Yes, I suppose I could have been what you would call ashamed, growing up so different from others of my clan. Luckily I have always recognized the intrinsic value of everything in creation. Though my Folk denigrate other beings constantly, they do not seem to feel this shame that you speak of. Some day perhaps, I will visit your world with more than my voice. There is much to learn there."

"I bet it was a shock for your Folk to find a Guardian Bollux among them," Rebecca said. "How did you ever manage to be born from two Bollux parents, if you don't mind my asking?"

"My father was not of this clan. As far as I know, he was some sort of vaporous fire being. I don't know much about all of that, since I only found out today when my mother was shrieking. I'm surprised I never heard it before."

"That sounds tough," Rebecca said sympathetically, profoundly grateful that she had her own parents back on Earth. "It must be hard to live among Bollux Folk and be able to relax."

"It's difficult at times," Liliar admitted, "but no more difficult than arriving on a strange planet and having to remember who you are in a short period of time."

"Thanks. It has been a real growth experience," Rebecca said wryly. "But the hardest part is not being able to communicate with Torin. I can feel he's worried, but I can't seem to reassure him and have him hear me. Plus, wherever I'm going next, it's not Griffin Country. I mean, there's something else I have to do first, but I'm not quite sure what yet."

"It's difficult to perceive through the veil of one's worry," Liliar observed. "I can show you how to tone sounds that he will feel, even through anxious thoughts. Singing will bring you into your body in whatever dimension you wish. Low tones will bring you more into third dimensional space while the higher notes help you shift to lighter spaces."

As Liliar began to hum deep in her chest, Rebecca became more solid. She joined Liliar in singing, and soon felt fully present in third dimensional space. The pain in her knee receded.

"Very good, your doubts are being sung out," said Liliar. "Now let's check your range and I'll help you open your musical intuition."

They began a series of exercises, and though Rebecca was rusty in areas, and her voice came out a little squeaky, Liliar reassured her.

"Your home language is missing some sounds," she explained kindly. "It is only a fragment of the Old Tongue. The more you use the old speech, the more your full range will return. Rebecca, you too have the ability to create with your voice, and to protect yourself with it. Listen and I'll show you."

The two spent the next few hours before dawn practicing sound creation. After they had redecorated Liliar's room three or four times by using their voices, Liliar pronounced her ready.

"I'm not sure exactly where you'll be going," Liliar said, patting Rebecca on the back, "but you are certainly quick at reminding yourself when it comes to tonal agility. I feel a lot better about Thianely knowing you're here. However, remember that even the most powerful voice may be affected by the great separation that has been occurring. You know how the walls turned that strange bog color as we sang? Some of my own songs have been a trifle discordant in places. Once I sang a marble into being that persisted in rectangularity. Haldane was very disappointed that it wouldn't roll. So keep in tune the best you can."

She waved as Rebecca chirped some high notes and began to fade again. "Take care, Rebecca, and I will tell Torin you are well. Whenever you're finished with whatever you're doing, we will meet in Griffin Country."

Liliar could still make out the edges of Rebecca's form, even though her new friend appeared to have dissolved right in front of her. She knew Rebecca could still see her even as the door burst open and a huge shaggy-haired man, rough and unkempt, pushed his way into the room. He looked a little like an upright boar without the tusks, and although Liliar was startled by his sudden arrival, she could not help but inwardly smile, as she always did, at the appearance of her brother Mosten. He had been particularly angry with her ever since she'd tossed him into the clear pool and contaminated him with clarity. He refused to believe it had been inadvertent and had taken to growing his body hair to obscure any accidental cleanliness that may have lingered. Now he stood glaring at her as Liliar smiled a friendly welcome.

"What can I do for you, Mosten?" she asked, smoothing out the indentation in the covers where Rebecca had been sitting. "You do realize you are uninvited, and you know it is punishable by death to be here."

Mosten began to rumble angrily. To Rebecca it sounded like the growling of a ferocious beast. She stayed, however, partly to give Liliar assistance if she needed it, and partly out of curiosity.

Mosten finally stopped thundering like a stormy sky and said roughly, "You can't harm me; it's against your nature. And that winged part-Griffin isn't here to help you either. Father told me what you did. After all my hard work destroying the mechanism that runs the Gates of Time, I return and find out that my wretched half relative has let the Griffin egg and its brother go, not to mention the fire boy."

"And," he said, smacking one brutish fist into the other, "we all know he's the heir of the Fire Lord himself, and commands the element of fire. You'd know it too if you ever bothered to join our little family feasts. I had it on highest authority that the firebrat is a danger to all of us. I dutifully warned everyone. Then what do you go and do? Sing him out to safety with that loathsome voice of yours. Because, of course, you can't stomach violence unless it's against one of your own family, like your older brother. Do you know that no rage sprite will have me any more ever since you polluted me? You've ruined everything!

What do you suppose will happen if this fool of fire finds out how much power he has? Especially if he manages to work together with all the elements, not to mention his water mate. You, Liliar, have unBolluxed things up for the last time! You have a choice."

He stepped closer to Liliar and stared down at her threateningly. "I will give you the opportunity to leave today, or I will go to Magbar, the Queen of the Bellorasps herself, and have her take your voice. She and her fellows are already climbing up from below ground. Several are on their way to us. Soon, my disgusting sister, you will be completely helpless and we will be rid of you at long last."

Liliar turned slightly pale. "None of you would willingly give up your life in order for her to take my voice, and you know, have always known, that this is what it would take. A life for a voice, just as it always is with her, and your soul as well. No Bollux has ever been born who would sacrifice him or herself for the advancement of the rest. Your threat is hollow, Mosten, as hollow as your heart. Now get out of my room before I sing you back into the pool."

"Don't be too sure, Sister," said Mosten softly. He turned abruptly and left, slamming the door behind him.

Rebecca eyed Liliar, who sat pale, but resolute on her bed.

"What will you do, Liliar? What are the Bellorasps?" she asked, becoming a little more solid so that she could give her friend a reassuring squeeze.

Liliar sighed. "The Bellorasps are nasty creatures that suck the sound right out of the space they inhabit. They are large, slimy, ungainly creatures with many mouths all over their bodies, several legs with suction feet, and a kind of dripping saliva, which streams out behind them. They cannot move that quickly, but they lay waste to everything in sight. Imagine, Rebecca, that we are all made of moving particles that resonate. Bellorasps eat the resonance in all living things. Normally they live deep below the surface of the planet, feeding on the ground resonance. It provides them the most sustenance with the least expense of energy. Usually they are difficult to budge from their underground caverns, since they are extremely lazy by nature.

There have been times in Thianely's history when they have been enticed above ground. The ruler of the Bellorasps can be provoked to action given the gift of the soul essence of a being or two. Each soul has a specific tone, a blueprint of sound that maintains itself throughout each incarnation. If a Bellorasp eats this essence, the soul may never reincarnate as itself. It becomes part of a Bellorasp's energy, making the Bellorasp more powerful. Luckily, few beings would be willing to sacrifice themselves in such a manner, even to gain the assistance of the Bellorasps.

To have one take my voice would make me vulnerable to everyone in my family. As I said before, Bellorasps must be bribed to act. Their price is high, much too high for anyone in my clan. Tehy gave me Meridwen's crystal to wear. I will follow it and go to him. Mosten's threats are not to my liking. He sounds too sure of himself, so it is time for me to go. I will bring my youngest brother Haldane with me, since he would not wish to stay here alone. Torin must learn of his origins also. To be the Fire Lord's son is a great responsibility. The Fire Lord was one of the first leaders of this planet, called here by Niaphani and Heric themselves. But you, Rebecca, where do you go?"

Rebecca smiled. "I need to go into a very nonphysical reality, sit quietly and examine the crystal wisdom that Alphumerian left with me. I have much work to do. Do me a favor and tell Torin I am well; I can feel him trying to find me." Liliar agreed, already gathering her things together. Rebecca soon faded completely.

Rebecca felt herself space traveling, rippling in and out of dimensions as she moved in a sort of spiraling wave. She pictured the place she had in her intention, and there she was, standing, or floating rather, outside an airy oasis of light. She passed what seemed to be an entrance, though no one was there to question her arrival. Inside the space she found a dome-shaped hall with different colored rays of light vibrating along the walls. She sat down on a segment of dense green energy, closing her eyes in concentration. All at once she was inside the crystals again, and running streams of information across her inward vision. There was so much multidimensional data, arranged in patterns of numbers, colors and sound, that Rebecca expanded her mind to make sense of it.

She saw numbers and letters, streams of light, and chunks of consciousness that grew as she changed the way she perceived them. As she allowed herself to expand over a great distance, the space between her cells widened. Suddenly, with a snap, she came together again into her usual three-dimensional body, still holding the images of crystal wisdom. Gradually she expanded back out again. She found that she could not only perceive inter dimensionally, but also control her vibratory pattern to the point where she could change form and density. She could twist herself into blobs of light or coalesce back into a coherent form. She played for a while, completely changing her shape and wondering what kept her together at all, mind or soul.

Suddenly she noticed pockets of distortions in space and time affecting her will, and realized that rifts in consciousness caused gaps in her intention. She struggled at first, singing to mend the tears, but even her greatest efforts could not stop the separation. It was a little like trying to sew and having the thread she was using unravel amid stitch. Even though she could visualize what she was trying to create, her will was being thwarted. She kept flickering from solid back to formlessness every time she experienced the separation, which seemed to be occurring on all levels intermittently. She stamped her foot in frustration at her inability to maintain her focus.

She finally had to chuckle. On her planet this intercellular play would be considered completely impossible, and here she was, annoyed that she hadn't gotten it under control. She remembered that once, long ago, everyone knew how to shift from matter to light and all the places in between, and that there was as simple an explanation for "miracles" as there was for making pizza. One merely had to be thinking and intending from a different dimensional perspective. It wasn't that she had forgotten how to move easily in and out of such levels; it was that something was definitely interfering on a large scale. Even Liliar, who had an extraordinary command of her vocal abilities, had mentioned difficulties she had been experiencing lately.

Rebecca laughed at her own expectations of perfection. "I keep thinking that if I sing the right note, or put together this information in my head properly, I wouldn't be so stymied. Here I am, doing things that are totally outrageous, and I'm mad that I can't do even more. Maybe I'm not capable of fixing the whole rip thing myself. It probably isn't even my responsibility."

Rebecca sat down, amid space and time, drifting through the creative capacity of her own thoughts. She decided to try humming sounds in tune with the crystal information moving across the screen of her mind, and spent the next few hours happily engaged in a brief history of universal theory, which bore absolutely no resemblance to anything hitherto discovered on her planet.

She discovered that as long as she didn't try so hard to hold onto one particular reality, the splits in intention didn't disturb her at all. In fact, she had a sudden insight into how the Bolluxes perceived their world and how balance itself could become inflexible if one became too attached to it. Any pattern could become constricting if one adhered to it like a barnacle. She felt an overwhelming sense of joy at the sheer freedom she felt and wished for a moment that Torin and her parents were there to share it with her. Again, just as she had at the top of the mountain, Rebecca let her body follow the movements of her mind, and she danced right in between moments of time.

## Chapter 14

Torin and Tehy stood in the nesting grounds beneath the mountain range that surrounded Griffin Country. Imposing in the starlight, the mountains were definitely a factor in the longevity of the Griffin Folk. They provided an almost impenetrable location.

Tehy sighed. "We did it. The egg is safe, we're here in Griffin Country, but Liliar's not. How do you and Rebecca stand it?"

Torin shook his head ruefully, and then patted his friend consolingly on the back. "It's never easy to leave one's mate, Tehy, but Rebecca doesn't feel the same longing. It's much more intense when it is experienced both ways. You know how the energy moves between mates and increases in intensity as it travels back and forth. You and Liliar will not be apart for long. I only wish I could say the same."

Tehy rubbed his shaggy head in disbelief. "Imagine loving a Bollux! Of all the mates for me to choose, why a Bollux? How could such a lovely being come through a mother like that?"

"It didn't seem to me you had much choice in the matter," said Torin. "As to how Liliar came out so well, I think it has more to do with her intrinsic nature than any Bollux form of nurture."

Tehy had to laugh. "Let's go find Mother. If I know her, she probably found the egg returned and immediately declared war on the Bolluxes. She's probably in council chambers, even at this time of night. Torin, have you been able to tel to Rebecca at all?"

"No, all I get is a wavering pattern of dissolution and integration, a field of energy that keeps forming and dispersing. It's frustrating."

"If she doesn't hear from us by tomorrow she'll be here soon anyway, you know. There are Air Folk at the Well of Pools that will be escorting her here," Tehy reminded him. "I can always fly to the Well of Pools in the morning and pick up both Rebecca and Leva myself."

"I know, but I don't like being out of tel range, and I can't feel her either. It's strange."

"Come on," Tehy said, as the two made their way between nests on the path through the nesting ground. "Let's go talk to Mother and check on the egg as well. We'll both feel better with a meal and some rest."

Tehy led the way to the edge of the nesting grounds where an enormous hill swelled above the ground like a large reclining beast. The hillside opened into several earthen passages, one of which led into an enormous crystal lit cavern. The center of it was immense, with many smaller caves on either side. The central cavern was large enough to house the entire Griffin population, which is exactly what it was currently doing. As Tehy had predicted, they could hear the rumble of angry Griffins as they entered, with the ruling council in front and the rest of the Griffins seated on individual stone seats to the rear.

The Griffin Folk varied greatly in appearance, some with huge shaggy heads, the bodies of cats, the claws of great dragons. Others had sharp horns, wings, tails, large golden eyes, or smaller slanted eyes like birds of prey. Most of them were huge, and for the first time Torin realized how different Tehy was from the rest of his mother's Folk. Compared to the rest of the clan, Tehy seemed almost small, and certainly not as wild.

In the front and center of the council was an enormous stone chair and in it sat a magnificent woman. Her fiery purple mane of hair cascaded down lightly furred shoulders to the midpoint of her wings, huge golden spans that must have been ten feet tall. Her face was a combination of fierceness and beauty. Torin could immediately understand why Tehan would have had a difficult time living apart from her. She had a pair of piercing turquoise eyes, a slender nose, full lips, and the brilliance of a quick mind. Her movements and her gestures were graceful, but sinuous as a cat. Her body was that of a woman, but her hands curved in talons and her feet, bare on the cave floor, were the paws of a lioness. She was clothed in a gown of scarlet woven material that draped her body decorously. Her snakelike tail coiled behind her, its tip moving slightly as she spoke.

Kerithan held up her hands for quiet as Tehy and Torin drew near. The rumbles died down to murmurs and Torin found himself being introduced to the Griffin Queen. It was a little like being examined by a contained whirlwind. The power in her gaze was unmistakable. She scrutinized Torin piercingly and smiled, revealing sharp teeth. As she stood to embrace her son, her wings flexed slightly, creating a small breeze.

Torin looked around, noticing Tehan sitting with the Air Folk on one side of the room. Tehan made his way to the front and congratulated both of them on securing the egg.

"I know it was gravely dangerous. Perhaps you could explain to the throng here how it came about that the egg arrived back in the nest so promptly. Kerithan has it safely covered in the Queen nest."

Kerithan nodded in agreement and had seats brought next to her so that Torin and Tehy could address the assembly. Again she raised her arms and the hall quieted.

"Griffinkind, my son and his friend, Torin of the Fire Folk, have returned from the stronghold of the Bolluxes." Kerithan's voice had the smoothness of velvet combined with the roughness of wild creatures.

"You all know that the egg has been returned safely, but the danger to our world remains. Now, we must decide our next course. Do we call upon our allies and go to war against the Bolluxes, do we remain here in the mountain regions of our breeding grounds and protect ourselves as best we can, or do we simply maintain our guard of the remaining Balance, sending scouts to all the Folk who require assistance?

She who fulfills the prophecy, Rebecca, is at the Well of Springs right now. Already the portents of the prophecy are coming to pass; the ground is unstable and the mountain beings awaken. I propose that we hear what my son and Torin of the Fire Folk have to say. Then we vote."

There was a murmur of assent as Kerithan motioned for Tehy and Torin to begin speaking. Torin explained how he had pulled Rebecca to Thianely, her progress thus far, despite Bollux attacks, and their journey to Bollux Country. They took turns describing their confrontation with Jierdan in the swamp and the arrival at the Bollux compound. Once they got to the meeting with Liliar, Tehy took over, describing the death of Jierdan and their confrontation with the Bollux clan. The entire assembly looked stunned at the thought of a Guardian Bollux.

"Not a pleasant position to be in," commented Kerithan wryly, glancing curiously at her son, for his voice shifted when he spoke of the singstress. "It is good to know we have an ally at the Bollux camp, but I pity her that family. They may be particularly eager to avenge their kinsman's death."

Torin shook his head. "They displayed little if any concern at all. They were more disturbed by the loss of the egg than by their son's passing. We were worried that they would take it out on Liliar, but she protected herself by singing them away. She's amazing."

"If this is as you say," Kerithan said, "perhaps her abilities will allow us to make a successful attack against the Bollux stronghold. We must find a way to get there with our force intact."

She surveyed her assembled people seriously. "You've heard the odds against us if we seek to destroy the Bolluxes. We have known that the air above Bollux Country is inhospitable to those who breathe clarity. At the same time, even if we take measures to protect ourselves from the separation that is occurring and choose to merely wait, we are in some sense shirking our duties as protectors of Thianely. I recommend that we confront the Bolluxes directly and neutralize them in order to keep them from causing any more planetary damage. If we vote and this suggestion meets with approval, I will charge a special brigade to stay and protect the children, the Nurturers, and the Queen egg. The rest of us will fight."

She turned to Tehan. "As our ally, your Folk may also have some say in this matter, and any of those who wish to avoid battle would also be safe here."

Torin watched as the Griffin Folk began to stamp their feet and raise their fists, simultaneously emitting loud shouts. Kerithan motioned for silence and insisted that they at least take turns yelling, while Tehan shook his head patiently and went to sit with the Air Folk. Tehy motioned to Torin as the Griffin Folk and Air Folk prepared to debate further.

"You notice how Mother makes her suggestion and makes it impossible for anyone to refuse? Spoken in true Griffin fashion. Hardly anyone votes against the Griffin Queen, except father, which is why she likes him so much. Come on, let's go get some food and some sleep. They could take awhile to reach a decision. The Griffin Folk are very noisy debaters and even though Mother likes to consider this a democracy, she will undoubtedly exert her influence. But Father and the Air Folk have always abhorred violence. I suppose I'm lucky I have Father's Folk to balance the fierceness of Griffinkind."

"It makes sense to have a Bollux for a mate then," teased Torin. "Liliar's probably the only being who could handle both sides of your family."

"That may be true," Tehy admitted, "but at least our Folk are of Thianely. Of the two of us, my friend, I think yours is the more difficult situation, though comparisons are often meaningless. Now, enough of this. Through here is the eating room."

Torin followed Tehy into one of the side rooms, which was full of tables laden with food. There were earthen shelves stocked with all manners of roots and fruit, both dried and fresh, and circular nest tables piled high with thick slabs of dried meat. Many of the Griffins enjoyed eating the slow, plodding barbest, a cattle-like creature with six legs. Nearby fields fed the roaming herds, so meat was always plentiful. There were several kinds of roasted grains, seared by the fiery tempers of Griffin food sorters to the consistency of mush. Torin avoided the meat, helping himself to some of the bowls of grains, roots, and fruits. Tehy loaded a thin stone platter with food and joined Torin at one of the wall benches.

"I doubt Liliar could be persuaded to act against her Folk deliberately," commented Tehy, after he finished chewing some dried meat, "even as forceful as Mother can be when she wants something. Liliar may dislike their basic natures, but she still cares for her family. I can't say I'm looking forward to meeting more of them, though I suppose she'll be bringing the little one, Haldane, with her when she comes. I didn't get a chance to prepare Mother yet. I didn't want to announce that my mate is a Bollux in front of the entire assembly, and oh, by the way, she's bringing another Bollux with her to live with us. That would have caused a total riot."

"We'll have to tell your mother soon if she didn't figure it out already. She did look at you curiously a few times when you mentioned Liliar. Your father too, or do you think he'll have an easier time accepting it?"

"Father usually does, but this may even be a stretch for him. I saw the look on his face when he realized I'd used a weapon to take life. He looked ill. Thank Rhiate; Liliar does not blame me fully for Jierdan's death! I still wish I could have defended myself without destroying him."

"I know. I was surprised that my fire shielding could be quenched by bog water, or I would've been more help. Bog matter must be very toxic. I think of the three of us, Liliar probably blames herself the most. She was so shocked when Jierdan lost his senses, she forgot to sing him away."

Tehy gulped down some flower juice. "That's it. I will not ask for her help, though I know Mother will try to persuade me otherwise. Liliar has had a difficult enough life without being asked to betray her family. She should not be asked to pay a price to live here; she must be welcomed completely."

"Would your Folk really destroy all of the Bolluxes if they could?" Torin asked. "Would that truly assist in maintaining Balance?'

Tehy shrugged. "Since the beginning times the Bollux and Griffin Folk have been at odds. We have killed several of them over the centuries, as they have us. Mostly it's been over really flagrant violations of spiritual law. For example, one of the Bolluxes, probably Etestian's great, great grandsire, stole a maiden from the Earthen Folk.

Her parents appealed to the Griffin Folk for help, so the Griffin Queen, Nerithan, demanded the girl back. After the old Bollux leader, Murdien, refused, two of his sons, Pustian and Dulsan, were later killed by Griffin warriors as they were attempting to snatch another maid. Queen Nerithan found out later that Murdien had eaten the first girl. Since then, even though Etestian has been known to devour uninvited guests, no Bolluxes have ever stolen another of the Folk to eat for dinner. It probably helped that Murdien died of acute indigestion. Anyway, Balance has always been maintained over the years, but lately, of course, everything's been strange.

Perhaps Father will talk some sense into Mother. He is much more interested in healing things than in slicing them into little pieces. At this point, none of us know what is truly causing the rifts in intention we have all experienced lately. Personally, I want to know what Rebecca has discovered. I wish we could speak with her before any major decisions are made. But they'll be talking all night, and I am already tired. I'll need a full night's rest to conference with my parents in the morning. How about some sleep?"

Torin yawned loudly. "I guess that answers your question. Lead the way to the sleeping rooms."

"Sleeping nests, actually," Tehy corrected. "We have to head back outside where the nesting ground is. Only mated folk sleep in cave."

## Chapter 15

Torin awoke to the sound of snoring Griffin Folk. He raised his head from the thick woven nest of yarweed plants and gazed about. The pink sun illuminated the entire nesting ground of sleeping Griffins, most still exhausted from the long night's debate. The nests were each large enough to sleep six to eight full grown Griffins, so the nest he shared with Tehy still had plenty more room. The walls of the nests were several wingspans wide, and half again as tall. Most Griffins climbed into their nests using their sharp claws, but Tehy had simply flown them to the top of the nest and promptly fallen asleep. Surrounding the field of nests were thick grasses, intermittent paths, and short bushes with sharp thorns. At the far end of one field he could see the grazing barbest herds.

Torin sighed and stretched, missing Rebecca keenly. He sat for a moment, checking to see if he could feel her and was immediately suffused with warmth. He took a deep breath, sighing with relief. He still could not hear her thoughts, but at least he knew she was well. She felt stronger to him somehow; her energy no longer flickered. He glanced over at Tehy, who was still sound asleep, and leaned over the edge of the nest to get a better view.

Inside the nesting ground he could see several small Griffinlings sharpening sticks to use as mock daggers. They were all very different in appearance. Some were winged, some had horns, and some resembled birds or reptiles. Many of the larger ones had long, snakelike tails, while others had only short furry tails. The few who had wings flexed them menacingly, whipping their tails back and forth and hissing ferociously. Torin watched as the entire group lowered their horns, bared their teeth, and attacked each other with great enthusiasm.

Torin shook his head in amazement. It was a wonder that Tehy wasn't more overtly aggressive if this was an example of his childhood. He didn't notice any of the Griffin offspring exactly sheathing their claws. If anything, they looked as if they needed an adult to intercede before they did some real damage to each other.

"I guess Mother won the vote," Tehy said, joining Torin at the edge of the nest. "I see the little ones are all getting ready for battle. Don't bother trying to break it up. They'll stop short of maiming each other," he added, watching Torin's expression of concern. "And yes, I spent quite a bit of time out here pretending to be a Griffin warrior when I was young. Then Mother sent me to Father's Folk and I had to learn other ways to solve difficulties. Some of the Griffin Folk think I've become too much Air. Of course, the Air Folk thought I was totally uncivilized at first."

He shrugged. "After my mentoring journey many of the old Griffin Guard assumed I would come to my senses and become a full warrior. I divide my time between Griffin Country and Father's Folk. I have to admit that until the mountain collapsed, being with the Air Folk was a lot more comfortable. No fighting, no shouting. Ah well, here we are, back to the old battling ground. I wonder how Liliar will fit in here."

"We'll know soon. Can you feel her from here?"

Tehy nodded. "Yes, the thread of song between us is very strong. I can also hear her thoughts occasionally, but not all of the time. It almost makes it harder to wait for her. Have you been able to sense Rebecca?"

"I could this morning," Torin said. "I can tell she's well, but she feels very different to me than before. Her energy has shifted. At least she's more cohesive, no more strange, undifferentiated wave pattern. I'm unable to pick up her thoughts though. For some reason I can hear Liliar occasionally. Do you think her voice allows her to tel even through the disruptions in space and time? Or maybe once you've heard her sing, you can find her anywhere. I think she was one of the original Guardians who first sang the creation of our planets into being."

Tehy turned to him seriously. "I trust her power completely, but I must admit I am not eager to inform my mother and the Griffin Folk of Liliar's arrival. It is completely against all Griffin tradition to have a Bollux, no matter how wonderful she may be, in Griffin Country. I do not wish to cause dissension among my mother's Folk, but Liliar is my mate. One's mate must be first."

"Your parents are mated; they will understand. Now how about some food? All of this traveling makes me hungry, yet you've been doing most of the work."

Tehy grimaced. "No wonder my wings are so stiff." He flexed them experimentally and leaped over the edge of the nest to coast gracefully to the ground near the fighting youngsters. The wild Griffinlings barely looked up from their battle, and soon went back to hurling each other into thorny bushes. Torin followed Tehy out of the nest, climbing down without the benefit of wings, while Tehy beckoned him toward the caves.

"Let's go have morning repast," suggested Tehy, "and hear the latest news."

Returning to the Great Hall, they quickly made their way back to the eating room. Tehan and Kerithan were the only two seated there, though the Griffin food servers were busily restocking the eating room for the morning meal. The Queen and her mate glanced up as Tehy and Torin entered. Tehan nodded resignedly at Tehy's look of inquiry.

"Your Mother is preparing her Folk to fight," he said. "As much as I would prefer any alternative, I don't see that we have that much choice. We've received word from some of the Griffin Guard that monitors the less traveled areas of Thianely. There is much activity in the northern regions. Skelric the Ice Lord has been meeting with the Bolluxes, for what purpose we do not know. Some of the Earthen Folk have reported Bellorasps on the move. We all know those creatures do nothing without some form of payment. The Bolluxes must have made some sort of arrangement with the creatures to destroy their enemies. We cannot sit back and do nothing."

Tehy turned pale as he and Torin exchanged horrified glances. "Liliar!" they both said at once.

"Tehy, you've got to bring her here immediately," Torin insisted. "If her Folk have got hold of a Bellorasp, even she won't be safe. The distortion one of those creatures makes will render her voice powerless."

Tehy nodded worriedly. "Mother, Father, Liliar is my mate, and I ask that she be welcomed here, immediately, as Torin says."

Kerithan snorted. "Welcome a Bollux! But wait, would she help us find a way into Bollux country, perhaps sing us there? I do not ask her to harm any of her kindred..."

Tehan slapped his palms on the table, turning to Kerithan angrily. "You mean ask her to make it possible for us to harm them? Make her welcome contingent upon her helping us? You would ask her to betray her own people! We would be no more balanced than they themselves if we stoop to their methods. What of your son's mate! You know the tie he feels, or do you forget ours so readily?"

Kerithan threw up her hands. "Very well, Tehan, we'll find another way to stop them." She glared at Tehy for a moment.

"This Bollux may be a Guardian as you say, but she is also a Bollux. No Bollux has ever been welcome in Griffin Country. You are certain she is your mate?"

Tehy nodded. "Yes," he said firmly.

Kerithan frowned. She wrinkled her nose in distaste and sniffed. "Does she look like a Bollux? I do not know how I am to explain this to Griffinkind if she looks and smells like a Bollux."

Before Tehy could voice his anger, Tehan reached over and clasped Kerithan's hand in his. "If what Tehy says is true, there is not time to debate the matter with your Folk. You are the Griffin Queen. You must welcome her yourself."

Kerithan scowled fiercely, but dropped her eyes. "So be it. I will welcome this Bollux to our Country, but do not ever let me regret this decision."

"There's one more thing," Tehy said, as Kerithan looked up again, daring him to speak. "Liliar brings with her a younger brother, Haldane. She will not leave without him. I said she could bring him as well."

At that moment Torin realized why Kerithan was truly Queen of the Griffins. The roar she let out could have felled half the trees in the Threshold.

"Actually she took that pretty well," Tehy said, as they sat finishing their meal. Tehan had hurried out after an enraged Kerithan, grinning unabashedly back at the two of them as he left. "Father loves it when he gets to boss her around. She'll get over it. It's the centuries of tradition she has to break that truly bothers her. At least she wasn't terribly angry."

Torin laughed. "I'm afraid to ask what happens when she is."

"Fire," replied Tehy shortly, around a mouthful of fruit. "It comes out her nose and mouth, igniting everything within a few feet. I soon learned to tell her bad news from a distance. The first time I learned how to use my wings was to avoid Mother's flaming temper."

Torin shook his head wonderingly. He remembered hearing stories from Tehy during their mentoring journeys, but it was different when they were actually sitting in a cave in Griffin Country facing the explosive rage of the Griffin Queen. He wished Rebecca were there with him. He longed to hold her again.

As Torin and Tehy got up to clear their plates, Kerithan stalked back into the room, closely followed by Tehan. "Tehy," she addressed her son abruptly, "this dew that enabled you to breathe the air in Bollux Country, did you say you received it from Meridwen of the Trees?"

"Actually, it was a gift to Torin, but yes, she provided the dew."

Kerithan nodded, her earlier anger already forgotten. "Do you think, Tehan, that you and Vinian could take a wing of warriors and fly to the Threshold of the Trees? If Meridwen would give us several vats of dew I think we could mount a reasonable attack on the Bolluxes. We would not need to bother your mate at all, Tehy."

Tehy smiled. It hadn't taken Kerithan long to find a way around the obstacle of Liliar's birth. He watched as his father agreed to fly to the Threshold, and a thought struck him. He looked to Torin to see that his friend was obviously thinking the same thing.

"Mother, we must fly to the Well of Pools to pick up Rebecca, and Leva of the Tree and Earthen Folk. Father, have you heard from them?"

"Yes, Leva will be arriving with Mehani of the Air Folk. She should be here later today, but I received word from others who have flown back from the Well of Springs that Rebecca is no longer there. Or at least, none have seen her after the first moments of her arrival there.

Leva has been especially concerned that she could not discover Rebecca's whereabouts. It's as if she vanished. I checked with the guides of wind and air currents, but she has not manifested in any space within their knowledge. Do not be alarmed, Torin, she has many abilities and much to recall. I would not be surprised if she had a very unique experience at the Well of Springs. There is much about Rebecca we cannot know, even if she is your mate..."

They were interrupted by a roar so loud Tehy had to look twice to make sure that it wasn't coming from his mother. They all looked at each other in a moment of stunned surprise and rushed out to the nesting grounds. There, ringed by a circle of furious Griffin Warriors, Griffin Folk, and many Griffinlings, were Liliar and a small Bollux defiantly waving his fists as Liliar tried to restrain him.

Kerithan strode forward just in time to stop one of the Griffin warriors from impaling the little Bollux on his blade while Liliar repelled him by humming a force field.

"Halt immediately," Kerithan bellowed, striking the lead warrior roughly on the arm. He dropped his weapon, but the other warriors kept theirs ready. "Down all," she insisted, and the warriors dropped their weapons instantly, though they looked at her in disbelief.

"It's a Bollux," the lead warrior insisted angrily, as if his queen were an idiot. The others banged their palms across their chests in agreement. "It needs to be killed, before it brings the stench of the bogs to Griffin Country."

"That Bollux and his sister," the queen said evenly, her sharp teeth bared, "have been invited. They are my guests."

The warriors went silent in shock.

"Thank you, Mother," Tehy said, pushing his way past the stunned guards to take Liliar's hand. "This is my mate, Liliar," Tehy proclaimed to all the Folk firmly. "This is her brother, Haldane. They are welcome here."

The small Bollux, who resembled nothing more than a hairy tumbleweed, shook his head in astonishment. "Liliar," he said loudly into the silence that greeted Tehy's announcement, "did you hear that? The fool has welcomed a Bollux. Doesn't he know any better than that? What sort of dim-brained halfling have you got for a mate?"

Tehy winced and ignoring the small Bollux, turned to Liliar. "I'm sorry about the Guard, Liliar. They are highly trained, with no love for most Bolluxes. But all will be well. I am heartily grateful to see you here safely." He placed one arm protectively about her shoulders, and glanced down at Haldane. "Come meet my father, Tehan, and then I'll show you both to the guest caves."

"One moment," Kerithan said in a particularly piercing tone. She stepped up to Liliar and reached out her hand. "I am Kerithan, Queen of the Griffin Folk." Sharp turquoise eyes stared into hazel. "I welcome you here as my son's mate, and as a Guardian and singstress."

She took Liliar's hand, placed the palm against her forehead for a moment, and bowed her head slightly. Liliar smiled politely, but did not look away, maintaining a direct gaze. Kerithan nodded as if satisfied with what she saw. She turned to the small Bollux who still held onto Liliar's other hand more out of excitement than any real fear.

The Queen bent down from her imposing height and bared her sharp teeth at the little creature. Haldane stared back, curious to see if she would try to eat him as his brothers had always threatened.

"You're not as ugly as I thought," he said finally, ignoring the gasp of outrage from the surrounding Griffin Folk. "Are you going to eat me?"

"You're too dirty," Kerithan snarled, trying hard to maintain a scowl. "I don't eat guests most of the time. You are welcome here as long as you behave yourself."

"I've never been welcomed before," Haldane said solemnly. "And I always behave myself, like a Bollux. I suppose you can't be too stupid or you'd never be Queen, but I do think it's a bad idea, welcoming me, I mean."

"I'll devour you, Bollux, if you disobey me," Kerithan promised. "Or I will give you to my warriors to tear into little bits and throw what's left of you into a fire pit. My first order is for you to be cleansed of that filth you wear. Deril and Bolaren, take this Bollux, give him a bath, and do something about his hair."

As two gnarled old Griffins came to take him away, Haldane turned to Liliar in horror, but she merely shook her head. "You wanted to accompany me," she said, "and the Queen commands this."

Haldane shook his head angrily. "I'll go. If I die from the clear water, it will be your fault. If you hadn't made my father so angry by stealing the egg, he wouldn't have tried to rip my head off for blowing up the dining hall and ruining his meal. How was I supposed to know your mate killed Jierdan and the bog sprites revolted and my father was already in a mood again? I'd just got back from being banished. If he wasn't so mad at you I wouldn't have had to get away. I wouldn't be in this unbolluxed place where they make you get clean!"

Haldane let himself be led away with only one retaliatory kick at a nearby Griffin, who promptly cuffed him on the head. Tehy reached for Liliar, and heedless of the watching Griffins, kissed her soundly. He led her over to Tehan while Kerithan soothed her still aggravated Griffin Folk. Tehan reached out to clasp Liliar on the shoulder reassuringly.

"We thank you for your assistance in returning the Griffin Egg," he said, as they walked to the nearby caves. "It took great courage to confront your Folk the way you did. I am pleased to welcome you for my son's sake as well. Now come and share refreshment with us. Kerithan may be occupied for some time."

Once inside the eating room, Tehan seated Liliar at a long table piled with food and drink. He handed her a plate heaped with food and sat down opposite her, with Tehy to her right. Torin, who had accompanied them as well, sat down on her left. He watched her eat for a few moments, and then said hesitantly, "Liliar, were you trying to tel to me earlier? I could hear you speaking, even though I could not hear Rebecca. Now that you are seated so close, there is a strange hum coming from your mind, like a familiar song without words."

Liliar turned to look at him in surprise. "I do not know what is happening, but there is some sort of resonance between us that I do not understand. Of course, I have been in contact with Rebecca, so perhaps you are feeling me through my connection with her."

Torin leaned forward eagerly, as Tehan and Tehy stared at her in surprise. "How did Rebecca wind up with you?" Torin asked. "How on Thianely did she arrive there safely? Where is she now?"

Liliar laughed. "I will tell you all that has happened since you left me. Rebecca is safe, and will rejoin you soon. But first I must return this crystal to you."

She pulled Meridwen's crystal from about her neck and handed it to Torin. "I think Rebecca will be able to follow this crystal here, which may make her journey easier. It was difficult enough to pull Haldane along with me even with the crystal's help. In the last nightfall there are more rips in the fabric of our reality that my songs cannot mend. Never have I found it so difficult to singtravel, though I must admit this is the farthest I've ever been from Bollux Country. My brother Mosten mentioned the Bellorasps as a threat as well. There are strange movements in the northern regions that I could feel as we traveled to you."

Tehan frowned in concern at this. "We too, have been hearing about activity in the northern region, Liliar. Skelric, the Ice Lord, has been seen meeting with several of your clan, and the Bellorasps have also been observed climbing up from the depths of their under holdings. I do not ask you to betray your people, Liliar, but we are in the night about what Skelric plans. He has never before deigned to speak with any Folk of Thianely and now he has made some sort of alliance with your kin. It does not bode well for any of us. However, any harm to Thianely is also destructive for your clan. What could be their motive for such devastation?"

Liliar shook her head. "I know that they have become increasingly chaotic. Before this recent separation they only acted to maintain their own interests. They were incapable of honoring any kind of alliance, even among themselves. We all live in separate quarters for this very reason. My brother Jierdan, I imagine Tehy has told you, went completely out of pattern, provoking his own death. It is as if they have all become the extreme of their natures, which were already quite extreme to begin with. It was becoming increasingly obvious that I would not be able to protect myself with the possibilities of Bellorasps in the area. I thank you for your welcome here. Now let me tell you of Rebecca."

Liliar proceeded to fill them in on Rebecca's arrival from The Well of Springs and her practice in singing creation. Torin nodded at Liliar's description of Rebecca's inability to maintain herself in solid form until she'd had more practice.

"That explains the intermittent patterns of energy that I perceived from her," Torin said. "Although she has felt much stronger recently, more cohesive, clearer, I still cannot grasp her thoughts."

"I'm not sure exactly what she does and where she is now," Liliar admitted, "but I think it may have something to do with the crystal wisdom that she carries. She must maintain a less corporeal form to access such information. She will come join us as soon as she is able. Now I must tell you of that which concerns you most directly. I heard it from my Brother of Threats, Mosten. He spoke of your parentage, Torin, as if he was certain. He said that you were the Fire Lord's son."

Torin merely stared at her, while Tehan whistled in surprise. Tehy noted his friend's shock. "It makes such sense," he said calmly. "You were found in an ash pit, and there's your ability to remain unharmed, your gift in traveling between worlds, even your fiery temper. Perhaps they're all gifts from the Fire Lord himself."

Tehan stroked his chin slowly. "Torin, such knowledge of your origins would not be given to you by the Great Tree. It must come from the Lords and Ladies of the Elements themselves. If the Lord of Fire is your father, you would inherit your gifts through him. You know the Lords and Ladies came from other universes to help the creators seed our planets. Latent abilities may manifest in times of dire need. What better time than now? Though I wonder how a Bollux came to know of it."

Liliar nodded. "Perhaps Mosten had it from the Ice Lord, Skelric. Mosten went to the northern regions quite a while ago. He told our father that he was going to practice earth rendings in frozen ground and chat up the local ice maidens. Something is going on there beyond a few earth movements. Skelric himself is on the move."

Torin paled, a queasy feeling in his stomach. Suddenly, he felt as if he was becoming someone other than himself, as if the words "Fire Lord's son" had somehow altered him. Where did Imanayon fit into such a picture? He felt such a kinship with Rebecca; he wished he could be with her in that moment. This is what it was like to be thrust into sudden awareness, rather than grow gradually into knowing as he had always been taught.

Liliar reached out a hand to comfort him. "I did not mean to shock you with such news," she said kindly. "I know how it feels to find out that you are other than you thought, but it is important to understand your abilities. I'm not sure exactly how Mosten learned of this, other than he seemed to think it a danger to him."

Tehan pushed back his chair and stood up. "There is much for you to tell Kerithan. She may know more of the Fire Lord, Torin. Much as I wish to hear what Rebecca may tell us, I did promise to lead a wing of warriors to Meridwen's Folk to request some of that dew you mentioned. Liliar, again, you are welcome among us. Tehy, Torin, Leva will be arriving shortly. Kerithan will wish to greet her as well. I will return as quickly as I may."

They bade Tehan farewell. Tehy and Liliar began to stare at each other longingly, so Torin excused himself. He still felt somewhat disoriented, as if the purple earth beneath his feet was shaking slightly. He went back out to the nesting grounds to take a walk, and saw the Griffin Folk finally dispersing for morning repast. Most still looked disgruntled at Kerithan's decision to allow the Bolluxes to remain. For a moment Kerithan stood alone in the nesting grounds, her tail whipping back and forth behind her in frustration. She turned as Torin approached.

"It is not a simple matter, throwing off centuries of enmity even to welcome my son's mate," she commented. "They will obey me, because I am Queen. How do you fare, with an otherworlder for your mate?"

Torin smiled. "I would not have another, though the waiting is difficult."

Kerithan eyed him curiously. "You are my son's friend. Has he told you of Tehan and myself? It too is a strange pairing. Tehy has had much to learn, for our ways are so different from the Air Folk's. He is both Griffin and Air, but I think the stronger for it. So too will you be, with such a mate."

Torin shrugged. "Liliar tells me that I am perhaps the son of the Fire Lord. Tehan told me that you may know of him. I learned nothing of my parents from the Great Tree."

Kerithan stared at him penetratingly, then reached out a hand to feel his forehead. "Open to me," she commanded. Torin found himself simply opening his mind to her gaze. Her palm felt cool and alive on his forehead. Suddenly he could see an enormous eye, like that of a bird of prey. He fell into its pupil and the darkness swallowed him completely. The next thing he knew, he was sitting on the purple ground with Kerithan beside him, roaring with laughter.

Torin looked at her questioningly, but it was some minutes before she stopped laughing and wiped red tears from the corners of her eyes.

"It is no surprise that you have known nothing of your origins," she finally said, remnants of amusement still in her voice. "I have some ability to internally scry Folk. But you have a built-in shield that is beyond a conscious mind defense. The barrier is composed of humor, thus resulting in paroxysms of laughter for whoever tries to pass beyond it. I count this a rare gift to receive, Torin of the Fire Folk. Whoever sired you is beyond my power to scry, but I do appreciate your parents' sense of humor. Obviously, when it is time for you to know more of yourself, you will."

"I thank you," Torin said simply. He got to his feet, stepping back as Kerithan stood up, fully extending her wings.

"I will leave you now," Kerithan said. "I fly to calm my mind and plan my battles."

She slowly flapped her wings, creating quite a wind. Within moments she was aloft, with her guard of winged warriors appearing in mid sky around her. Torin watched for a moment, admiring the easy grace with which they flew.

Since the Griffin Folk were in cave eating, Torin had the nesting grounds to himself. He sat on a small clump of grass, pulled a leaf pad from his backsack and began to draw Griffin Country. He thought of his Grandfather and tried to reach him in his mind, but all he received was a blurry picture of Imanayon mounted on what looked like a furpaka, traveling in some densely forested terrain. He sighed, realizing that for the first time he felt cut off from his Folk and friends, not to respect their privacy, but simply because he could not break through the barriers of mind disruptions. He felt the separation from Rebecca as a physical ache in his chest and when he looked down he could see the glow of his heart spiral signifying mourning.

He looked up as two small specks in the sky came closer. He recognized two of the Air Folk as they landed close by. He stood as Leva unclasped her hands from around the neck of woman named Mehani. Mehani's mate Brillim nodded to Torin and immediately the two Air Folk set out for the eating caves. Leva greeted Torin enthusiastically, hugging him fiercely.

"How are you?" Torin asked, noting Leva's healthy green skin tone. "You look like you've been to visit your home tree."

"I feel as if I have, but it's just the Well of Springs," Leva said. "It has a way of clarifying things, both within and without."

She looked at the faint glow of his chest visible through his tunic. "I know Rebecca's fine, Torin," Leva said. "Although she wasn't at the Well of Springs, it doesn't mean she's lost."

"I know; I can tel that she is well. But I want her with me. Also, much has been happening. I feel like I've been turned upside down and my mind's been stretched."

The two sat down side by side while Torin explained recent events to Leva, who had some information to impart as well.

"This all makes sense," she said excitedly. "At the Well of Pools I went inside the ground of Thianely, like Imelina taught me, but even further. The very center of Thianely is shifting, which is having an extreme effect on energy fields. The disruptions are coming from within Thianely herself. I also know more about gateways than I thought. I think with all the Folk's help, particularly with Liliar and Rebecca singing, we can repair the Time Gate. It actually has a mechanism that exists in another dimension, but it is accessible from here. I know how to fix it. Did you know I used to help engineer Time itself?"

Torin idly picked up Leva's hand and examined her palm distractedly. He shook his head. "It seems like we're all discovering more abilities than we imagined. Here I thought I knew myself."

"If you think about it," Leva said, reclaiming her hand and wrapping her arms round her knees, "we're all odd, aren't we? I mean Tehy is half Griffin and half Air, Liliar is half Bollux and who knows what, I'm half Earth and half Tree and you're turning out to be a direct relative of the Fire Lord. Rebecca, she's from another world. It must be important or we wouldn't all be together this way. I suppose the Great Tree couldn't tell us everything at once or we'd explode from learning too fast."

"Don't forget Haldane," Torin chuckled, "even though he's all Bollux, from what Liliar tells me, her brother is a master at destruction. He may come in handy at some point, if he doesn't completely dissolve in clear water first."

It was Leva's first visit to Griffin Country, and since Tehy and Liliar were completely engrossed in each other, Torin decided to show Leva around. He gave her a tour of the nesting grounds and the caves. The two spent the remainder of the day wandering about observing the Griffin Folk making ready for war.

It was strange to Leva, whose Tree Folk spent as much time as possible nurturing growth, that a whole people could be prepared to protect Thianely by violent means. She was especially surprised at the bloodthirstiness of the Griffin children, as her own brothers and sisters were considerably gentler in their play.

Tehy and Liliar finally surfaced for evening repast, accompanied by a very surly Haldane, who looked presentable in some borrowed finery from the Griffin Folk. Actually, most of the Griffin Folk wore as few garments as possible, and Haldane was thrilled to be wearing only a waistcloth, even if it was of the finest woven plants. He had a shock of golden hair under the years of accumulated dirt, and was almost handsome in the right sort of light. His temper, however, was less than attractive. Kerithan finally banished him to a private cave to eat by himself after he continued to interrupt the meal by throwing food.

Liliar unlocked her gaze from Tehy long enough to greet Leva. They all listened to Leva describe her experiences at the Well of Pools, her newfound abilities, and the separation originating within the depths of Thianely. Kerithan delineated her plan to drop Meridwen's dew over Bollux Country. The Griffin Queen suggested that Leva lead a group to the Earthen Folk to seek Imelina's assistance in repairing the Time Gate.

"The Earthen Folk have the most experience with the Gate since it's located near their village," she said. "Although they've lost connection with the ground shifts, they have expertise in such matters. I will be able to spare a few Griffin Folk, if necessary, though most will be stationed on guard duty all over Thianely." She turned to Liliar. "Do you think you will be able to sing yourself and your companions to the Earthen Realms even with the disintegration in time and space?"

Liliar thought for a moment. "I could not guarantee that we would all arrive safely. The separation is becoming more extreme every nightfall. I have enough awareness to anticipate rifts when I singtravel myself, or even send an object. Days ago singing Torin and Tehy here was not a problem, yet I had some difficulty singing Haldane. I think it would be safer to travel overland, or at least have Tehy or the Air Folk fly us there by more conventional means."

"Very well," Kerithan agreed.

They finished their meal in silence, and soon bade each other good night. Torin escorted Leva to the nesting ground to find a place to rest. Long after Leva had curled up to sleep in a nearby nest, Torin sat up gazing at the stars, pondering the nature of his parentage. What did it mean to be the Fire Lord's son? Who was his mother?

He thought how ironic it was that all of his life he had spent letting go of the need to know his parents, and now he was confronted with the importance of discovering them. What were his abilities? He recalled explaining them to Rebecca, but now he didn't fully know. It was unsettling. He calmed himself with a ritual that he'd learned as a child. He closed his eyes, focused on the spiral in his chest, and pictured himself following the spiral to its center and back out again. He finally fell asleep, smiling at the image of Rebecca he'd found in his heart.

## Chapter 16

Rebecca sat in stillness, watching her thoughts float in the vastness of space without any physical movement to distract her. She felt, when she checked on the level of her senses, that this was the most restful state she'd ever experienced. There was a quiet joy in it, though her feelings arose and dissipated as quickly as her thoughts. She brought herself back to the level of thoughts sweeping across her mind, back into her body, feeling her legs and arms, feet and hands returning to her as hesitantly as estranged relations. She felt a tingling in her limbs, a sudden sense of purpose. She looked down and found herself standing in a dense grassy area atop a hill. It was bright sunlight and although she didn't recognize the area, she felt at home there, completely content.

As she stood quietly, blinking her eyes to accustom them to the brightness, her vision began to shift. It was as if a series of filters were flipping through her mind, resulting in different levels of perception. First the hillside became interconnecting lines of radiant gold energy; then they coalesced into a mass of swirling colors. In moments, Rebecca's vision had telescoped out into space in order to observe Thianely and its neighboring planets, Torildian and Hevald, rotate around the pink sun. The images shimmered, and Thianely turned into a ball of golden light, an oscillation of energy lines, and finally a symphony of sound. The magnification of her vision increased until she could pinpoint any spot on Thianely and see it so distinctly it was as if she were there. When her perception changed again, she saw rifts in space, their dark jagged forms sundering the golden white energy lines.

She observed the internal structure of the planet, with its tectonic plates moving in synchronicity with the lines of energy. She was amazed to note that in the exact center of its landmass, the area that Torin had called Belathgarin, a huge structure lay buried deep within the planet. It looked like a giant, many-faceted crystal that had been compressed too tightly and required assistance in expanding to its full capacity. Part of the earth shifts across the surface of the planet seemed to be resulting from the efforts of the structure to free itself.

Rebecca moved her awareness deeper into the structure. She asked for entry with her mind, but felt some sort of obstacle in the way. All she received was an image of herself floating above the ground. She imagined entering the structure and suddenly, she felt a prickling of her skin, an enormous jolt of energy, and she was hurtling through space at an alarming rate. She landed with a jarring thump, opening her eyes to find herself sitting in a large field under the dim starshine of late night. There was the shadow of a tall mountain range nearby. She had landed in some thistle-like grass that pricked her through her clothing.

She quickly stood up and looked about trying to figure out where she was. The starshine was only bright enough to get a general impression of the landscape, but nothing looked in the least bit familiar. The mountain range extended for as far as she could see in all directions, as if she were in a valley. She could make out the shapes of some structures a short distance away. Rebecca paused, trying to navigate by feel, and stopped in astonishment. She could feel Torin very strongly. She began to walk, following the pull of his energy as if it were a visible path in the shadows.

Torin awoke to what he thought was a dream, the sound of Rebecca's voice in his ear, the feel of her hand on his shoulder. For a moment he forgot to contain himself, and Rebecca found herself pulled close to what felt like a Torin-shaped furnace. His lips were on hers, his arms were holding her firmly as his chest began to vibrate and turn bright orange red. Energy began to shoot through them like a vibrant spring. Rebecca felt it as a wave through her entire body and flushed deeply, unprepared for the swirl of emotion, the sheer passion that swept through them both. For a moment she was overwhelmed, unable to think as Torin kissed her more and more deeply. He shook himself, pushed her from him firmly, and sat up, taking a series of slow deep breaths to regain some sort of control.

He reached over to her, running one hand over her face gently, and grinned. "I am very pleased to see you, as you may have noticed. I was not expecting you and lost my containment for a moment. I hope you weren't frightened."

Rebecca was glad the starshine was not bright enough to reveal her embarrassment. She didn't know what to say. She was still shaking slightly from the energy moving through her body. Now she knew what Liliar had meant about mating on Thianely. She sat up, hugging her knees to her chest and tried to find something to say.

"I'm not scared," she said finally. "I'm glad to see you too. I have a lot to tell you. But I was feeling so purposeful and mature and confident. Now I feel really young. I guess we'd better talk about sex."

Torin looked at her in surprise. "You are not comfortable with being female in this lifetime?" he asked.

Rebecca blushed. "Not that kind of sex. I mean what you call mating. It's kind of intense."

Torin reached over and put his arm around Rebecca, drawing her closer to him in the nest. "I know you are not ready for physically mating yet, Rebecca. I lost my containment for a moment. Now you can be close to me and nothing will happen, or at least nothing like what we just experienced. I must admit I do not regret feeling our energy moving together. I've missed you. Now tell me, how did you find your way to Griffin Country?"

They spent the next few hours filling each other in on what had transpired. Rebecca looked forward to seeing the rest of her friends again and meeting the Griffin Queen. She could barely make out the outlines of the other nests, but Torin promised to show her around Griffin Country the next day. Rebecca wondered why she hadn't met any of the Griffin Guard as she traveled through the nesting grounds, so Torin explained that they had Air Folk flying sentry on the mountains.

"They all recognize you," he assured her, "and though I'm sure Kerithan knows of your arrival, she would not interfere between mates who have not seen each other for many days."

"Oh," Rebecca said shortly, "about this mating thing, Torin. Liliar said you would be feeling kind of like how you're obviously feeling. I don't really know how it works, I mean..."

Torin laughed out loud. "Yes you do. It's the same as on your Earth, Rebecca. The difference is the flowing of soul energy between mates. When I'm in the presence of my mate without any need for containment, my heart spiral glows first, then all of our energy centers line up and we move through each other. I get very hot as I move into you, and you feel like warm water flowing into me. I'm not sure what additional abilities will be revealed once we mate fully, for there are some gifts that only may be opened in the presence of another. One's mate is an important catalyst to move more deeply into full awareness. That time is not yet. I still do not even know what it means to be the Fire Lord's son, or who my mother may be."

"I'm not that tired, Torin," Rebecca said, laying down next to him and looking up at the stars. "Will you tell me about the Fire Lord, what you know of him?"

Torin nodded, reclining as well, and pulled Rebecca closer to lie with her head on his chest. She listened to the steady beat of his heart as he spoke about the arrival of the Elemental Lords and Ladies to Thianely.

"Since the beginning times, the creatures of air, including the devas and sprites and faeries, were all tied to the Lord of Air, Dariel. From what I've been told, he's one of the beings your people call angels, or perhaps an archangel. Though I've never seen him, he is said to be very tall, with white flowing wings and a very commanding presence. He resides in the skies above Hevald, the planet of air, watching over his home planet. The Lords and Ladies only manifest in times of great purpose. Because of all of the rendings on Thianely, there are those who say the Lords and Ladies will soon appear again.

The Fire elementals, Fire Folk, and other creatures of fire are tied to the Fire Lord. He has been seen even more rarely than the Lord of Air, and the name by which we call him is Torienmar. He is called upon in times of great need only, for he spends much of his time on Torildian, the planet of fire and the place he calls home. It is too hot for those of Thianelian flesh as it is much closer to our sun.

The Lady of Water, your own elemental tie, is Meruane. She wears garments of the sea, rare vines and flowers, often appearing to the merfolk to give them counsel. Naiads and Water Folk pay homage to her as well. You probably know more of her than I from the times you were born of the merfolk.

The Lady of Earth, Emera, lives deep within the center of Thianely. As strange as it sounds, none have seen her, for she lives in a crystal palace and will only show herself on the day that Thianely needs her most, or so it is said."

Rebecca sat up excitedly, accidentally jabbing Torin with her elbow. "I saw it, the crystal in Thianely's center. Torin, she must have thrown me here! Remember I told you I arrived here without consciously willing it? I tried to enter the crystal with my energy and got tossed here immediately!"

Torin rubbed his chest where Rebecca had bashed him with her enthusiasm. "That confirms that it's close to the time of the prophecy coming to pass. I wonder if Emera will be emerging soon, and what that will portend exactly. One thing you have to say about the prophecy, it's not very specific."

Rebecca leaned over and kissed him in apology for her elbow. "Sorry about that. I thought you were impervious to physical harm."

"We are all somewhat more vulnerable with our mates," he explained.

"What about the other Lord, the Ice Lord?"

Torin rubbed a hand tiredly over his face. "Skelric, the Ice Lord, is the most often encountered of all of the Elemental Lords and Ladies. He stays primarily in the northern regions, turning everything in sight to ice, fighting the seasons and Yarwen, generally creating havoc. Before now, even the Bolluxes would have little to do with him. Almost every traveler to the northern regions has had some sort of skirmish with the Ice Lord. His mate is the Queen of the Drenics, and she is said to have a very harsh way of dealing with unwanted guests. Only Fire Folk and the dwarves of the northern caves manage to emerge unscathed from the northern region.

I have often wondered why of all the Lords and Ladies, Skelric spends the most time on Thianely. I suppose it must have to do with elemental balance. In any case, those are the Lords and Ladies of Thianely. Now, my heartling, I am becoming weary. Let's sleep."

The two lay quietly for a time, holding each other closely and listening to the guttural snores coming from neighboring nests. Rebecca sighed in contentment, happy to be near Torin and at the Griffin stronghold at last.

## Chapter 17

"Time to wake up, Rebecca," Torin said into her ear the following morning. He kissed her nose playfully. "Tehan has returned with great vats of dew from Meridwen, Leva, Liliar, and Tehy are all in the eating caves, and I'm hungry."

Rebecca sat up and stretched, surprisingly well rested on the bed of moss and grass. Torin moved over to the edge of the nest, looking out over the nesting grounds as flanks of Griffins mobilized for flight.

"Come here," he said, pointing to the marvelous sight of dozens of Griffin warriors preparing to leave. All of those Griffins with wings and at least twice as many of the Air Folk were lining up, hoisting heavy sacks of Meridwen's dew. Torin assisted Rebecca in climbing down from the nest, where Tehan immediately spotted them.

Tehan trotted over, embracing Rebecca and welcoming her to the Griffin compound. "Perfect timing," he said. "We're getting ready to neutralize the Bollux bogs. Kerithan lost no time in ordering her warriors. Torin, I spoke with Imanayon at the Threshold. He left the Fire Folk in order to answer Meridwen's call for healing assistance for her Tree Folk. He gives you greeting and wants you to know that all is well at home."

He left them to find Kerithan and make last minute decisions about organizing the deployment of the dew. Torin led Rebecca to the Great Cave, where they joined Tehy, Liliar, and Leva for a leisurely breakfast of hot roasted grain meal and fruit. After greeting her friends, Rebecca spent most of the time between mouthfuls updating everyone on her adventures.

"Where's your younger brother, Haldane?" Rebecca finally asked Liliar. "I've heard so much about him, but I don't see him."

Liliar smiled, while Tehy groaned slightly. "We had to send him outside to the nesting grounds," she explained. "He seemed to think he had some say in our mating since our offspring will be his nieces and nephews. It didn't matter how many times we told him we have no intentions of reproducing yet."

"Or how many times I told him we needed privacy," Tehy grumbled. "So I had Mother's guard take him outside and keep him nested. I'm surprised we haven't heard from him. He's not exactly quiet."

"I was a little concerned that he would be upset when he found out about the dew," Liliar admitted. "But he seemed to think the idea very amusing. He thinks it will serve our relatives well to be drenched in cleansing, probably because he had to take a bath. Perhaps one of us should go and look for him."

"That won't be necessary," Kerithan said, as she approached their table. "I have him outside training with the other young Griffins. We'll make a warrior out of him yet; what he lacks in discipline he makes up for in ferocity."

She inclined her head to Rebecca, and said, "I am pleased at your timely arrival, Water Maid. You are most welcome here in Griffin Country. I have heard much of you from my son and his friends. Now I would like you to accompany me to my resting chambers where I would speak with you privately."

Rebecca bowed to the Griffin Queen with great respect. The Queen looked tired, as if she'd had little sleep, but her eyes were clear and her authority unquestionable. Rebecca excused herself from her companions, leaning over for Torin's kiss as she left. She followed the Griffin Queen to her quarters.

Inside Kerithan's cave was a beautiful nest trimmed with colorful, silky feathers and soft pillows of woven grass. The room was well lit by fire tapers and the glow of large rose crystals. Her nest took up much of the room, but there were several viny chairs grouped about a hearth, and Kerithan indicated that Rebecca should sit in one of them, while she made herself comfortable in another.

Kerithan sat silently for a moment, observing Rebecca with her intensely brilliant eyes. Rebecca looked calmly back, for some reason completely unintimidated by the Griffin Queen. Kerithan finally smiled, shaking her head ruefully.

"It is as they said," she commented. "You are the one of prophecy, Rebecca. Yet there is much in yourself still undiscovered. It will be a very compelling journey for you, this lifetime." She glanced down at her hands, the green and blue scales smooth as a snake's. Finally she looked up.

"I will ask you some questions that you will answer from a place deep inside yourself, a place of old wisdom and foreteling, perhaps answers that you did not know you have. I am asking your soul these questions. You will find, as you age, that your soul will be that which guides you more and more. Your personality will become merely a framework for the wisdom of your deepest self. Trust this process."

Rebecca nodded. The Griffin Queen had just very neatly explained the sense she had of being both extremely old and physically young simultaneously.

Kerithan continued, "Tell me, Rebecca, are the Lords and Ladies returning to Thianely?"

Rebecca found herself answering without a pause. "They will return, but elsewhere than Thianely. We must contact Hevald and Torildian and call upon the Lords of Fire and Air for assistance. The Earth Lady Emera will emerge from the innermost depths of Thianely only when Time is sung aemethra. Lady Meruane will flow as water, and Skelric's reign will melt like ice in patterns of light. The gift that was given so long ago will be returned to this purple earth and all will be changed within no-time."

Kerithan looked at her in surprise. "Aemethra? That is an ancient word for the weaving of the crystal bridal knot. Dwarves in the Northern caves weave crystals together at their formation so that they grow into intricate knots that symbolize the coming together of individuals within the Great Pattern; the marriage of the physical within spirit. Mates keep the crystal knot until the death of one of them, when the crystal is buried with the body. Tehan and I have one, and Liliar brought one with her that she sung herself, for her own mating with Tehy. But how could time be sung so?"

"The Gate of Time must first be repaired. Time must then be sung from all the planets at starpoint from Thianely, including Torildian, Hevald, Thianely itself, and my own Earth. There are those beings whose purpose has always been to sing creation, and these know the song of aemethra. We will enlist their aid. In the meantime, we must keep the Bellorasps from completely distorting the song of Thianely. Your people must keep the Bolluxes and Bellorasps in check while we repair the Gate and coordinate help all over Thianely and beyond. I will return to my planet, and assist from there."

Rebecca stopped in dismay, realizing what she'd said. For the first time, she understood that she didn't want to go back and leave Torin or Thianely or her friends. She couldn't even imagine how she would fit in on Earth, though she still longed to see her parents.

Kerithan reached over to clasp her hand reassuringly. "You will not be separated from your mate, Rebecca. Thianely is as much your world as is your birth planet. You must trust where your journey takes you, as you have so far. I will not question you further. Sometimes knowing too much of the future prevents one from being focused in the present.

For now, we of the Griffin Folk will marshal our forces to deal with the Bolluxes and Bellorasps. Tehan and I will enlist the aid of all the Folk on Thianely. Liliar must sing to Hevald and Torildian to call on the Lords of Air and Fire and their Folk. You must accompany Leva to the Earthen Folk and see about fixing this Gate of Time."

Rebecca stood up, slightly disoriented from the speed at which everything had been decided. She needed to talk to Torin. Before she could leave, Kerithan motioned her over to her nest.

"Would you like to see what it is that your mate and my son risked entering the Bollux Compound for?"

Rebecca looked down at the huge egg softly nestled in the Queen's beautiful nest. From its original gray-blue color it had changed to a bright magenta mottled with green. She reached over to touch its outer shell and found it smooth as leather with a slight give to it. It pulsed faintly with the heartbeat of the creature inside, and for a moment Rebecca felt its mind touch hers, a faint whisper like wings brushing sky.

She turned, surprised at the gentleness of the touch, as Kerithan gazed down in pride. "She will be a true Warrior Queen!" Kerithan said. "Strong and commanding and wise. The hope of Griffinkind's survival."

Rebecca decided that now was not the time to mention that the being inside the egg seemed more kind than commanding. "It's beautiful," she murmured instead. "I'm glad Liliar returned it safely."

Kerithan nodded in satisfaction. "She is a fine mate for my son. We owe her much. Now let us go and tell the others what must be done. I will bid my Folk farewell before they leave with the dew."

They returned to the eating caves, only to find that everyone had gone outside to watch the last of the preparations for flight. Rebecca soon caught up with Torin, who stood a little to one side as mates bade goodbye to mates, and parents hugged their children. The mood of the people was somewhat somber, for none had ever returned safely from Bollux lands before. Barnel, one of the chief warriors, led the large group of Griffin Warriors while Vinian, one of Tehan's most trusted messengers, led the Air Folk.

Torin grasped Rebecca by the hand and pulled her inside the Great Cave as Kerithan began her formal send off.

"Come here a moment," Torin said, tugging Rebecca by the hand into a small cave off of the main passageway. "This is our room, now that we've been acknowledged as mates. No more nesting caves for us."

Rebecca looked about at the small room. The nest where they were to sleep was at one end. Several woven mats covered the floor in colorful array, while huge glowing crystals shed pink light on the surroundings. Torin's backsack was tossed on the floor, nearby her own backsack and a small pile of books. She smiled, thinking how nice it was to have their own room, and how short a time they'd probably spend there.

"Now," Torin said, after giving her a few moments to look around. "What did Kerithan want, and what's next?"

Rebecca sat down on the floor by the bed, since there were no chairs. Torin immediately sat down next to her, green eyes intently scanning her face, while she brought him up to date.

"While Liliar is singing to the other planets, you and I and Leva will go to the Earthen Folk?"

Rebecca nodded. "I think I need to be reminded of the nature of Earthen elements. Remember I told you that when I tried to enter that crystal structure in the center of the planet all I saw was an image of me floating? I don't think I'm grounded enough yet to be allowed entry. I had some trouble remanifesting myself after I met Wilowren. She recommended that instead of emotional states I use pure will to keep me in physical form, but then Liliar reminded me how to sing myself present so I sort of skipped the pure will part. It seemed so, I don't know, completely lacking in humility."

"How do you mean that?" Torin asked curiously.

Rebecca shrugged. "Well, it feels awfully arrogant to decide I'm here because I choose to be and that's it. No permission needed, no reason or higher purpose other than because I want to, with no particular usefulness to anyone."

Torin leaned over and kissed her temple. "How about if I kiss you because I feel like it without any great purpose behind it? Is that less of a kiss? Are you of less value if you're here because you simply wish to be, perhaps for pure enjoyment?"

"On my planet, if you're not doing anything useful or being successful at something, you're not particularly valued," Rebecca explained. "I guess it's hard to let go of even such a silly idea, because I'm so used to it. At the Well of Springs I did feel how responsible I am for my own perceptions, thoughts, feelings and so on. Being responsible for your own existence seems like an awful lot to swallow."

"It does sound difficult," Torin agreed, "unless you decide it can be a truly delightful experience. If it makes you feel any better, you're not responsible for anyone else's perceptions but your own. Think how freeing it is to know that everyone has free will to be or not."

"Hey, wait a minute, this is beginning to remind me of Shakespeare in ninth grade English. I always thought 'To be or not to be...' was a depressing soliloquy. There you have it, it was only my own perception again."

Torin stood up, pulling Rebecca to her feet. "Let's do something completely for the sheer joy of it, Rebecca, because we choose it. I could use a break too, before we have to plunge back into fixing Time Gates and dealing with long lost Fire Lords." He looked at her face, which had immediately flushed bright red.

"Did you know your face turns color whenever you think about mating?" Torin said mischievously.

Rebecca put a hand up to her face, blushing even harder.

"That's not what I meant, but I'm willing to change my mind," Torin teased. Rebecca shook her head, waiting for the flush to subside before she spoke.

"So you never blush at all?" she asked, changing the subject.

"Parts of me turn orange and red when I lose my containment," Torin said. "Remember?"

He laughed, as Rebecca turned red once more. "See, now wasn't that completely fun and without purpose? I was going to suggest we play a game of skifpen, but watching you turning colors was even more enjoyable."

Torin had begun to explain the ancient game of skifpen to Rebecca when Liliar stuck her head in the door. "Sorry to interrupt you both, but Kerithan and Tehan are trying to establish a time line. Tehy has offered to fly you and Leva to the Earthen Folk. There is another whole wing of Griffin and Air Folk who are going to attack the Bellorasps near the Bollux stronghold and try to force them back underground. Kerithan wants me to sing to the neighboring planets, and then meet you at the Earthen Folk's dwellings to help with the Gate. We're going to leave Haldane here with the Griffin warriorlings. She wants to know if you can be ready to leave at the sun's next rising."

Rebecca and Torin both nodded, as Liliar made her way into the room.

"Skifpen, is it?" she asked. They motioned for her to join them and within minutes Tehy had arrived, looking for his mate. Leva soon wandered in and the small cave became somewhat crowded. Rebecca found herself embroiled in a fast game of skifpen, a mind game in which teams of two to three people tried to telepathically send sounds and images to one another, while the other team tried to interfere. Torin explained that on Thianely, it was a children's game meant to teach the importance of mind shields and concise imagery.

The company of friends soon found that although Rebecca had the least amount of experience at the game, her images rapidly improved with practice, and when it came to sheer intentional volume, she was so loud her thoughts were unmistakable. The four others were finally forced to band together to blot out her inner voice. Liliar teased her that when it came to range, perhaps Rebecca should be singing to the other planets.

"I may be loud in my mind," Rebecca replied, "but I'm not sure my voice carries that far. Besides, I'm still not sure what you mean that my thoughts are mind piercing. It seems normal to me."

"We know," Tehy said, still mentally wincing. "It's just that your will is connected to your intention and your intention is connected to your thoughts. When you want something to happen it gets broadcast very widely and intensely. We experience that as loud, when it's really like an intentional tide sweeping over us."

"You have a really big will," Torin said. "Remember when you got angry at council, we could all feel it, even those of us who were far away? That's probably why you had that emotional training in the Great Tree."

Rebecca looked around at all of her friends. "I'm scared of it," she admitted. "That's why it seems so arrogant to will something and have it happen. Because I know it could, and it scares me to have that much influence on things. I'm sorry if I hurt your heads."

Liliar put an arm around her shoulders comfortingly. "It is meant for you to have such a large will, Rebecca," she said. "It is only that you need to learn to use it properly. If you're too afraid to learn, it will come out when you least expect it, like a willful child. Speaking of willful, here's Haldane."

Haldane, who'd managed to lose most of his waistcloth and a few tufts of hair during his Griffin skirmishes, poked his head in the room interestedly.

"You're loud," he said to Rebecca approvingly. "We had to stop playing battle because the Griffinlings got head pains. I like it. Can you teach me?"

"No!" Liliar and Tehy said simultaneously.

That night after evening repast, Kerithan asked Liliar to begin her marathon of singing. Liliar had estimated that the songs would take days to complete, and several more days to reach Hevald and Torildian. She would pause every few hours for breaks. Two of the Air Folk would see that she had food and rest when she needed it. Haldane wanted to help, and became very angry when Liliar told him he could help best by being quiet, not one of his innate abilities. She stood in the Great Cave, its resonance perfect to magnify her voice, and had opened her mouth to begin, when Haldane interrupted yet again.

"Haldane, I have to sing really far and loudly, to speak to others on distant planets. You really must be quiet now."

Haldane planted his feet and a mulish expression stole over his features, but he did close his mouth. Liliar stood tall and with arms lifted, began to sing. As they listened, even Haldane stood silently, for the song was a stillsong, of notes so resonant and clear that the fabric of creation paused, and the sound traveled through time.

Liliar seemed to grow and expand before their eyes. The quality of the song shifted and flowed until they could see the planets she called, Torildian of orange skies and fiery air, too hot for Thianelian lungs, and Hevald, an airy oasis whose atmosphere was thinner than Thianely's, but yet supported life. Liliar's calling was worded in fire and in air. The Torildian and Hevaldian Folk's histories were woven into the song so that it seemed all of a piece.

One by one the entire company of Griffinfolk and Air Folk made their way into the Great Cave, following the swells of sound that swayed and danced in the air around them. For hours the people stood listening, learning of the Folk who lived far from them, their ways of life, and even the separation that affected their own planets. Without stopping to think about what she did, Rebecca rose to stand beside Liliar, and she sang home.

The sound of the Earth filled the cave, mingling and somehow blending with the song of Torildian and Hevald. For some of the assembly, it was the first glimpse they had of cultures and a planet vastly different than theirs. They listened, mesmerized by the song of the Earth in her pain and longing. The beginning of the planet, through the first people, world wars and the desolation of the present, all poured from Rebecca's throat. The song shifted, as she called to all of the Guardians slumbering, forgotten on a planet that needed them without delay. The Folk of Thianely could feel them, the masses of heart-starved, weary Guardians who'd been waiting, waiting for the call to awaken on Earth.

Finally Rebecca's voice faded, and she went to stand beside Torin, who hugged her to his side. Liliar's song continued, rising and flowing through the room and out to worlds beyond.

Tehan tugged Kerithan from the Great Cave, down the hallway to her room. He pulled her gently into his arms, as the beauty of Liliar's voice swept on.

"It will go well, my Lady, our Folk are sensible fellows. They will return from the Bollux lands. Tehy will return safely from the Earthen Folk. His companions are both powerful and wise, and we have much to do here."

"I must confess I am grateful I did not know of his journey to the Bolluxes beforehand," Kerithan said, looking deeply into her mate's eyes. "I know he knew of the egg's loss, but I would not have approved."

"I know," Tehan said. "For such a fierce Queen, you are still his mother. But I foresaw success, of a sort. So I bade him go. His mate is a wonder, isn't she?"

Kerithan nodded. "You know as well as I that the Bellorasps are on the move, as well as the Bolluxes. The Earthen Folk are in much danger from earth shifts and I prefer to have my son closer to home. His mentoring journey was long enough. He lived half his years with you."

She sighed, holding him tightly for a moment. "There are some times when the leadership of the Griffin Folk, and the burden of enforcing spiritual law lies very heavy. I will not mourn my office when the Queen egg hatches."

"Will you come to me then?" asked Tehan quietly.

Kerithan smiled at him. "I will, if Thianely yet exists. And now I need my rest. Join me."

## Chapter 18

Rebecca awoke the next morning, sprawled half over Torin, who still lay sleeping. The lilting sound of Liliar's voice could be heard through the walls, and Rebecca wondered if she'd sung all night without respite. She smiled, imagining that neither Haldane nor Tehy would have put up with that. She looked over, and was admiring Torin's profile when he opened one eye sleepily and mumbled, "Gaze more quietly."

Rebecca sat up, scoffing at the idea of having her eyes be too loud. It seemed that Torin could tease her even half asleep. She got up, still full from evening repast the night before, and began to pack for the trip to the Earthen Folk's village. She changed her clothes, appreciating the shimmer of the comfortable silvery tunic Torin had brought her. She brushed her hair with the shell comb the merfolk had given her and turned round to see that Torin was awake.

"How long have you been up?" she asked, flushing slightly.

"I won't answer that so we can give your face a rest from that particular shade of red," he said, "but don't worry, I didn't see anything I didn't like."

After a brief tickle fight, in which Rebecca discovered that Torin was not the least bit ticklish, they met Tehy and Herien, one of the Air Folk, out in the Great Cave. Liliar was resting quietly on a chair, eating some fruit and drinking a lot of fluids to keep her voice supple. Haldane bounced up and down nearby, demanding to be flown to the Earthen Country.

Tehy had one large hand clasped on the little Bollux's shoulder, trying to keep him from bothering Liliar. Rebecca and Torin grabbed some fruit to snack on as Tehy and Herien, a tall slender youth, planned the journey. Leva soon arrived, carrying her backsack.

"There will be no need to worry about a space to stay," she assured them all. "My grandmother Imelina lives in a multiroom dwelling. She will be expecting us. I know the way very well. I went there to learn from my grandmother. My father took those of us who were old enough to travel far from the tree."

Torin pulled Leva somewhat abruptly over to the side of the cave. "Leva, before we leave, I want to tell you something I did not speak of before. You remember when I tried to prevent you from accompanying us?"

Leva nodded. "I did not understand you at all. You knew Imelina was my grandmother, and that Rebecca would eventually need to meet the Earthen Folk. You must have known I was a Guardian, even before I did."

"I knew from the moment we met. It is easy for me to recognize other Guardians, but sometimes they must learn to recognize themselves first. I wasn't sure if you were ready to assume the responsibility, Leva."

Leva stared at him. "It is not your right to determine that. Why would you try to prevent me from discovering all that I am?" she demanded. "That is not the way of a Guardian."

Torin reached out and held Leva by the arm. He slid his hand down to hers and tugged her toward him. He turned over her left palm until it lay face up.

"Remember when your palms were running with sap, after the Great Tree died? You let me fire cleanse them for you. Look at your destiny line, Leva. See how it intersects your line of life?"

Leva examined her palm closely and turned a slightly paler shade of green. "But it doesn't necessarily mean that following my purpose will result in an early death, does it?"

"One does have the ability to alter one's destiny," Torin replied. "Besides, that's your left hand, merely what may happen. If you look at your right hand you'll see that the lines do not quite intersect. I was trying to prevent you from reaching your full responsibility before you could handle it, but it looks as though the Well of Pools has given you the knowledge as well as the ability to carry out your purpose. I apologize for discouraging you from accompanying us. I truly have valued your companionship, as well as your help."

Leva nodded, still somewhat shocked. "How could I not have noticed this before?"

"Everything that happens changes us," Torin said gently. "Our palms reflect our choices. There is still time to decide if you wish to stay or go."

Leva shook her head. "I know I must be there. I remember how to fix the Gate, and from what Rebecca said, it has to be working before time can be sung aemethra, right? So, I go. You don't have to watch me all of the time either. I can take care of myself."

Tehy tapped Torin none too gently on the shoulder. "We need to leave soon, you two, if we're to get there quickly. Flying pairs is more difficult than with one passenger, you know, and it's a long journey."

Torin and Leva joined Rebecca in saying goodbye to Liliar, who promised them she'd be there to help as soon as she could. One of the Griffin Folk held a howling Haldane as they all trooped out to the nesting grounds to prepare to leave. Each of them carried a backsack filled with provisions and clothes. Torin and Rebecca grasped Tehy's shoulders as his wings spread fully, lifting them aloft. Leva held fast to Herien, and the two followed close behind Tehy. Rebecca and Torin looked down as the nesting grounds receded and Tehy's huge wings carried them safely over the nearby mountains.

The flight was very long, as the Earthen Folk lived at the southwestern tip of Thianely's landmass. They were forced to stop and rest several times. They flew directly over Fire Folk country and spent a night in Imanayon's house, though he was still at the Threshold of the Trees. Tehy and Herien rested, while Rebecca, Torin, and Leva lay out among the trees, soaking in the sunshine and peace of the ground. Leva felt renewed in the garden, and spent time with the Devas, speaking of healing plants and tree lore.

Inside the house, Rebecca found her old raincoat and rain boots waiting for her on a shelf in the living space. She looked at them fondly. It seemed strange to see something from Earth in Imanayon's house, but she decided to leave them there. She and Torin slept in his room, while Tehy and Herien took Imanayon's and Leva slept in the room Rebecca had once occupied. Leva had wanted to spend the night in the garden, but the Devas were watering and she would have been drenched.

They left early the next morning and Torin, who had never been so far west before, watched the scenery flash by with great appreciation. Rebecca was reminded of pictures of Arizona she'd once seen, arid and sandy, though the Thianelian ground was a deep purple. Herien seemed to take the changing landscape in stride, while Tehy was more focused on finding a place to land. He needed a great deal of food to compensate for the effort of flying pairs for so long a distance.

To Leva, flying over the flat plains and deserts was like coming home, and when they stopped for a break, she quickly gathered some mesot roots to quench their thirst.

"We could ask the sky for rain I suppose," Leva commented, "but these are as watery and much easier than asking the weather to change." As they all sampled the crisp roots, they had to agree. Torin dug up several to store in his pack, and they were on their way again.

Finally, as the pink light of the sun was beginning to fade, they reached what Leva called "The Place of the Earth Dwellers." They landed on a flat open area that looked like high desert to Torin, although Leva seemed to be able to see something he could not, for the moment they alighted, she left them, stepping into what looked like a small depression in the ground.

Leva raised her arms and chanted, "I call to my family, the Earthenkind; I am Leva of the Trees, Daughter of Lenton and Morlina, Granddaughter to Reabus and Imelina. Soil of the ground, sap of trees, flow through me. Earth of my people, open to me."

As her companions watched, Leva began to spin around. The ground beneath her rose up and up, so that in a few moments she was dancing on top of a large hill. Finally she stopped and slid down the hill on her bottom, landing on her feet directly in front of a small opening, which continued to grow as they waited. They stood in amazement, as similar hills began to rise up out of the ground around them, so that soon the flat desert was covered with earth-dome structures. In each an opening appeared, and from inside the homes poured out hundreds of Earthen Folk, all wearing thick robes of some root-like material.

They all made way for a woman who had come from the home upon which Leva had done her calling. Imelina, for it was she, embraced Leva fiercely and greeted Torin, Rebecca, Tehy, and Herien. She was a small woman, though like many of her folk, powerfully built, and her brown eyes gazed at them shrewdly from under her thatch of straw-colored hair. She motioned them to follow her back inside her dwelling. Torin turned to catch a glimpse of the other Earthen Folk, who seemed content to sit outside on the ground and chat with one another.

Imelina led them into a large, welcoming homemade of earth and roots and woven ferns. The only light came from a rose quartz crystal that glowed brightly, lending a pink glow inside the room. The quality of light was nearly as bright as daytime. Outside the day was growing chill and dark, though Rebecca noticed that Imelina's robe was thick enough to keep away the cold. Seeing Herien shiver, however, Imelina tossed him a garment of some fleecenest material and he pulled it over his head, finding it thoroughly comfortable. They sat on some packed earth chairs covered in soft vines, in front of a small tree table that grew in a circular branching configuration. Leva seemed to know the tree well, for she patted it gently and spoke to it for a few moments.

Imelina set some refreshments before them; root drop tea and desert rose cakes, and sat down next to Leva and Rebecca with Torin, Tehy, and Herien opposite them. She spoke of the earth changes and the disintegration of the Gate of Time.

"The ground of Thianely cannot always hear us anymore," she said sadly. "I know from Imanayon it is so with the other elements as well. A number of us were working on the Gate of Time, trying to keep the mechanism centered, but one of the Bolluxes came and set off a sound implosion, which severed our connection completely. Our homes usually are above ground, but we have been staying below, deep enough to avoid the Bolluxes and the time distortions that rippled across the desert after the implosion, but not so far down as to be completely vulnerable to core fault earth shifts.

The Time Gate, as you probably know, helps keep the seasons and elements in harmony, as well as making earlier lifetimes distinguishable from the present. There have been reports of many beings losing awareness of their present selves. Imagine the complete confusion of personalities and life purposes if the boundaries between lifetimes are not maintained! Several of the Water Folk have completely lost their minds, unable even to remember that they are Water Folk. I know you believe you can assist us in restoring the Gate. I truly hope you are correct, for it is dangerous to remain here much longer with things as they are.

Yesterday one of the children fell into a crack in time and space. No matter how we call, she cannot hear us, or at least we are unable to communicate with her wherever and whenever she has gone. Perhaps we can bring her back. I do not know. But now, what may I do to help you?"

"Grandmother," Leva said, "I am a Guardian of Thianely, and I helped build this Gate. I did not know of this until I went to The Well of Pools and remembered. But it is true; I do recall how to repair the Gate. I will need to speak with the Earthen engineers who have worked with it. Grandmother, we must bring the Gate back to working order, and we must sing aemethra as well. I can fix the Gate, but I do not know how to sing so."

Tehy said reassuringly, "Liliar can sing anything in creation. She may not know a lot about engineering, but she built a room with her voice and she can tel-sing as well as remove unwanted beings from the vicinity. She will be finished singing to the other planets soon, and I will bring her here. You know what the Bollux response will be to our fixing the Gate and halting unwanted Earth changes. They'll be furious."

"Yes," commented Torin, "especially when they find out what Kerithan and Tehan are doing to their swamp land. Your Earthen Folk may bear the brunt of the Bolluxes' anger. We also hear that the Bellorasps are on the move."

Imelina snorted in disgust. "We've heard of the creatures, crawling out of the ground like huge mouthy worms. There's a nest of them west of here. We think they helped that Bollux blow the Gate. Now," she said, staring at Rebecca curiously, "you're the one we've been waiting for. I imagine being you can be quite a trial at times. Don't you worry; there's a bit of the prophecy we've kept apart from the other one. I'll show it to you in the morning."

She stood up briskly, "I'll let you get some rest. You have your choice of rooms. I have mats to sleep on if you like and I'll be down below if you need anything."

She made her way gracefully out of the room.

"How many floors does this home have?" asked Torin, surprised that there was a downstairs at all.

"I think, all told, about seven or eight floors," replied Leva, settling herself down on a mat. "The Earthen Dwellers give a separate floor to each generation, or maybe two floors if the family is large. Each lineage has its own dwelling. That is partly why everyone knows who is who. My great grandparents live well below ground and no longer come to the surface at all. My aunts, uncles and cousins live on another floor. You know that my father left to go on his mentoring journey and fell in love with my mother, a tree woman. He stayed at the Threshold."

Leva was silent for a moment in longing for her tree. "I can live here longer than most because my father's people have a strong affinity for trees. Not every family here has one in their home though. I lived here for many months during my training, but then I needed to return to live in trees once more. Earthen Dwellers are the only beings I know of with multistory homes."

Tehy and Herien took one room on the first floor, while Torin and Rebecca took another. "How do they get air downstairs?" Rebecca wondered aloud. "The lowest floors must be many feet down. Think about the air pressure on your ears."

"Don't worry," Torin said, settling in next to her, "you won't have to go down there. I imagine Air Folk would find it a bit oppressive too. Did you notice the look on Herien's face? Now, let's get some rest," Torin added sleepily. Rebecca nodded, grateful to have a respite from flying and glad that Torin's shoulder cushioned her from the thin mat and hard earthen floor.

## Chapter 19

Rebecca awoke curled up next to a sleeping Torin. She got up quietly, left the house, and walked for a while, finally sitting down near a sand dune. The ground beneath her seemed to be murmuring in earthy tones and she had a flash of arriving back on earth only to hold lengthy conversations with concrete sidewalks. She laughed, wondering what she was doing, but knowing at the same time that part of her knew.

As she sat, contemplating the elemental qualities of earth, and sifting the purple sand between her fingers, she saw the ground beside her begin to sink. Attempting to rise, she felt herself being sucked right into the earth, down into the ground, gasping deeply before the purple sand closed over her face. Rebecca held her breath, afraid to open her eyes for fear of getting sand in them. She came to a stop abruptly, and the suddenness of landing made her open her eyes and breathe in reflexively. She looked about in surprise. Deep beneath the dunes of sand was a whole network of tunnels. She was sitting in the narrow passage of one of them, and by the faint light of a crystal embedded in one wall, she could see where the tunnel branched out in more directions than she could count. She took a deep breath, relieved to find that there was plenty of air, though it did smell like old musty clothes. Above her she could see no opening at all. Near her was the small pile of sand that had carried her down, and as she watched, it sank into the hard surface of the tunnel floor like water into parched soil.

Rebecca stayed sitting since the tunnel ceiling was so low she'd have to crawl to get anywhere, and she had no idea of where she would go anyway. She ran a hand over the tunnel wall, and the murmuring sound she'd heard before became magnified. She heard it inside her mind, a voice of depth, soothing and compelling at once.

"Feel the density, the weight of your own body, the pressure of the air on your skin, the thick compression of spirit in form. Remember that your physical nature is but one expression of your soul. Do not carry your body about as if it were unwanted bulk, but revel in the sensory joy of it! It is of no less value than the fullness of awareness, of mind, of spirit. The earth provides many things, the foundation of growth, the nurturing of living creatures, and the embrace of renewal after death. Without the element of earth you would not exist in the form you have chosen. Lie still, Child of Knowing, and become the ground beneath you."

Rebecca lay back, breathing deeply, as the soil came alive under her body. Her arms and legs grew heavy, and her head sank slightly into the floor. She was completely supported in the most comforting fashion. All at once she began to experience tingles up and down her spine, traveling along her arms and legs, head and neck. She grew very warm. Pulsing with energy, she felt as if nutrients from the soil were being absorbed right into her pores. It was like being fed directly from the ground.

"Now I know how a tree feels," she thought, and watched as her lower limbs grew tendrils and roots. "Or maybe an earth worm," she added, chuckling as her lower form took on the aspect of a wriggling worm. She turned onto her side, putting her ear to the ground to better hear the sound of roots seeking moisture, the scurrying of soil dwellers, the wise voice of Thianely singing wordlessly to her inhabitants.

Rebecca's body felt vibrantly, radiantly alive. Each cell expressed itself until she was humming, humming along with the tune of Thianely. Suddenly she felt a wave of awareness flow through her. "I shift in tune with my thoughts when I'm really grounded. What would happen if I shifted between thoughts, in the space between willingness and intention?" She played, within the depths of Thianely, with the power of her mind fully present in her body.

Imelina had woken early and gone out to harvest roots. When she returned it was to find Rebecca sitting at the table while the others slept. Imelina bowed low, seeing in Rebecca's arms the child who'd gone lost in the ripple of time.

"I traveled between thought to find cracks in time," Rebecca whispered softly so as not to awaken the sleeping child, "and found that she followed me here. I think this little one is very talented, and should be trained."

Imelina nodded and took the child from Rebecca, hurrying outside to take her home. Rebecca sat and waited, as first Leva, then Tehy and Herien, and finally Torin joined her at the table. After they'd eaten, Rebecca described traveling between thought to find the child. As she started to explain what she'd done, Imelina returned, bearing a small purple scroll made of some resinous material that had been mixed with earth and crushed stone. Rebecca looked at her questioningly.

"We have part of the original prophecy here." Imelina put it down upon the table so they could all see. Tehy and Leva crowded next to Torin and Rebecca while Imelina traced the letters with one finger.

"Here there is the prophecy that most of Thianely knows, but down at the bottom there is an additional part, added on much later. A bit of a phrase really. I had it from my mother who had it from hers and so on, back to the first Timekeepers of Thianely." She read to them in the Old Tongue, slightly accented by her earthen tones:

"Lords and Ladies, Guardians bring
Together starpoint planets sing,
Twining time in a crystal knot
Loving all that will has wrought."

Rebecca looked down at the scroll. "There's my favorite word, "will" again. This confirms that the problems here on Thianely are completely interconnected with other worlds. Our restoring the balance here cannot happen without the others' help."

"I know this is off the subject, Rebecca," Torin said, "but could you explain how you traveled thought without being affected by all of the separations that have been occurring?"

Rebecca smiled. "I traveled between thought, rather than elementally or intentionally. I came through the center where all the elements meet, where nothing exists at all, therefore I could not be affected."

"Rebecca," said Leva softly, "listen to what you've said. You traveled through the center where nothing exists at all. You've done it."

Rebecca stood still, slightly shocked, while Tehy and Torin clapped her on the back. Herien looked somewhat befuddled. Imelina flushed in excitement, "Why, it's so, Lady, you told me yourself, and the little one followed you here the same way. Why then, perhaps you could teach us all!"

"I traveled through the center," Rebecca repeated wonderingly, sounding a little bit surprised at her own success. "It's really not that difficult at all. One merely needs to let go of the idea that there is a right/left, good/bad, centered/uncentered at all. The funny part is that first they must be distinct enough to let go of. I realized that on some level we have been playing roles, and even knowing that we still must act according to what feels right. I can show you what I mean. You have to think before you can let go of thought enough to travel between."

"That means the Bolluxes will never figure it out," Torin said dryly.

"Does this mean you can bring Liliar here without me having to fly back?" Tehy asked, interested in practical applications.

"Perhaps you could send me back without me having to levitate the whole way," Herien interjected. "It would really save me time and energy."

"I think so," Rebecca said. "Let's try it. Herien, why don't you think of your destination and let the thought travel along right out of your mind. Now, I'll give you a little push..."

Herien vanished right before their eyes. There was no blurring at first, as when he became part of the element of air, he simply disappeared.

"I like this," Tehy said excitedly. "Let's see if you can bring Liliar here as well. She should be finished singing by now."

Within moments, Liliar arrived, with an ecstatic Haldane clutching her arm.

"I had to bring him with," she said. "I barely had time to blink, I got here so fast. What was that anyway? You certainly didn't sing me here. I saw no interruptions in space at all."

Rebecca tried to explain. "I think it's because between thought there's no time, so if you travel between thought, the effects on space and time here don't affect the travel."

"You're going to have to teach everyone how to do this," Liliar said. "Even my singing has been thwarted. I think most of the songs got to Hevald and Torildian, though we'll have to wait and see. I tried to sing them around any gaps or separations, but it was difficult."

Leva motioned to Liliar to come and sit down at the table. "I know how to repair the Gate of Time; I have the template for it inside me," Leva informed Liliar. "However, I do not know how to sing aemethra, and that is where we need you to help us."

"I think I have the knowledge, but it will take many of us to create the necessary resonance, including those of other worlds."

"My mother said that she will be contacting all of the Folk of Thianely to help," Tehy said.

"Imanayon sent word to many already," Torin added.

"And," said Rebecca, "it will be much easier when we have cleared away some of the clouds of confusion around Thianely. I saw these gray amorphous blobs of old thoughts and beliefs when I was in between things. They haven't helped keep minds clear. I think teling will be easier if we first sing a clearing song, Liliar. It might be something Thianelians need to do regularly. I'll have to go back to Earth soon to do the same and to coordinate singing efforts there."

Torin stood silently, acknowledging to himself that he knew that one day she would have to return. Rebecca reached over, placing her hand over his.

"Not without you though! You have to come with me, Torin. Earth needs all of the help it can get, and so do I. The Guardians on Earth need to awaken or our efforts will be useless. Liliar, I'm still a little confused about this aemethra. How do we sing time into a knot without that knotting things up?"

"I think the literal translation of the old word means "arising from the same foundation". The crystal strands all grow from the same origin, then entwine to create a whole crystal. "Knot" on Thianely means entwined, not stuck. Mates choose to be entwined, while remembering we are all distinct yet from the same source."

"Oh," Rebecca said, thinking of all of the images of tying knots, including matrimony, she'd learned on Earth. "That makes sense. On my planet everything has to do with ego, so people do get knotted together. I wonder if it will even be possible to sing aemethra there. I suppose we can try."

"I want to come," broke in Haldane, who'd been listening in fascination. "I want to go to Earth. Royden said it's the best Bollux place. They have lots of things to destroy, and they like us. Royden said they even have a word that sounds like us, in honor of our ancestor in the beginning times who went there to create chaos. Take me!"

As Liliar shook her head, Haldane began to pout and stomp his hairy little feet. "When I'm big you won't have anything to say about where I go or what I do. I'll go to Earth like Royden and Haldar and Jierdan did. I'll travel all over the universe and blow up whatever stars I want and do whatever I like."

For Rebecca, the thought of the Bolluxes loose on Earth did much to explain the state of her world. As Haldane appeared to be in the beginning stages of a full-fledged tantrum, Imelina, who'd been standing nearby, grasped the little Bollux firmly by one pointed ear. Still shouting in anger, Haldane was escorted outside.

Rebecca reached over and tugged Liliar to her feet, motioning to her to come outside. Then, the two singers stood on the purple earth outside Imelina's dwelling and while the Earthen Folk and their companions watched, they began to sing a clearing song for all of Thianely. The sounds poured from them in waves of rainbow colors as the ground shook slightly and resettled itself a little more brightly.

They all felt it, the shifting of the ground beneath them and the subtle change in the air, as if something had left. It was clearer both inside and outside them. Each of them noticed that their minds felt sharper, and at the same time more detached, as if emotions could flow through without becoming fixed.

The five of them sat down on the warmth of the ground and discussed how to organize the next few days, and soon Haldane came back with Imelina, wiping crumbs from his face.

"What was that song?" he asked, with a puzzled expression on his face. "I heard it before once, when I was outside laying on the ground. I thought it was a bog sprite playing tricks on me, but they don't sing, they only shriek. It makes me feel funny somehow, like my insides are tickling me."

"That's what it's supposed to do," Rebecca said, "It's the song of Thianely when she's happy. Are you going to help us sing sometime?"

"I don't think I'd better," Haldane replied, "I have a voice like a sick bog sprite with something stuck in its throat. But I am good at scaring things away."

"That may come in very handy," said Rebecca, "you never know. Anyway, all voices together are what we need, because everyone has a particular tune that is their very own. Even your family's voices are important."

Haldane stared at her rudely. "You don't know them if you think they'll sing, especially if you want them to. They might yell though. They all sound worse than me."

"That's okay," Rebecca said. "Everyone is always vibrating at some level anyway. I bet they'd get good and loud if they were angry enough."

Haldane looked at her hopefully, "Can I help get them really angry? I am good at that."

"I'll bet you are," said Rebecca, as the others began to laugh. "Actually, I heard that Bollux country is having a bog party any time now. I imagine there will be even more clarity over Bollux Country. Leva, if you get to work on the Time Gate, we'll be ready to sing when it's fixed."

Leva nodded. Liliar left with Imelina while Tehy offered to fly Leva above the Gate to check on any damage visible from the air. Haldane rushed away to see if he could raise a dust storm in case any of his family came looking for him. Rebecca and Torin walked out among the sand dunes for a while, holding hands.

"When do you think we'll have to leave Thianely?" Torin asked, as they walked along.

"I think we may be done here sooner than I thought," Rebecca said, shaking her head in amazement. "It certainly is easier to get people to come together here than it is back home. And you don't even have satellite communication here. I've already gotten a sense of what it will take back home. There's such a blanket of confusion and fear over everything, it seems monumental."

"Hey, for the woman who walked through thought, it won't be that hard." Torin commented.

Rebecca looked at him, shaking her head slightly. "Earth has been asking to heal, Torin, but no one can make people be ready to understand, or to want to remember themselves. All anyone can do is help create an environment in which they have more choices. The people on Thianely are used to being one with the elements, and you know what it was like for you on earth; you know how weird everything is there."

Torin put an arm over her shoulders gently, hugging her close. "Rebecca, any work we do here will be having an effect upon earth, and besides, think of all of this as part of your training. There are Guardians there as well as here. They merely need to be reminded.

Did you know that right now there are other Thianelians on earth learning about your world? They will help us. You're piercing enough to be heard three planets away, so we know they'll contact us.

Let's concentrate on Thianely first. I've been getting a very familiar feeling lately, as if we've done this many times already, on many different planets. Hopefully somewhere in our memories are old primers for planetary evolution practices."

Rebecca shrugged. "I hope so, though it does seem like whenever I really need to know something, there it is! I wonder what my parents will make of all this. I'm not even the same person I was when I left. Sometimes I wonder where I'll fit."

"Anywhere you want to," Torin said. "Though I must say that my sojourns on earth were difficult at best, and highly draining. I found it took more effort to do the simplest things. Remember you don't have to take it on all by yourself; there are other Guardians there, even if they haven't quite remembered themselves. Yes, you are different from how you were when you left Earth, but your parents will be so happy to see you."

"I think so too," Rebecca said. "I miss them a lot and I'm ready to go back. As soon as the Gate is finished will you travel between thought with me?"

"Of course," said Torin, putting his arm about her shoulders. They walked on, enjoying the day, as the sun cast pink shadows in ripples of dunes. It amazed Torin how desolate the place appeared, despite the hundreds of Earthen Dwellers who lived nearby. Aside from the occasional row of high dunes, the area was fairly flat, allowing one to see for some distance. Torin pointed out some of the insects and small animals indigenous to the area. Rebecca was amazed to see some small lizard like creatures skating down the sides of the sand dunes. Torin called them sand skippers. Apparently they could fly as well, but enjoyed sliding downhill so much they rarely flew except when in danger.

Finally, they circled back around to Imelina's dwelling, where Liliar had organized groups of Earthen dwellers so that they could practice singing. Torin and Rebecca took their places in one of the outer circles and listened as Liliar tried to convey a sense of singing aemethra. Most of the Earthen Folk were familiar with the practice of bestowing the crystal knots on mates, but translating the idea into song was entirely different. Liliar explained that some of the process would be completely spontaneous, as every living being had his or her own internal song. There would also be a harmonic overlay, encompassing and emphasizing both the collective consciousness and each individual as well.

Rebecca turned to Torin. "Can you imagine trying to express that in Earth terms?" she asked in dismay. "I know what she means, but it isn't due to any rational explanation. Part of it's because I heard her singing to Hevald and Torildian."

"Don't forget your own song to Earth," Torin pointed out. "I know that will be felt by many. Remember what you said before about each being resonating all of the time."

It was interesting, Torin thought, as Rebecca closed her eyes and began to hum from the ground up through her body, that even though everyone hummed a bit differently, it was the difference between them that brought harmony to the sound, simply because the intent was similar. Torin, too, closed his eyes and began to hum. The sound began beneath them and spiraled around the circles. It spread out until the ground was vibrating, and the air came alive with the pulsing. The entire gathering of Folk began to sway with the song until they were all rocking in their places on the ground.

Leva, meanwhile, was checking out the extent of damage at the entrance of the Time Gate. It was several minutes flying distance away from Imelina's and was obscured by a large sand dune. Tehy had flown her above the old portal, but it winked in and out of view so much that neither of them could see much at all. Tehy flew back to join Liliar, while one of the old Earthen engineers took Leva to the large portal that led to the Gate. The portal was a huge shimmering dome that wavered as she watched.

"Used to be solid as a stone," the engineer commented. "Bolluxes turned it to a flicker of itself."

Leva nodded, wondering if she ought to enter such an obviously damaged entryway. Finally she realized she'd have to step through if she wanted to examine the Gate. The old engineer shook his head.

"None of us have been inside since the implosion. We don't think it's safe."

Leva thought for a moment. She remembered what Rebecca had said about traveling through thought, and in a moment found herself standing inside the portal beneath the huge energetics of the Time Gate. It was very high and oval shaped, of alternating currents of energy. The outer frame was of a milky white density, while the inner core, where time flowed past, was transparent. It definitely had substance though, as ripples appeared across its surface in undulating waves. Leva reached deep inside for the knowledge she needed to assess the damage, and got to work.

## Chapter 20

After a long session of singing, Liliar motioned everyone to silence. They were all exhilarated as well as fatigued by the intensity of the singing practice. They were heading for their homes when they heard a tremendous crash. It was the horrendous shriek of thousands of injured Folk screaming, the hideous rending of uprooted trees, the metallic clash of weapons, the heavy tread of menacing giants. The entire gathering raced homeward in alarm. Nothing could be heard above the noise, so Torin merely pulled Rebecca along with him after the fleeing Earthen Folk.

Tehy and Liliar appeared at Torin's elbow. Rebecca soon found herself grasped firmly about the waist and swept up into the air. Tehy's great wings beat slowly under the heavy weight of his three companions, but he rose high enough into the air for them to get a clear view of all of the Earthen Folk ducking into their dwellings. Within moments every dwelling had completely submerged under ground.

Tehy flew higher still, and over the ridge of a sand dune they could see the cause of the ghastly noise. Six enormous Bellorasps were crawling like huge purple slugs over the sand toward the Earthen Folk's village. The creatures left thick, slimy trails behind them. With their vast bulk they moved slowly, but the noise they made traveled a far greater distance.

As Rebecca looked down she could see hundreds of slender stalks protruding from the gelatinous bodies. At the end of each stalk was a large opening with huge lips. She shuddered, realizing that each Bellorasp had thousands of mouth stalks all over its body. The horrid creatures were completely blind, causing them to wave their hungry mouths about in the air as if hunting for prey.

Rebecca, completely disgusted, glanced over at Torin and found him shaking beside her, his body quivering so violently he nearly fell out of Tehy's grasp. As she reached out a steadying hand to soothe him, she saw blue fire flow up his throat and burst out the top of his head. Red flames shot from his arms and through his palms. Tehy winced, barely able to hold onto his fiery friend. Liliar clung to Tehy's back while Rebecca clutched Tehy's arm with one hand and tried to hold Torin with the other. Torin glowed a brilliant yellow. He became so bright that Rebecca closed her eyes, while Tehy hovered blindly and Liliar buried her face in Tehy's wing.

At once they heard a loud hissing sound and a shrieking wind blew past them, thick with dust and the acrid odor of souls finally released from long confinement. The horrible noise ceased. In silence, they opened their eyes and saw below them the singed, blackened corpses of six Bellorasps, twitching feebly as they died.

Tehy flew past the grisly sight, setting them all down close to the still submerged Earthen village. They hovered over Torin, who'd collapsed exhausted on the ground. Sweat poured from his skin in increasing droplets, finally stopping abruptly. He opened his eyes wide, and seeing their concerned expressions, tried to smile reassuringly. Wiping his forehead with a corner of his tunic, he sat up.

"I'll be fine," he said, still pale from exertion. "I didn't know I could do that. I did not intend it at all; the fire simply came pouring through me. I've never shot flames that way. I suppose the singing attracted the Bellorasps. Excuse me, I need to go sit somewhere by myself."

Torin got up to his feet unsteadily and walked away. Rebecca started to go after him, but Tehy stopped her. "Not now, Rebecca. He's never caused harm to another being before, let alone six deaths. He had absolutely no control over it. That's a lot to accept. Let him be. He needs some time alone to grieve."

Rebecca sighed, but remained where she was. "What was that strange noise and the wind that blew by us? It felt conscious somehow."

Liliar answered with a shudder. "Remember how my brother Mosten threatened to send the Bellorasps after me? They suck the energy, the vibration right out of a person. What we felt were all of the beings those Bellorasps had eaten finally being freed."

"So Torin did a great service even beyond protecting us and the Earthen Folk," Rebecca concluded, shaking out her stiffened fingers. Holding onto Torin had taken all of her strength.

Tehy flexed his wings, trying to stretch the tired muscles of his upper back. As Liliar went to rub his shoulders he said, "Yes, that's true, but I'm not sure if Torin would see it that way. He has been well trained, Rebecca. To simply ignite living creatures without any particular provocation is not acceptable to him. The light pouring from him was incredible. I'm surprised our vision suffered no ill effects."

"I closed my eyes," Rebecca admitted.

"So did we," Tehy replied. "Still, he was incandescent, like a shooting star, although once the light came he felt surprisingly cool to the touch."

Rebecca turned round as Leva, who'd missed the whole thing, rushed up to update them about her success at traveling between thought. She'd only heard the Bellorasps faintly, as the portal to the Gate had blocked much of the wretched noise. She was astonished that Torin had been able to destroy six Bellorasps at once. After recovering from her surprise, she announced that the Time Gate was repairable, but would take longer than she had hoped.

"I'll need help from the engineers too, but they won't go into the portal at all without Imelina's permission. I think now that I've returned unharmed they might be more willing."

The Earthen Folk soon resurfaced their dwellings and Imelina sent some tunnelers to bury the Bellorasps. Everyone was amazed that Torin alone had been responsible for the creatures' deaths. Not even the Griffin Folk had been able to kill Bellorasps that quickly. Leva wondered aloud if the creatures' destination had been the Time Gate, rather than merely the Earthen Village.

"There's been so much damage already that the sound emitted by one of those creatures inside the portal would demolish the rest of it," Leva pointed out. "I think we're going to need a lot of protection while we work on repairs."

Liliar looked worried. "My voice won't be that effective in the midst of their terrible shrieking. I tried to sing them away, but I wasn't even audible. At least they didn't take my voice."

"I don't think we were close enough to them to be in that kind of danger," Tehy said. "I made sure to stay far enough away. They sound terrible enough as it is."

Imelina turned to Tehy. "We will have one of our telers contact your mother's Folk. My telers have informed me that long distance teling is again possible since the clearing song was sung. Perhaps the Griffin Queen will send a Griffin Guard to assist us."

She hurried off to organize the long distance telers. Later she called a small meeting at her home after evening repast. Several of the most proficient engineers were there and Torin had finally returned right before the meal, but Rebecca had had no time alone with him.

They all sat in Imelina's living space drinking fermented cactus juice, except for Rebecca who couldn't tolerate the brew.

"Long distance telers have been reporting from places all over Thianely." Imelina said. "The clearing song has helped their reception immensely. Kerithan the Griffin Queen has reported that the Bollux Bogs have been rendered inert. The mission to drop Meridwen's dew has been a complete success, though I hear the Bolluxes are quite outraged. A guard of Griffins is patrolling the perimeter of Bollux country to keep an eye on them because they have threatened to retaliate for the cleansing of their bogs.

I do have grave concerns over some other news I've been hearing. News of the Bellorasps' deaths has already traveled far on Thianely. Magbar of the Bellorasps is livid about the deaths of her creatures. She knows that only one of the Fire Lord's lineage could have done this. The Bolluxes and Skelric himself may target you as well, Torin. Your grandfather, Imanayon, has left the Threshold to help protect the Fire Folk. I would suggest you find yourself off world for a time, until things settle here."

Imelina turned to Leva. "I hear that the Gate may be fixed, but will require more help than we thought. I'll post my most experienced engineers, and they will enter the portal without balking. We'll need a guard for you while you're working. The Griffin Folk have offered to send some warriors to assist. I also want to comment on the fact that a very small Bollux is tucked down behind a chair over there, listening to everything I'm saying. I have no objection to Folk asking to attend this meeting, but I do object to sneaking about."

Tehy reached over and grabbed Haldane by the back of his neck. He lifted him up, despite his wiggling and squirming, and removed him from the room.

"At this point, young Bollux, you are leaving. Next time you will ask before entering the room, or listening to our plans. Now, go find something to do outside. No uprooting Imelina's herb garden."

He returned a few moments later, and sat down with a sigh. "That child. I can hardly imagine a whole family of them, and he's not even full grown. At least he seems to appreciate you, Liliar, so there's hope for him yet."

Liliar smiled. "He's young, and much kinder at heart than the rest of them. He needs to be kept busy and out of mischief. Perhaps I can put him to work helping Leva fix the Gate. It would be fitting, I think, since our family members helped break it."

Imelina spent the next several minutes conferring with Leva and her engineers. After the meeting broke up, Rebecca took Torin by the hand and led him out into the darkening sky. They walked quietly for a time, their feet sinking slightly into the purple sand. Finally they stopped to rest and Torin began to talk.

"I know killing the Bellorasps was helpful to those of us they would have harmed," he began, idly running his fingertips over the back of one of Rebecca's hands, "including protecting the Gate from further damage. But what disturbs me is that I had no thought of doing anything; it simply happened. It was as if I were mindless, thoughtless, reacting in anger like a small child, only there wasn't any anger. I have no singe marks at all, even though the elements are unreliable. Remember how I burnt myself making a meal at home?"

He shook his head in disbelief. "I am not really a warrior, Rebecca, though I remember having had warrior lifetimes. This was beyond anything I remember. Six Bellorasps completely destroyed, instantly."

Rebecca regarded him compassionately. "Torin, I don't think what you did falls under normal conditions. You looked like a human laser beam. The light you gave off was incredibly intense, and didn't really seem like fire in the usual sense. You only got physically hot at first, and then you became cool. You grew too bright to look at."

"I wish I could meet my father," Torin said suddenly. "If I had the proper training, I wouldn't be caught by surprise like this."

"I can certainly relate to that," Rebecca said. "Maybe you get to learn as you go, like me."

Torin reached over and hugged her closely. "I know it's been difficult, Rebecca. You've been very brave about everything, you know. I'm relieved I'll be going with you to Earth, although it always gives me separation sickness at first."

Rebecca looked at him in concern. "What's that?"

"The atmosphere of any planet includes the thoughts and feelings of all of the people who live there. In the case of your people, there's such a cloud of fear and suffering that it feels very oppressive. Separation sickness is the state of forgetting one's connection to all of creation. One becomes sad or angry, lonely, physically ill, and what many of your people call depressed. The connection to one's inner knowing is weakened and one's mental, physical and emotional health is compromised. It creates more suffering and feeds the atmosphere with despair which keeps getting worse."

Rebecca stared at him in astonishment. "What you call separation sickness, most people call the human condition. How do you maintain balance when you're on Earth?"

Torin shrugged. "I have to create a very strong energetic filter system when I'm there. Sort of like an energy space suit to protect me from the environment. I bring things from Thianely to remind me of where I come from, and I ask the spirits of the elements there for help. The few times I went there before, I contacted other visiting Thianelians for support. I usually bring a few plants from home to comfort other travelers as well."

"Some time you're going to have to tell me about your experiences on Earth more in depth," Rebecca said. "I wonder if I'll get sick when I get back. I never thought of our normal state of affairs as symptoms of separation sickness before. Oh well. I suppose we should get back to Imelina's house. It's probably not too safe out here, although at least I don't have to worry about being sucked up by any Bellorasps while you're around."

Torin winced, pulling her to her feet. "Rebecca, you certainly have a way of helping me achieve more clarity. I can't wait to see what will happen next. Actually, up until the last couple of years, most of us led relatively peaceful lives."

"Me too," Rebecca said, as they headed back to the Earthen dwellings. "But mine was peaceful in a dull sort of way. When I look back, it feels like I've been sleepwalking up to now. Or living in black and white and switching to living in color. Of course, you'd have to add in sound and senses that I didn't even know existed before. It certainly makes life more interesting."

They returned to Imelina's dwelling and found Haldane outside the door digging what looked like a large trench. He informed them that he was making a trap for the Bellorasps to fall into and while Rebecca and Torin complimented him on his industry, they kindly pointed out that the location was more likely to trap an unsuspecting Earthen Dweller. They helped him fill in the deep hole before it became too late to stay awake, and suggested he make one nearby the Gate of Time to help the Griffin Guard when they arrived.

Haldane nodded. "I better do it soon if I'm going to be traveling to Earth with you. I'm all ready to go whenever you want to leave."

Torin shook his head and Rebecca decided she'd better have a chat with Haldane in the morning. "We'll talk about this another time," she said, escorting a somewhat besmudged Haldane inside to put away his digging implements. Everyone else had already retired for the night, apparently unaware of the small Bollux's nighttime activities.

"It must take a lot of work to raise a Bollux child," Torin commented as they arranged their sleeping mat more comfortably. "I'm not sure what kind of training he's received, but at least he hasn't destroyed anything yet. Liliar has a lot of patience with him."

"He's really kind of charming in a scruffy sort of way," Rebecca agreed. "He is trying to help."

The next morning they were all interrupted at morning repast by the arrival of six Griffin warriors. They reported directly to Tehy, insisting that the Queen had requested that her son act as wing leader. Tehy quickly finished his meal and left with Leva and the Griffins to decide where they would best be posted. Liliar went back to training the Earthen Folk in singing, and they were surprised when some nearby Cactus Folk joined them to assist in the chorus. Rebecca had never seen any Cactus Folk before. They had very knobby jointed bodies, rough purple skin and thick tufts of hair on their faces and bodies. Torin explained that they rarely came above ground, for they were cousins to the Rootlings, an entirely submerged Folk, and very distant relatives of the Earthen Folk.

"We call them Nortam Folk in the old tongue," Torin explained. "That means root bound. They cannot be far from the roots of their plant homes for more than several hours or they start to dry up. The only moisture and nutrients that they can tolerate are those that come from far below the surface. They have many tunnels deep under ground that they rarely leave. It is very brave and generous of them to offer to help. You'll notice the tones they sing are very low. I'm sure Liliar appreciates the added range."

Rebecca made a point of meeting the Cactus Folk, to thank them all for allowing her to visit their tunnels. Without that experience, she wasn't sure if she would have learned to shift between thought.

Rebecca and Torin spent the next several days singing, chasing Haldane around to keep him out of trouble, and listening to growing reports from the long distance telers all over Thianely about Bellorasps on the move again. Torin listened to one of the Fire Folk telers in growing dismay. He turned to Rebecca after an especially long session with his grandfather.

"There are strange changes in the weather, Rebecca. Skelric is affecting seasons up North, and Grandfather says they've experienced autumn, Yarwen, and spring in the space of a few weeks. Yarwen has not restored balance, and the healing garden is suffering. Beings are reporting damage to trees and plants all over Thianely. It's as if no one's will makes any difference. Everything is out of control. The simplest request is often being denied. Rebecca, the Bolluxes and the Bellorasps have made no secret of the fact that they will harm either of us on sight. I think it's time to go."

"Won't they attack your village, and our friends while we're gone? I mean, in order to get us to respond more directly?"

"I thought of that," Torin admitted. "But Grandfather said that Kerithan has already sent several of her warriors to guard the Fire Folk. Meridwen sent more dew, and Grandfather has been grilling me about how I destroyed the Bellorasps. He thinks that the Fire Folk can set up a perimeter of flames to keep the creatures out. Our singers have been coordinating with Liliar to sing aemethra. Grandfather said that the merfolk are also lending their voices to Liliar's efforts. The only problem is that sound attracts the Bellorasps even more. No one is really safe when they're about."

Rebecca sat and thought for a moment. "If we could somehow get Earth to sing more clearly, if I can sing a clearing song there so that we're not so clouded over, then singing aemethra will happen more quickly. I mean, Hevald and Torildian will help; it's Earth who's not able to yet. So I suppose we can do the most good there, even though I don't feel good about leaving everyone in the middle of vengeful Bolluxes and Bellorasps. I guess you're right. We should go."

"Imelina believes that if we leave, the Bolluxes will focus their revenge on the Griffin Folk, rather than trying to hunt us down here. She'd appreciate it if we left today, Rebecca."

Rebecca leaned forward into his arms. "I knew it would have to be soon. Hold me for a moment, Torin. I'm more nervous about this than I thought."

Torin obliged, pulling her closer and wrapping his arms about her.

"I wonder sometimes, myself," he confessed. He brushed a lock of hair from her face and rested his cheek against hers. "I imagine it may be difficult for you to return to your world after all that has happened. As it will be for your parents to see how much their daughter has changed, not to mention having me along."

They held each other for a while, drawing comfort from each other's nearness. Rebecca leaned back with a sigh. They got to their feet, and hand in hand, made their way back to Imelina's home to pack up their belongings. Torin pulled a blue garment out of his pack, tossing it to Rebecca. It was her old raincoat. She clasped it to her for a moment, thinking of home, and then realized she no longer needed it.

"I'll leave this for Leva," she said, taking the boots Torin handed her and laying them aside as well. She made sure she had her flask of the life-giving water, the root from the great tree, the crystal necklace Liliar had returned to her, her mercomb, and the wristlet from Torin. She tucked the leaf pad into her backsack, adding an extra set of Thianelian garments and some dried food. Torin finished his packing as well, and they went out to find the others to say their goodbyes.

Imelina, knowing they would leave immediately, had already gathered everyone together. They waited outside Imelina's home, in agreement with Torin and Rebecca's decision to leave as soon as possible.

"I will miss you, Rebecca," Liliar said simply. She reached into her pocket and pulled a smooth marble from her gown. It was mottled in swirls of colors, blues and reds, purples and oranges.

"I sang a toning marble for tuning things. Hold it in your palm and sing when you need it. It will help with the clearing song of your planet."

Rebecca took the marble and carefully put it into her tunic pocket. Liliar stepped forward to hug her and Torin goodbye.

Haldane, who had stood watching the exchange, rushed over to Rebecca and presented her with a strange, dried up object. At her look of puzzlement, Haldane said, "Here, it's a petrified bog sprite, guaranteed to scare anyone away. All you have to do is add water and it moves. I usually spit on it. It's not really alive, but it looks like it enough to scare people. You might need this since Liliar said I can't come with you now, but maybe later." He eyed her solemnly. "I will come to Earth some day. I have business there."

Rebecca nodded, and carefully accepted the shriveled gray mass as if it were a precious gem. "Thank you, Haldane. I may need this. I think I'll wait to use it when it's really necessary." Much to Haldane's disgust, she bent down and kissed his forehead.

"Thank you again," she said, "and don't forget to sing with Liliar, even if your voice sounds bogworthy."

She added Haldane's gift to her tunic pocket, and smiled as Tehy stepped forward, bowing low. "Safe journeys, you two," he said. He reached up and plucked a feather from his wing, presenting it to her with another bow.

"Rebecca, this is to remember your gifts from the air. Take care of my fiery friend here." Tehy pulled both Rebecca and Torin into a furry embrace, hugging them soundly. Imelina had packed them some food for their journey, although if everything went well they would arrive in Rebecca's room and have no need of extra provisions, but Imelina insisted, so they accepted gratefully. Finally Leva approached them.

"Some day, Rebecca, I will have to go to your world and meet the Tree Folk there and see how they fare. For now, I would like you to take this leaf from the Threshold of the Trees, and this bottle of tree sap I collected. I hope you can use them. And Torin, I brought an extra tunic for you, made of leaves to protect you from homesickness. May you be well in all travels."

Torin packed the items into his backsack, along with Imelina's provisions. He and Rebecca took turns embracing Leva.

"We will return when it is time," Torin said finally. "May Rhiate bless your efforts here and ours on Earth. We'll work as quickly as we can and try to get word to you through song. Farewell!"

Rebecca looked about her, at the pink Thianelian sky, the dusky purple earth beneath her feet. She gazed into each of her friend's faces and realized how much she loved them, how much she'd learned from each of them. She felt a sudden sense of loss, and worry that somehow she would never be able to return. But she knew she would. She had to come back because Thianely was home now too.

She and Torin stood close together with their friends clustered about. Rebecca smiled at them all. “Thank you so much for welcoming me, for being so helpful, and reminding me of who I am. I know I’ll see you all again soon. Stay safe.”

Liliar sang a departure song, a gentle, lilting melody that soothed and comforted. When the rest of them joined in, Rebecca had to smile a little at the froggy sound of Haldane’s voice. She bent down, scooping a little of the purple earth into her hand, and poured it carefully into her pocket. She held one of Torin’s hands, and looked once more at their friends’ kind faces.

After Torin nodded his readiness, Rebecca closed her eyes, picturing her home on Earth as fully as she could. She visualized her room in great detail, the blue carpet, and every piece of furniture, even the windows. She imagined being there, the feeling of waking up under soft covers, peering out under the canopy of her bed. An intense longing to see her parents, to be home, swept through her. She let all thought dissolve, and focusing on nothing at all, she pulled Torin along through the still spaces between thought. The sounds of Liliar’s song faded, blending into the liquid light that they’d become. Suddenly Rebecca felt the familiar sensation of carpet beneath her feet, Torin’s hands clasping hers, and knew that she was home.